BROKEN WINGS

*Also by Terri Blackstock
in Large Print:*

Evidence of Mercy
Justifiable Means
When Dreams Cross
Blind Trust

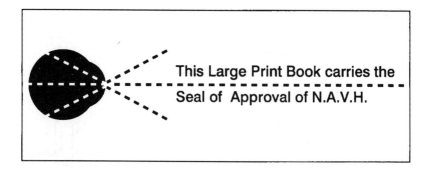

BROKEN WINGS

TERRI BLACKSTOCK

Thorndike Press • Thorndike, Maine

Published in 1998 by arrangement with Zondervan Publishing House.

Thorndike Large Print® Christian Fiction Series.

The tree indicium is a trademark of Thorndike Press.

The text of this Large Print edition is unabridged. Other aspects of the book may vary from the original edition.

Set in 16 pt. Plantin by Al Chase.

Printed in the United States on permanent paper.

Library of Congress Cataloging in Publication Data

Blackstock, Terri, 1957–
    Broken wings / Terri Blackstock.
      p.   cm.
    ISBN 0-7862-1468-6 (lg. print : hc : alk. paper)
    1. Large type books. I. Title. II. Series: Blackstock, Terri, 1957–   Second chances.
    [PS3552.L34285B76 1998]
     813′.54—dc21   98-4364

*This book is lovingly dedicated
to the Nazarene*

ACKNOWLEDGMENT

Special thanks to the commercial pilot in my life — my father, Sam Ward — for spending hours and hours answering my endless questions about commercial-airline piloting, crash investigations, industry problems, and so on.

This book could never have been written without his patience and enthusiasm.

Dear Reader,

The book you've just bought from my "Second Chances" series is truly evidence of the second chances God gives us. The books in this series have been published before, by Dell, Harlequin, or Silhouette. I was a Christian when I entered the romance market in 1983, hoping to take the world by storm. What I found, instead, was that the world took *me* by storm. One compromise led to another, until my books did not read like books written by a Christian. Not only were they not pleasing to God, but they embraced a worldview that opposed Christ's teachings. In the interest of being successful, I had compartmentalized my faith. I trusted Christ for my salvation, but not much else. Like the Prodigal Son, I had taken my inheritance and left home to do things my own way.

I love that parable because it so reflects my life. My favorite part is when Jesus said, "But while he was still a long way off, his father saw him . . ." I can picture that father scanning the horizon every day, hoping for his son's return. God did that for me. While I was still a long way off, God saw me coming. Early in 1994, when I yearned to be closer to God and realized that my writing was a wall between us, that my way had not been the best way, I promised God that I would never write anything again that did not glorify him. At that moment, it was as if God came running out to meet me. I gave up my secular career and began to write Christian books.

Shortly after I signed a contract for Zondervan to publish my suspense series, "The Sun Coast Chronicles," something extraordinary happened. The rights to some of my earlier romance novels were given back to me, and I was free to do whatever I wanted with them. At first, I thought of shelving them, but then, in God's gentle way, he reminded me that I was free to rewrite them, and this time, get them right. So I set about to rewrite these stories the way God originally intended them.

As you read these stories, keep in mind that they're not just *about* second chances, they *are* second chances. I hope you enjoy them.

In Christ,
Terri Blackstock

CHAPTER ONE

She was about to snap. Addison Lowe knew all the signs, for not so long ago he had been on the verge of a breakdown himself. From the descending stairwell that led to the rainy airport runway, Addison had watched her, the shadows rendering him inconspicuous. He'd seen it all: the plane taxiing into the hangar for an unnecessary inspection of its wing, the petite first officer debarking as fast as the crew would allow her to, the long wait until a replacement pilot could be found. And then he had followed her through the rain until she was back inside Shreveport Regional Airport, and observed her as she stood, wet and pensive, staring with haunted eyes out at the congested runway.

Flipping back the page on his clipboard, he jotted down a few notes about her behavior, shifted against the rail at his side, and focused on her again. A look of controlled misery settled over her features, but her posture straightened, as though she might allay that misery with sheer physical effort. Hugging her rain-damp arms, as if to comfort herself, she stepped closer to the

9

rain-splattered window and followed the upward progress of a 747. She shivered noticeably as the plane became nothing more than a light against the opaque darkness, then turned from the window.

Across the corridor at the Southeast counter, a young ground clerk gave her a compassionate look. "It's okay, Erin."

Erin, he thought. *That's what they call her.* He took a few steps up the stairs and saw the expression of defeat flit away as if she had chased it. He could see that she didn't want pity or gentle pats on the back. And she didn't want to be afraid. He knew. He had been there.

Brushing her damp, ruffled bangs away from her forehead, she looked past the ground clerk to the door that led to the office of Frank Redlo, the assistant chief pilot. And with all the determination of a woman about to turn a major corner in her life, she started toward the door.

Addison waited a beat after she'd gone in before he followed her. He shouldn't trail her like some spy waiting for a glimpse of impropriety, he told himself, but some instinctual compulsion drove him on. Instincts were a major part of his job, after all, and if one of Southeast's pilots was showing symptoms of instability, he, above all people, had the right to know. It wasn't just idle curiosity or a need to follow the pull of whatever it was in her eyes that had moved him. He was simply doing his job.

Besides, he had an appointment with Redlo, anyway.

She was already in her boss's office when he stepped into the waiting area outside it. Through the open door he could hear the sound of Redlo's low, angry mumbling, and then her voice rising above his, her tone defensive, desperate.

"You don't have to give me the third degree, Frank, because it doesn't matter anymore."

"What do you *mean* it doesn't matter? You're one of our pilots! You're on our payroll, aren't you?"

"Not anymore," she said without hesitation. "I came in here to resign."

The words came too easily, shaking Erin up. Had she really said it? Had she meant it? Bleakly, she realized she had.

Frank's face mottled into various unsettling shades of crimson. "Resign! Are you nuts? You can't resign!"

"Why not?" Erin argued. "I can't fly. You said yourself that a pilot who can't fly is of no use to an airline."

"Don't twist my words!" Frank said, one hand flailing in the air as he shook his index finger at her. "I said there's no room for a pilot who *won't* fly. You can and will!"

"No, I *can't!*" she shouted. "I froze, Frank. I was cleared for takeoff, and I froze!"

Frank clutched his head with both hands, as though to keep it from splitting right down the middle of his bald spot. "You can't do this," he said, lowering his voice to a reasonable level. "You're tougher than this. You've flown dangerous missions for the FBI and the Justice Department, for heaven's sake. You've had bullets flying at you, and you didn't bat an eye. Erin, you've got to get a grip. This is not the end of the world. You're just depressed, but you'll get over it." He slammed his elbows on the desk and raked back what remained of his hair. "You were up for a promotion soon. You were ready, Erin. I was gonna recommend you be moved up to captain." He dropped his hands and leaned across his desk, his silver eyes punctuating each word. "You're a good pilot, and I won't allow you to throw a career away because of a senseless crash that had nothing to do with you. For pete's sake, you weren't even on that plane."

Tears stung her eyes, but she blinked them back, determined not to let this conversation turn into a wearisome summation of the crash. It was over, behind them, and she didn't want to talk about it. "You can't stop me, Frank. I quit. That's all there is to it." The words held only harsh finality. Stiffly, she stood before him, waiting for acceptance.

"Okay," Frank said. He slouched back in his chair and rubbed his forehead. His face looked as fatigued and wrinkled as old bedsheets. He swiveled to the window at his back and peered out of it, shaking his head. "Okay. Let's say that I accepted your resignation and you walked out of here, gave up everything, and did something else. What would that be?"

Erin laughed bitterly. "I'm not stupid, Frank. I can do a lot of things."

He swiveled around, his sagacious eyes assessing her. "But you're a pilot, Erin. Sure, you can do any number of things. But would you *like* doing them? Would you be able to do them for the rest of your life?"

"Yes." She bent over his desk, bracing herself with her hands, and met his gaze squarely. "And without being terrified. Without nightmares. It would be worth it."

Frank clasped his hands in front of him and leaned forward, shaking his head. "Know why I don't believe you? Because I remember the little brunette who marched into personnel years ago and demanded a fighting chance at flying for this airline. You didn't take no for an answer, and in the years since I hired you, I've learned a few things about the strength and power of your will. Erin, three weeks ago you weren't terrified. You weren't having nightmares. Three weeks from now you might be over it. I won't accept a snap decision from you."

Fiery frustration colored her neck, and her hands coiled into fists, their rigid tightness matching her mood. "Frank, please. You just don't understand."

"I do understand, Erin. I understand that Mick was the one who convinced you to work for this airline. I understand that he was about the closest friend you've ever had. I understand the uncertainty of not knowing what caused the crash. And I understand the grief that you — that all of us — feel now. But you can't throw away your career for that. You just can't."

"If I do it in writing, Frank, you can't deny it."

"No, but I'm a real flake when it comes to paperwork. I'll probably lose it. Just like I'll probably forget this conversation the minute you leave. I'm funny that way."

"I could go to Bill Jackson. He's the chief

14

pilot, Frank. He'd have to accept it."

"He's out of town until the day after tomorrow, Erin," Frank said with feigned regret. "Looks like you're still employed, at least until then."

Erin's hands trembled, just as they had trembled in the plane as the tower told her she was cleared for takeoff. Cold dampness coated her palms, while her lips seemed dry and unsteady. "What are you going to do? Force me back up? *Make* me fly?"

Frank stood up, his back as rigid as his tone. "You have to go back up, Erin. You have to fly again to overcome this. Believe me, you *will* get over it."

"Frank, making me go up now would be dangerous and irresponsible. I wouldn't force it if I were you!"

"I won't force it, Erin," he said. "That's not my intention. I'll wait you out. But you're still one of my best pilots, and I don't plan to lose you."

The firmness in his voice robbed her of her energy as she stared at him in disbelief. There was no way to make him understand. What was the use? Nothing she said would change his mind. The proof would be in her performance — or her inability to perform.

Frank came around his desk and set his hands on her shoulders, the fatherly touch making her despair even more. Tears pricked at her eyes. Erin concentrated on the prints of relic airplanes on the wall, the enlarged snapshot of Frank's new grandchild, the clutter of books stuffed in their shelves . . . anywhere but on the eyes of the man who seemed to read her so clearly. "Erin, you really will get over it. You'll wake up one morning — maybe tomorrow, or next week — and want to fly so badly you'll be able to taste it. I've been through it myself. I know what I'm talking about."

Erin looked at him dully. She was too tired to argue.

"There's another consideration, Erin, and I don't want to put any more pressure on you, but you should be thinking about it."

"What?" she whispered.

"The takeover. I know you've heard rumors . . . we all have. Trans Western is probably going to buy us out any day now. Their owner, Collin Zarkoff, is the hardest-nosed jerk you've ever laid eyes on. If you're off the payroll when he takes over, I can't promise you a job will be waiting when you get back."

"I'm not asking for special favors," she said, her voice cracking.

"You're not resigning, Erin," he repeated quietly. "Now go home. Work through it.

I'll catch you in a day or two. Meanwhile, I'll cover for you with the chief. Tell him you've been under a lot of stress. Need some time off. Maybe some counseling."

"Counseling," she said tightly.

"We all need it sometimes," Frank said. "That's why the company has a psychologist on staff. There's no crime in needing to talk."

Too weary to argue about it, she nodded. "You're right. I'll look into counseling." Then, because her emotions were too close to the frayed edge of self-control, Erin wiped her eyes and turned to leave.

Addison Lowe rose when she started back through the waiting area, and he nodded a polite hello when she caught her breath and looked at him, startled. The molten gold color of her eyes was unexpected. Funny, he hadn't noticed them from a distance, or the trim, feminine fit of her uniform, or the delicate features that made her suddenly appear more like an attractive woman than a pilot on the edge. That hollow, abysmal look still sparkled in the depths of her eyes, tugging at the scars inside him that reminded him how far down he had once fallen himself.

"Mr. Lowe." Frank came out from the

office, hand outstretched. "I didn't know you were waiting."

Addison shook his hand, keeping an eye on Erin. "We did have an appointment about ten minutes ago, didn't we?" Addison asked. "I had a few more questions about the crash."

Resentment washed over Erin's features, and that broken, weary look was replaced with a brief flash of anger. Without saying hello, good-bye, what-were-you-eavesdropping-for, *anything,* Erin vanished through the doors that led to the main terminal.

The door to her house was unlocked, and Erin stopped short of opening it. She dropped her forehead against the casing and closed her eyes, reluctant to go inside. If the door was unlocked, it meant that Madeline hadn't left for the studio, or Lois hadn't left for her flight yet. It meant that there would be questions . . . concerns . . . even panic at the latest failure in Erin's life. But she couldn't escape the inevitable. Her roommates would know all the sordid details about her aborted flight as soon as Lois got to the airport and heard the gossip. Erin might as well tell them herself. Trying her best to look cheerful, Erin pushed the door open and went inside.

The sound of Lois's blow-dryer in the living room whistled a deafening note as her roommate bent at the waist, drying her blond bob upside down. The movement at the door caught her eye, and Lois snapped her head up. Her silky hair fell miraculously into place, attractively contrasting the black of her pilot's jacket. The dryer cut off, and an ominous silence settled in the room. Lois's blue eyes rounded in dread.

"Oh, no . . . Erin . . ."

Erin smiled, the effort straining her cheeks, and raised a hand to stem Lois's outburst. "Don't start, Lois."

From the other room, she heard Madeline's voice. "Erin?" In seconds, Madeline was rounding the corner into the living room. "Erin, you're supposed to be on your way to Washington."

Erin dropped her small suitcase next to the sofa and ran her fingers through hair that had been in better shape before she'd tramped through the rain. "And you're supposed to be at the studio, getting ready for a trip to New York. And Lois, you're supposed to be on your way to Atlanta."

"Not for an hour," Lois said, throwing her dryer into her bag and snapping it shut. She leveled her gaze on her friend again. "Erin, what happened?"

Erin's smile lost its life. "Nothing happened."

"You couldn't fly." It wasn't an accusation, but a statement. Erin waited for the lecture that was certain to follow.

"Did you even try?" Madeline asked.

Erin laughed mirthlessly, and noticed that her fingers were still raking frantically through her hair. Self-consciously, she dropped her hand back to her side. "I got in the cockpit," she said, turning away from them. "I taxied down the runway." Her mouth twitched as she spoke, and she held her eyes still to keep the welling tears from falling. "I was even cleared for takeoff."

She turned back to her friends, and saw that Lois had covered her face and was shaking her head balefully. Madeline's eyes were as round as quarters as she stared at her. "Oh, Erin."

"And then I froze," Erin went on, "and Jack, my new captain, the one whose confidence I needed, had to cover for me to keep every pilot on the runway from hearing what I was doing. I got off the plane. I couldn't fly."

Lois's eyes glimmered with sympathy, and she came to her distraught friend and embraced her with the strength of years of friendship. "You'll get over it, Erin. You'll work through it."

Erin wiped at her eyes and tried to find some semblance of a smile to reassure her. "I know, I know. No big deal. Meanwhile, you're going to be late if you don't get out of here."

"I could call in sick. I'll stay with you if you need me."

"No," Madeline said. "*I'll* stay home. I was just going to recruit animators from the art school, but I'll get someone else to go for me."

"Absolutely not. Sam was going with you. You've been looking forward to this trip for weeks." She knew the last thing in the world Madeline wanted was to lose the opportunity to spend time in the company of the man she was in love with. And if Erin knew Sam, he wouldn't be crazy about the idea, either.

"But he was going to visit friends there, too. He can go on and I can go in a day or two, when Lois gets back. Really, Erin, I want to stay."

Erin picked up Lois's suitcase and Madeline's bag and handed it to them. "Go. I'm just going to take it easy, try to get some sleep. Keep busy. Don't worry, I'll be fine."

Lois sighed deeply and studied her friend. "You're a survivor, Erin. Survive, okay?"

Erin nodded. Sometimes surviving wasn't

21

the best thing, she thought miserably.

Madeline and Lois started reluctantly for the door. "I'll be back the day after tomorrow," Lois said. "And I'll be praying for you constantly."

"Me, too," Madeline said.

"Thanks," Erin said. "Don't stop."

Madeline looked a little forlorn, and turned back to Erin, who stood hugging herself in the big, quiet house. "Erin, are you sure you'll be all right?"

"I'll be great," Erin said, affecting a smile. "By the time you get back, I'll probably be back in the saddle."

"I hope so," Lois whispered, then with one last, hesitant look, the two women left Erin alone.

Erin stood in the open doorway, watching each of them drive out of sight. She couldn't help envying her roommate's lack of fear in going up. Would Lois feel the same fear as Erin if it had been *her* captain who crashed . . . *her* close friend? The warm October breeze caught her hair, swirled it over her shoulders, and swept it into her face. It had stopped raining, and the temperature had dropped a few degrees. Louisiana summer still hung on, but a pleasant autumn coolness laced the air. The feel of the wind reminded her of freedom — the freedom she used to feel when she was far above the clouds, soaring through a sky so blue that it made her eyes water. Why couldn't she anticipate that freedom again, instead of feeling the bars rise before her eyes and the vises lock on her wrists and the noose tightening around her neck as soon as she thought of flying?

Catching her breath, Erin closed the door and went back inside. She'd spent more time in this house in the last two weeks than she had since she and Lois had moved in with Madeline. Lush and massive as it was, it was feeling more and more like home. Safer all the time.

The phone rang, but she didn't want to talk, so she let the answering machine pick up on the fourth ring. The message was for Lois, and after it had clicked off, she lifted the phone off the hook and stuck it in a drawer in the china hutch.

She sat down on the velvet sofa that Lois had brought with her and turned on the television with the small remote. Harold Monroe, the local television news anchor, was reporting the new tax laws. Erin's mind wandered as she stared blankly at the set, recalling the night two weeks ago when she had sat in this very room, watching this same man, with Madeline playing amateur nurse to her injury. It had been no big deal, Erin had insisted. The minor car accident she'd had on the way to the airport that evening had caused her to hit her head — a concussion, the doctor had said, and she was grounded for a few days. Because of her injury, she had been replaced on the round-trip flight from Shreveport to Dallas.

As Madeline clucked over her, making her head ache worse, she had heard the news report about the crash. *Flight 94 from Dallas. No survivors.*

As vividly as if it had just happened, Erin remembered the panic that had taken hold of her as photos of the wreckage played across the screen: the plane in a million, indistinguishable pieces, the fire billowing here and there, the bodies being pulled out . . .

Her pounding heartbeat had deafened her to the reporter's message, and to Madeline's rapid-fire prayers, but the two most important words seemed indelibly grafted in her mind . . . *No survivors . . . no survivors . . . no survivors . . .* She had sprung up from the couch, intent on rushing to the airport to somehow prove that the report was a mistake. It wasn't *her* flight. Not *her* friends. The newscaster had gotten the information wrong. Not Mick. Not all those people. Not dead!

But there had been no mistake. And Erin didn't think she had stopped shaking since that night.

The reality of the crash hadn't been the worst part, however. It was what came later — the speculation about the cause, the media's interviews with witnesses and ground victims who'd survived, the funerals that came one after another, the shock on the faces of Mick's wife and son — that had made the ordeal seem endless. And then when the press began hinting that neglect had been the cause of the crash . . . it had just been more than she could take. No one could tell her that Mick, the man she had flown with almost exclusively for the past five years, could have made a mistake and flown the plane straight into the ground. There was some other explanation. There had to be.

". . . National Transportation Safety Board officials still refuse to release excerpts of the tapes . . ."

Tonight's news report hauled Erin's attention back to the television, and she sat rigid, listening, as a still portrait of Mick in his uniform dominated the screen.

". . . pending investigation. However, sources at Southeast Airlines tell us that it's possible that pilot error caused the crash that left 151 people dead, including four ground victims. Forty-eight-year-old Mick Hammon, captain of Flight 94, was a retired Air Force colonel who had flown with Southeast for ten years . . ."

A malignant rush of fury heated Erin's face, and she turned the set off and covered her mouth with her hands. It *wasn't* his fault!

But whose was it? On the heels of the question came the faint, reckoning voice that had haunted her since that night. *I should have been there!*

The thought made her stomach turn, and she stumbled to the kitchen sink and splashed cold water on her face, then leaned over the sink to steady herself as tears flooded her eyes.

"Lord, help me," she whispered aloud. "I know that no one could have stopped it, because no one caused it. My being there wouldn't have changed things." But the words sounded hollow in the still house, and no matter how many times she uttered them, Erin knew she would never be convinced.

CHAPTER TWO

The persistent ringing of the doorbell penetrated Erin's thin, shallow sleep, and she
opened her eyes and sat up. Through the
haze of grogginess, she realized she had fallen
asleep on the couch, wearing her faded jeans
and an old sweatshirt. There had been too
many ghosts to sleep in the bed. The couch
kept her from falling too deeply into a sleep
from which there was no escape once the
dreams started.

The doorbell rang again, and Erin stood
up and looked around, prepared to destroy
any evidence that she'd slept on the couch.
People were already beginning to question
her mental state. But then, she was beginning to question it, too.

Pushing back her sleep-tousled hair, she
stumbled to the door and opened it. The
man she had seen waiting outside Frank's
office last night stood before her, clad in an
ivory sweater that deepened the rough tan
on his seasoned face. "Yes?" she asked.

"Miss Russell?"

"Yes," she said again, irritated.

"I'm Addison Lowe. I was in Mr. Redlo's

27

office last night . . ."

"I remember, Mr. Lowe," she cut in, crossing her arms with a decided lack of tolerance. "I hope you found my conversation with my boss interesting."

"I wasn't eavesdropping. I had an appointment."

"Regardless," she said, still blocking the door with her body, "you listened to a private conversation that was none of your business."

"That's where you're wrong, Miss Russell," he said.

"Wrong about your listening? You don't expect me to believe —"

"No," he said. "Wrong about it being any of my business. It's very much my business. It's my job to know when a pilot's stability is waning, though I generally find out after it's too late."

All the murky grogginess in Erin's head vanished, and molten fire rose up in her eyes. "I beg your pardon."

Addison reached for his wallet and handed her a card. "I'm with the National Transportation Safety Board, and I came from Washington to investigate the crash."

"The National Transportation . . ." The words faded off into nothingness before they were completely uttered, and a foreboding sense of panic descended. Had she really admitted to being afraid to fly in the presence of an NTSB official? Had he heard *everything?* She tried not to look as defensive as she felt. "What . . . what do you want from me?" she asked weakly.

"I understand you were Mick Hammon's first officer," he said. "I thought maybe you could answer some questions for me."

She glared up at him, weighing one consequence against another. He didn't exactly look menacing. In fact, those dark green eyes sparkled with soul. The normal impulse would be to like him at first sight. But Erin didn't want to like him. Not if he was the one sifting through the remains of Mick Hammon's crash.

On the other hand, she asked herself, what choice did she really have? Sighing loudly, she stepped back from the door to let him in. She was still an employee of Southeast Airlines, after all, and when it came to an investigation, the NTSB might as well be the FBI. She looked around for signs of her emotional state that could quickly be discarded, cluttered clues that she was at her rope's end. "You might have called first," she said, gathering a pile of wadded Kleenex from the coffee table and rushing into the kitchen to throw it away.

"I tried," he said. "The phone was off the hook."

Erin swung around, saw him standing in the kitchen doorway. His green eyes probed mercilessly, seeing far too many things that she wasn't prepared to reveal. Guiltily, she glanced at the china hutch, where the phone was still buried. "I guess I forgot to hang it up last night."

"No problem," he said. There was an almost amused twinkle in his eyes, but beneath that twinkle lay something else. Something like . . . concern. "I leave mine lying around all the time. Just forget to hang it up."

"All right." She stared coldly at him, resentful of the way he was trying to corner her about something that was none of his business. "I took it off the hook on purpose. I was in a bad mood." Impertinently, she held out her wrists. "Go ahead. Cuff me and haul me in."

The deep laughter that erupted from his throat took her by surprise, and her anger began to diminish by degrees. For the first time she noticed the strong texture of his short black hair, the thick lines of his brows, and the startling contrast of those laughing, smoky emerald eyes. The corners of her rigid mouth softened, and she smiled when he rubbed his mouth, as if the gesture could wipe away his condemning grin.

"Sorry," he said, his laughter dying. "I don't mean to drill you. If you want to leave the phone off the hook, it's your prerogative."

"I appreciate that," she said dryly.

"I'm also sorry I woke you," he added.

She looked down at her wrinkled sweatshirt, at the jeans she'd slept in. Self-consciously, she raised a hand to her tangled hair. "I . . . I wasn't asleep. I had just gotten up."

"Had you?" he asked skeptically. The look of amusement vanished from his eyes, replaced by that annoying look of concern. Erin wished that just once in the past two weeks she could have looked in someone's eyes and not seen concern. "Well, whatever . . . I realize I haven't come at the best time. But I really need to talk to you before I can go on with my report."

Erin turned to the coffeepot, groped for the can of grains, and mechanically began filling the percolator. "I don't know why you have to talk to me. I wasn't there."

Addison shifted his weight to one hip and leaned on the counter. Subtly, the scent of woodsy after-shave drifted to her senses. "No, you weren't there, but you were usually

31

Hammon's copilot, and, I hear, his closest friend at the airline. I need a lot of background on him if I'm going to come to a fair conclusion about the crash. You can give it to me."

His words served as sparks to ignite her tinder-dry emotions, and Erin swiveled and glared at him across the small kitchen. "Fair conclusion? Are you kidding me? You just want more evidence to nail him. Why not? He isn't here to defend himself, is he? You can say just about anything you want to about him."

"Erin, I'm looking for accurate —"

"You can call me Miss Russell."

"I got your name from your file," he said, all warmth gone from his voice. He quietly assumed an authoritative tone. "And I'll call you whatever you like, *Miss* Russell. As for your hysterical accusation, I am not trying to 'nail' anyone. I'm trying to do my job and make certain that the cause of that crash is known so that it doesn't happen again."

Silence continued between them for a series of eternities as the smell of perking coffee intruded on vexed senses. Finally, Erin turned back to it, poured two cups, then grudgingly added the cream and sugar he politely requested. A frown cut deep into her forehead as she handed him a mug, then set a spoon in her own and stirred the dark liquid. "I don't . . . I don't want to talk about Mick with you. Or the crash. Or anything else."

Addison sipped the coffee and leveled those poignant eyes on her again. "You have to," he said quietly. "If you don't, I'll have you subpoenaed, and you'll have to talk about it in front of a board of my superiors. Believe me, you don't want to do that."

She gulped her coffee, scalding her tongue. Frustrated, she set it back down too hard. It sloshed onto the counter, but she scarcely noticed, for she was staring at Addison with scathing eyes. "Well, do you mind if I brush my teeth first? Change clothes? I didn't expect to wake up to an interrogation this morning."

"I'll wait," he said, leaning back against the counter. "Take your time."

Seething, Erin pushed past him and slammed the door as she went into her bedroom.

Addison braced himself for a moment, waiting for another slam or the crash of a glass hurling against the wall, but none came. When he was confident that she wasn't violent, he wandered out of the kitchen to the living room. Quietly, he regarded the coffee table. Moments before she had cleared it of those wadded Kleenex. That, in itself, disturbed him. He lowered himself to the couch and felt that it was warm. And she'd had on those rumpled jeans and sweatshirt that looked as if they'd served their time. The mottled patches on her skin when she'd come to the door told him he'd awakened her. Had she been sleeping here in her clothes after falling asleep crying?

The thought gave birth to an uncomfortable ache inside him. From what he'd seen of her already, she was teetering on the edge. Her display in Redlo's office last night had been evidence enough. She couldn't fly since the crash, and now she couldn't sleep in her bed. So much fear in such a small package. What was she afraid of?

Even as he asked the question, he knew the answer — not in words really, but in his gut where memories came in pangs instead of images. Only once had he come so close to being in the same state Erin was in today. Once . . . but that was four years ago. How clearly he remembered sleeping on the bedspread of his bed, fully clothed, sometimes without even shedding his shoes. Or the even worse nights, the ones when he dropped off to sleep in the recliner, unable to face the lonely act of preparing for sleep by walking into the bedroom, knowing he'd awaken to a lonely day. His grief over his wife's death had made mere life an ordeal. It had taken months for him to get his life back to normal, even after his father-in-law had talked him into moving from his office job at the NTSB to the position of field investigator, to channel that grief into something worthwhile. But still, late at night when he was all alone, that pain came back to him.

Was Erin Russell experiencing that now? Had she been in love with Mick Hammon, even though he was married and at least twenty years older than she? The thought tightened his stomach inexplicably. Why did that idea bother him? He didn't know this woman, and he hadn't known the man. What did he care if they'd had an affair? Besides, he told himself, it probably wasn't true. Maybe it was simply — as her boss had said — the grief and denial over the death of a very close friend.

Whatever the cause of her distress, he thought, he would go easy on her. She was near the breaking point, but he could see the strength in her eyes. It was the same type of strength that had brought him through his wife's death. He admired anyone with that kind of soul-deep, there-when-it-counted substance.

He looked around the room, at the trinkets that she and her roommates had no doubt collected during their travels. On the walls were framed and matted landscape scenes with Bible verses inscribed beneath them. In a prominent place just inside the door was Philippians 4:13 stitched in needlepoint. "I can do everything through him who gives me strength." Did her strength originate where his did? Or did that picture belong to her roommate?

The door opened, and Erin stepped back out. Her hair was brushed in soft waves, and she had changed clothes. A baggy pair of slacks hung from her trim figure, gathered at her small waist where a white blouse was tucked inside. Even without makeup she looked lovely. It had been a long time since he'd seen the just-awake freshness of a woman. Much too long.

Still, her eyes were tired, wary, and he knew she would never let her defenses down easily. He would have to work at that.

"All right," she said, standing before him, arms shielding her stomach. "Interrogate me. I'm ready."

Addison smiled like a man who'd been misunderstood. "This is not an interrogation, Erin —" He caught himself and held up his hand to stem her unspoken protest. "Excuse me. I meant Miss Russell. It's an investigation. And I'm afraid it's going to take a long time. I hope I can count on your cooperation."

"I'll do the best I can," she said. "But let me warn you. If I start feeling that you're trying to pin this crash on my friend, who was the best pilot I've ever flown with in my life, you *will* have to subpoena me, Mr. Lowe."

"I'm just after the truth," he said.

"So am I," she replied. "No one wants the truth more than I do. No one. But the crash wasn't Mick's fault."

"You've made yourself clear," he said quietly. "Now, I suggest we go someplace nice for breakfast. You obviously need to eat, and it wouldn't hurt me, either. We can continue this there."

"Fine," Erin said without enthusiasm. Grabbing her purse, she led him brusquely out of her house.

The moment they were seated in the Crown Room restaurant at the airport, Addison wondered if his wisdom in choosing it had failed him. While she hadn't objected to coming here, he could see how self-conscious she was around so many who knew

37

her. How quickly had word of her freeze in the cockpit gotten around last night? Were they all whispering about her state of mind, laying wagers as to when — or if — she would overcome her fear? He hoped not.

Addison watched her pick at her eggs Benedict. Her gaze moved from her breakfast to the window to the runway and far beyond to the place where the wreckage had lain for days while the NTSB team had gathered pieces of debris for various types of analysis. There was fear in her eyes each time a plane landed, but what she felt was more complex. He could see that she experienced a deep yearning, almost an envy for the ones that launched into flight. She wanted to fly, but couldn't. She wanted to say good-bye to Mick Hammon, but didn't know how.

Addison tried to give her time to eat before he began his questioning. He had mistakenly believed that bringing her to her own turf, the airport, might make her loosen up. Now he wondered if he should suggest some other, more neutral place, some place that would be a comfort to her rather than a distraction.

Her expression changed, as if she was beginning to puzzle something out.

"What is it?" he asked, his attention fully captured.

She hesitated for a moment, struggling with her thought. "You have the tapes," she said finally. "The cockpit tapes of the crash."

He nodded and sipped his coffee. "They're part of my investigation."

"I want to hear them," she said, too quickly.

Addison sighed and set down his cup. How many times had he heard that same request since he'd come here? The phone calls came at all hours of the day and night — mostly from the media. "The cockpit voice recorder was damaged in the crash. I've sent it home to Washington to be repaired. We have experts who can salvage damaged tapes. But even when I get it back, I can't release it," he said. "Not until I've filed my report."

"Yes, you can," she argued. "I've seen it done over and over."

"Not when *I'm* conducting an investigation, you haven't."

She sat rigid, trying to look composed. "Mr. Lowe, whenever there's a crash that interests the public, the cockpit tapes are splashed all over television. Look at the crash on the Potomac a few years ago . . . even the space shuttle explosion. Why can you release them to the media and not to someone like me?"

Addison was calm, unperturbed. "Have you heard this tape on the news?"

"No, but . . ."

"That's because I don't work that way."

She leaned toward him across the table, her face paling with the argument, but her gaze piercing him. "Then let me just hear an excerpt when you get it back. Just the few minutes before the crash."

"Absolutely not."

She leaned back in her chair, her golden eyes searching him in frustration. "Why not? In every other case —"

"Not the ones I handle," he repeated firmly. The matter was non-negotiable. He looked out the window, frowned at the orchestrated order on the runway, and thought for a moment of how much could go wrong out there. The burden of his job was great, and he handled it the best way he could, the most ethical way he knew. He brought his gaze back to her. "Look, you said yourself that you want the truth in this case. You want your friend to be treated fairly. So do I. I don't happen to subscribe to the idea that the last few moments of a man's life is any of the public's business. It's spectacle, it's great news, and the media loves to exploit that kind of thing, speculate on what happened, pin blame on somebody. But I won't allow it. I'm after the truth, and I won't let some half-baked dramatization bring up the network ratings."

The wary look she'd worn all morning diminished a degree, and a sparkle of something — surprise? respect? — shone in her eyes. "All right," she whispered after a moment. "I suppose you're right about the media. But I was his copilot. I would have been in that airplane if I hadn't had that car accident. I *need* to know what went wrong."

Addison leaned back in his chair, wishing she hadn't used just those words. Hadn't he used them himself, just four years ago?

I need to know what went wrong.

It won't change things, Addison. You've got to let go of her.

For my peace of mind, man. Don't you understand? My wife was on that plane!

He raised his eyes to the woman across the table from him, the woman with pain and grief in her eyes, the woman embracing her fear like it was her dead friend. And he understood. "I know what you're going through," he said softly. "But I can't share the tape with anybody until I've finished the investigation. I've heard a few pieces. There are too many ambiguities, too many places where the wrong conclusion can be drawn. And while I haven't heard the end of the

41

tape, I feel pretty sure that those last few seconds were not something that can give you peace of mind."

Tears filled her eyes, and she looked out the window again, unseeing. He knew what she was thinking. She didn't even have to say it.

I never said good-bye. He'd thought the same thing himself, so many times. But even worse than that was the recurring thought that had hit him at the most innocent of times those first few weeks. *I should have been there.* Somehow, in sharing those last few moments with Mick through the tape, she thought she could live them with him. But she couldn't die with him.

"Before we start," he said quietly, "I feel I should ask you a very personal question. It's none of my business, I know, but I think it might have some bearing on how I look at Mick Hammon."

"What?" The question came out flattened with pain.

"Were you in love with him?"

The reaction that passed over her face startled him, for it was quite the opposite from what he expected. It wasn't defensiveness or guilt or sadness or confession. It was pure, unadulterated fury.

"How dare you?" she hissed. Then,

snatching her purse, she got up and stalked out of the restaurant as fast as she could move.

Stunned, Addison glanced around for the waitress, then threw down a twenty and darted after Erin with his clipboard clutched in his hand.

The airport corridors were crowded with people scurrying in various directions. In the confusion it took a moment for him to find her. She was running away from him against the flow of people. He broke into a trot, dodging and bumping people as he went.

At last, he caught up with her. "Erin," he shouted breathlessly, grabbing her arm and turning her around to face him.

"Let go of me!" She jerked her arm free and backed away. "I'm not going to answer any more of your stupid questions. Subpoena me, sue me, do what you have to do. But I won't sit there with a man who can't understand the grief of a friend over a friend without drawing smutty little conclusions."

Addison felt as if he'd thrown sand in a baby's eyes. His thick brows arched with apology. "I'm sorry," he said, dropping his hand helplessly to his side. "It's just that I don't know you, and I didn't know him. I'm trying to get a grasp of this situation, and all I have to draw on are my own impressions. You seem so shaken by his death, I thought —"

"You thought wrong!" Erin glanced around her, at the people shuffling past, oblivious to the scene, then glared back at him. "Mick was a family man, and he loved his wife. She doesn't deserve that kind of sleazy speculation, and neither did he. And if that's the kind of fairness you plan to give him in this report of yours, then forgive me if I don't have a lot of faith in it!"

"I made a mistake," he admitted loudly. "I'm sorry."

"Have you ever had a friend, Mr. Lowe? A real friend? One who was there when you had problems, one who gave you advice that you rarely listened to and always discovered was good after it was too late, one who encouraged you and helped you and believed in you? That's the kind of friend Mick was to me!" She lowered her voice, her lips quivering in pain. "I miss him. But he was not my lover!"

"I believe you," he said, suddenly jealous that Mick Hammon, whatever kind of man he was, could have had a friend as devoted and as caring as the woman standing before him. He didn't answer the question she had

44

flung at him, about his ever having had a friend like that. But deep in his empty soul, he knew he hadn't. "I was out of line," he whispered, one hand roughing up his hair. "I'm sorry. Really. Can't you accept that and start over? If for no other reason than just to make sure I don't come to any more inane conclusions? Just to keep me on track?"

"I'm not sure I can do that, Mr. Lowe."

He threw up his hands. "*Please* call me Addison. I can't stand this Mr. Lowe stuff."

Erin stood still and didn't call him anything.

"Can we try again? Please?"

She turned away from him for a moment. Sighing deeply, she said, "If you'll get me out of this airport. Just take me someplace else, and I'll . . . I'll try. I've just got to get out of here."

"All right," he said, quenching the fierce instinct to comfort her. "This way." He led her to the nearest exit.

The breeze outside lifted her hair, releasing the feminine fragrance of violets. He swallowed and hoped the feelings she'd stirred weren't apparent in his voice. "Where would you like to go?" he asked, his heartbeat still pounding in his ears. "Back to your house? Another restaurant? Where?"

She thought for a moment, then looked up at him, a spark of frantic longing in her eyes. "The lake," she said. "I want to go to the lake."

CHAPTER THREE

The smell of lake water and wind assaulted Erin's senses. She stood on the bank of Lake Bisteneau, just outside of Shreveport. Her arms engaged in a self-embrace as the wind rippled across the surface of the water. The lake, for heaven's sake. She hadn't been here all year, even though she lived less than thirty minutes away. Why had she thought of it today?

The answer was clear. The wind sweeping across the water tasted of freedom. There were no engines rumbling beneath her, no places to fall, no memories from which to hide. The water was as close to the sky as she could be without going there. It was as close to peace as she could find.

The warm wind whipped her rich hair wildly around her face, and she squinted. If only this man weren't who he was, she thought. If only Addison Lowe were someone who could grab her hand and take her running along the shore, make her forget instead of demanding that she remember. If only she could laugh with him, skip a few stones, take a boat ride . . .

Addison stood quietly beside her as she breathed in the peace the way an asthmatic breathes in oxygen. He hadn't uttered a word. It seemed that he was waiting, compassionately biding his time until she gave him the go-ahead. Erin turned to him and looked up into eyes more sensitive than she wanted them to be, softer than she would have imagined.

"I love the water," he said, his gentle tone lightening the mood, comforting her. "I lived about a mile from the beach when I was growing up. I had a little sailboat, and I must have spent hours a day fighting the wind and the waves. All my life I've planned to go back, find a little seaside house with big windows that have an Atlantic view. Just never have."

Erin looked out over the water. A speedboat arched past them, causing the water in its wake to thrash against the shore. "I hardly ever come here. I'm always so busy. But I should come more. It's peaceful."

"Is that why you started flying, Erin? For peace?"

Her eyes gravitated toward the sky, and a tentative stillness seeped into their golden depths. "Maybe. The first time I went up it was in a little single engine plane that a boy I was dating had rented. He had just gotten his license, and I had to sneak out to the airport because my mother absolutely forbade me to fly with him." Erin laughed softly and glanced down at the sand. "When I saw the clouds below me and the ant-sized people and the cars inching along, I remember thinking that that was where I wanted to be. Up above it all, soaring free and fast, like a seagull."

Addison's smile was one of genuine pleasure. "How did you talk your mother into letting you take lessons?"

"I didn't tell her," she said, a mischievous grin pulling at the corners of her mouth. "My father paid for them and swore me to secrecy. For years, she thought aviation was a science elective in college and that everyone who graduates from LSU has to learn how to fly. She finally figured out that I wasn't going after a master's in art when I went to Emery Riddle to train to be a commercial pilot."

Her lilting laughter joined his on the wind, then quickly died. Erin dropped her gaze, reminding herself why they had come here . . . reminding herself that it was no time to drop her defenses. "I'm glad she wasn't alive to hear about the crash. Thinking I was on it would have killed her." Silence lay between them, heavy, dark. "Go ahead," she said with false bravado. "Ask me your questions. What do you want to know?"

Addison looked at her for a moment, as if assessing the resolution in her face, or measuring the strength in her features. He didn't try to change her mood, she realized, and that endeared him somewhat to her. "Let's sit down," he suggested.

Obediently, Erin dropped onto the grass with no regard for her clothes. He lowered himself next to her, dropped his clipboard on the grass, and set his wrists on his bent knees. "Erin, when was the last time you saw Mick before the crash?"

The question demanded a direct memory, one she had tried to avoid for two weeks. She forced herself to answer. "The day before, I guess. I took his son to a wrestling match."

"A *what?*"

His amused tone made her smile again. "A wrestling match. Hulk Hogan, The Undertaker, the works. What's so funny about that?"

Addison chuckled again. "I'm sorry. I just find it hard to imagine you at a wrestling match. Did you like it?"

"Of course I liked it," she said. "It's very entertaining. I'd elaborate, but I don't really think we came here to talk about wrestling."

"No." Addison seemed to regroup his thoughts, and his smile faded. "Okay, so you took his son to this match. Did he come, too?"

"No. He and Maureen stayed home. It was their anniversary. Twenty-seven years." Erin looked out over the water, remembering the candlelit table and the polished silver and the Cornish game hen Maureen had roasted for the occasion.

"What about when you brought him back? Did you stay?"

"Only a few minutes."

"You said it was his anniversary. Had he consumed any alcohol that night?" Addison asked, picking up his clipboard and making a notation.

"That was at least twenty hours before the flight."

Addison began writing furiously, which vexed her further. "Did he or did he not drink that night?"

"Maybe a glass of champagne," she admitted defensively.

"One glass?"

That smothering feeling closed over her again, and Erin felt her defenses erecting around her. "I don't know how many glasses. I told you I was only there about ten minutes. He wasn't normally a drinker . . ."

Addison propped his wrist on a knee and regarded Erin intently. "Erin, this is very important. Do you think he had had any to drink before you got there? Would he be inclined to drink after you left?"

"I said Mick was not a drinker!" she snapped. "He did not get drunk that night, and if he drank a toast with his wife, it couldn't possibly have had any bearing on his performance the following night."

Addison was too busy making notes to argue with her. "His anniversary," he mumbled absently. "Then he and his wife were probably up pretty late that night."

"That is none of your business," she blurted out, astonished. "What difference does that make to your investigation?"

"How much alcohol he consumed and how much sleep he got has a bearing on his fatigue the night of the crash. It's policy to ask those questions."

"Then your 'policy' stinks. That flight didn't leave until 7:00 P.M. He could have slept late or taken a nap."

"Did he?"

"How would I know?" she shouted, rising to her feet. "Didn't you ask his wife?"

Addison's silence spoke volumes; his pencil stilled. "I haven't spoken to her yet. I was hoping to put that off until last."

Erin studied the man still sitting in the grass, the hard breeze scampering through his black hair. Was it sensitivity that had kept him from Mick's family, or guilt? Did he want to avoid drilling them or avoid having them drill him? Was it compassion or cowardice? "Is that 'policy,' too?" she asked.

"What? Interviewing the family, or putting it off?"

"Either."

"Unfortunately, it is policy to interview the family," he admitted. "One that I'm not fond of. I always put it off until I have enough facts so that I don't have to drill them on everything." He looked down at his notes again, dismissing the subject.

"Did you speak to him at all the day of the crash?"

Still standing, Erin closed her eyes. The sound of the wind across the water calmed her anger a degree, and she tried to remember, despite a protectiveness that urged her not to. "Yes. He called me that morning about our schedule. He wanted to trip-trade one of our flights the next week — you know, drop one of our flights and replace it for another at a different time — and he wanted to make sure it was okay with me. You see, we always buddy-bid for our flights. That way we could always fly together instead of getting split up. Some pilots fly with a different person each month, but we always stayed together." That wasn't the question, she knew, and yet voicing those tame memories aloud seemed to make the more painful ones less forbidding.

"What time was the call?" Addison asked.

"I don't know. Late morning. Around eleven maybe."

He paused as he wrote, assembling the facts on a yellow sheet of paper. Finally, he studied her again. "Tell me about your accident," he said.

Erin shrugged, but a look of pain — or guilt — returned to her eyes. She dropped to her knees, then sat back on her heels. She tore out a blade of grass and folded it into tiny sections. "It was nothing, really. A fender bender on the way to the airport. It was raining that night, and I slammed on the brakes, and my car slid. I hit my head, so they wouldn't let me fly."

"Concussion?"

"Just a slight one." Erin rubbed her head, the spot where the bruise had stopped being tender over a week ago. "I tried to talk them out of grounding me, but Frank insisted. He replaced me." She pulled a deep breath and looked him directly in the eye. "You know, I was supposed to fly that night. We alternated, Mick and I. I would fly one leg of the trip, he'd fly the next. If I'd been there, I would have been flying instead of him."

The concerned frown between his brows bespoke genuine concern. "You were lucky to have had that accident," he said.

Erin regarded him blankly, as though the word *lucky* was beyond comprehension. Had it been luck? Not for a moment since Mick's death had she felt a sense of relief that it hadn't been her. Instead, she felt as if she'd left something unfinished. There was a hole someplace where she should have been, and it didn't feel right not filling it.

"You flew with Hammon for five years," Addison said, as she looked out over the water with vacant eyes. "In that time, did you ever see his performance under stress? Any emergency situations or problems in the cockpit?"

A hard, protective glaze drained all emotion from her expression. "You have his records. Read them."

"Everything in his career won't appear on those records. I'm looking for other things. Things that may not have been reported. Things that maybe only you would know about."

Erin shook her head balefully, and her barely audible laugh held more anger than mirth. "If you're expecting me to provide you with smutty details about Mick's past mistakes, then you've got a big surprise ahead of you."

"I don't want smutty details. I want facts. If you don't answer me, you'll have to answer —"

"I know, I know. A board of your superiors. But you know as well as I do that I'm not going to help anyone — no matter how powerful — nail my friend. If you or your superiors want to know about Mick's past performance, then read his records."

"Why are you so defensive about him?"

She looked up at him, her eyes alive again. "Because I know his family. I knew him. And I know how easy it would be for you to take some past foul-up in-flight and his reaction to it, and turn the information into so-called indisputable evidence to support whatever you want it to."

Addison stared at her for a moment, as if amazed at her suspicious reasoning. Erin felt his eyes probing deeply into her, seeing things she wanted buried. "Then there *were* incidents?" he asked.

"You're a smart man, Mr. Lowe. You must know that occasionally things go wrong. Weather, instrument failures, communication problems, illnesses on board.

Mick handled those things with as much finesse as you could ever imagine. And you won't get more than that from me."

"Erin, I'm not trying to 'nail' him. I'm simply trying to determine if there's anything to indicate that he could have functioned in a real emergency. Your information could have a positive effect on the investigation. Why do you assume I'm looking for something negative?"

"It will have whatever effect you want it to," she said, clipping each word. "The man was an ex-fighter pilot in the Air Force. He flew in Vietnam. He was a colonel when he retired from the service. That fact alone should prove that he could function under stress."

Addison set his clipboard down and rubbed his forehead. "All right. Here's an easy one. Tell me about Mick's temperament. His personality. Will you answer that?"

A soft smile crept across her lips. "Yes, I'll answer that. He was funny. Always laughing, cracking corny jokes. He said he liked flying with me because I always appreciated the punch line."

Addison smiled weakly.

Erin stared into the distance. "Mick was the kind of person that you could turn to, you know? With a secret or a dream or just an observation. He never made fun of me. And he loved to fly. More than just about anything." She looked at Addison, a thought occurring to her for the first time. "Are you a pilot, Mr. Lowe?"

"Yes," he said. "I flew for an airline for six years before I came to work for the NTSB ten years ago."

"Then you know what I mean."

There was awe in the tone of her voice, and he heard the desire just behind the fear. "I know that feeling," he said. "But I wonder if you still do."

"Of course I do." She tore out another blade of grass, vaguely aware that he watched her tear it into pieces.

He lowered his voice cautiously. "Then what was that all about last night in Redlo's office? You tried to resign. Said you never wanted to fly again."

Erin felt her lungs constricting again, but common sense told her not to address the subject with total frankness. Addison might not be as understanding as Frank was. And what if Frank was right and she could work through her fear . . . overcome it somehow? As much as she wanted to escape flying again, she didn't want to throw away the option. "I was upset," she said. "I'm having a little trouble getting my confidence back. I keep thinking of the crash." She dropped the blades of grass and dusted off her hands. "It's the uncertainty that's driving me crazy. The not knowing what went wrong. If I just knew. If I could figure it out, I feel like I could get a grip on it."

Addison looked down at her hands. She was shaking. "Are you going to get help?" His question was asked so quietly that she almost didn't hear over the sound of the water.

"You mean by seeing a psychologist?" she asked, sounding vulnerable for only a moment before her voice took on a hard edge. "I plan to, even though I'm not sure it'll do any good. I know where my fears come from, and they're well-founded. I can really work through this on my own."

"Can you? It seems pretty serious to me."

"But then, you don't know me that well."

"True."

They stared at each other in truce for a moment, each measuring the other's ability: hers to confront her ghosts, his to know the truth when he heard it.

He rubbed at the lines webbing out from his eyes, apparently struggling with the words he wanted to say. "What if I told you that I'd had someone close to me who was killed in a plane crash and that I'd suffered similar anxieties? That I feel so strongly about my job because of my own loss? If I told you that, would you stop looking at me like the enemy and see that I really am on your side?"

Erin appraised him from behind her self-erected barriers, testing his expression for a sign of authenticity. It was there, in the softness of his eyes. "How long ago?" she asked quietly.

"Four years, to be exact," he said, and the pain that flitted through his eyes testified on a deeper level that he, indeed, knew what she suffered. "And I'll tell you something. You don't ever forget. Ever."

Erin dropped her gaze back to the grass. "Does the fear go away?" she asked quietly.

"Yes," he whispered. "It did for me, but it took a lot of faith and relying on God. The Bible says, 'Perfect love drives out fear.' "

"First John 4:18," Erin said softly. "I've been using that verse like a mantra."

"You're a Christian?" he asked.

"Yes," she said. "Not that I've done much relying on God lately. I guess I've been wallowing in all the emotions. It's hard to pray when you're grieving."

"I know. That's when you need others to pray for you."

"I have that. My roommates are in close touch with the Lord."

"Good. Then give it some time, Erin. God will drive out the fear."

Erin looked at the sky, breathed a great, deep sigh, then brought her gaze back to his. "I hope so," she whispered. "I really hope so."

CHAPTER FOUR

The ride home was quiet, tense, and Addison rebuked himself for not being able to make her smile. She was traveling through her own personal vortex, and it was his job to make sure she dwelt there until he'd gotten the answers he needed. She was right. NTSB policy stank. The whole thing stank, he admitted, and not for the first time. Why hadn't he met her under different circumstances where he could turn on the charm and ask her to dinner? Why did this pall of death and despair have to hang over them now?

He glanced over at her, leaning against the car door, and saw that her cheeks were colored pale pink from the sun. *What do you think about when life is normal?* he wanted to ask. *Who do you see? Where do you go?*

But the defensiveness in her hunched posture told him he would get nowhere with her. She saw him as the enemy, and for all practical purposes, he probably was. He leaned forward and flicked on the radio, set the dial to a station with a relaxing tune, and sat back, hoping to see the tension drain out of her. But it didn't seem to affect her at all.

She raised her elbow to the window and gazed off into the distance. The song on the radio finished, and the local news came on. He reached for the dial to turn to another station, find another song that might do a better job of soothing both their tensions, but stopped when he heard the name "Mick Hammon" spoken by a deep-voiced announcer.

Immediately, Erin perked up and turned her full attention to the radio.

". . . Officials are expected to complete the flight report soon, citing evidence of pilot error in the crash that killed 151 people . . ."

Erin's eyes flashed accusingly to Addison's, and he shook his head. "They're grasping, Erin. I didn't tell them that. I wouldn't tell them anything, so they're making things up."

Her lips tightened into a thin line, and he knew the sting of her angry eyes again. "You can stop it. You can tell them it *wasn't* pilot error and that the cause is still undetermined. It is, isn't it? Because in this country, a man is innocent until proven guilty."

Addison pulled into her driveway, cut off the engine, and laid his head back on his seat. "Erin, this isn't a question of guilt or innocence. Even if it was Hammon's fault, no one's condemning him. It's a question of human error. Human beings make mistakes. That's no crime."

"Yeah? Well, tell that to the kids at Jason Hammon's school . . . the ones who are calling his father a killer and spreading malicious rumors about how he was addicted to drugs and how he was hallucinating when he drove the plane into the ground. Tell them about human error and see if it stops the rumors or gives Jason any peace."

"Drugs? No one ever said he was on drugs!"

"No one has to say anything for a rumor to start. All they have to know is that it was pilot error, and imaginations go into full gear manufacturing reasons."

"I can't do anything about the cruelty of kids, Erin. You can't blame me for that."

"Kids?" Erin laughed caustically and leaned closer to make her point. "It isn't just kids. It's adults, too. If you'd spoken to Maureen, you might know that she's been getting calls from anonymous people who say they're family members of those who died in the crash. They're calling her husband a murderer and saying that he killed people they love. And why? Because of your belief that it was pilot error. Think about it. What does that mean? That he was drunk? That he fell asleep? That he forgot how to fly? If you say it was pilot error, then for every hundred people out there you'll find a hundred different, ready-made reasons. None of them will be accurate, and none of them will be kind. Does that matter to you at all, Mr. Lowe?"

He looked out the window, feeling his own defenses rising up. "Of course it matters. I'm sorry for Mrs. Hammon, and I'm especially sorry for her son. But where does that leave me? I still have to find the truth, and I still have to report it. If I altered my report, a lot more people than those two could be hurt. Another pilot in similar circumstances could make the same mistake, and another crash could occur. I'd have to live with that. I'd sure rather live with telling the truth and hurting two people, than shirk my job and hurt hundreds more."

Disbelief colored Erin's eyes. "It's black or white to you, isn't it?"

"No," he said, turning his head back to her again. "There are grays, too. But you aren't too anxious to help me find those gray areas, the ones that could change my mind. Until you're willing to give me honest answers about his past performance, you have to accept a little of the blame for the speculation."

Erin's face stung, and she swung open the

car door. "I think we've said enough for one day, Mr. Lowe. You'll understand if I don't invite you in."

Addison only watched, embracing his own anger, as she slammed the car door and bolted up the steps to her front door.

Tears charged to Erin's eyes when she was safely inside the house. Rage choked her, and a whirlwind of guilt and regret blew through her heart. When would this be over?

She stumbled to the couch, collapsed onto it, and covered her hot face with her hands. Addison was right. Some of the responsibility *was* hers. But how could she tell him everything, only to allow him to come to the wrong stupid conclusions?

She wiped her face and tried to think rationally. Would anything she said really make him draw negative conclusions about Mick?

She thought of the time their radar had indicated another flight was coming toward them, although the tower couldn't locate it. The controller had ordered him to stay on his flight path, but Mick had defied him. He had avoided a midair collision with a private jet by bucking orders. The episode hadn't gone on the record simply because the controller didn't want to call attention to his own mistake.

There were countless other incidents, some on record, some not. Missed approaches in bad weather, when minimum visibility requirements just weren't good enough. Safety precautions that bordered on the rebellious. And she was certain Addison had read about Mick's stubbornness the time he'd practically thrown two Federal Aviation Administration inspectors off the plane when they'd tried to ground his flight because one attendant hadn't posted the latest pay incentive update in her manual. Mick had a fiery temper, that was no secret, and he operated more on his instincts than from any flight manual. That alone could indict him. But he was the best pilot she'd ever flown with, and she would have trusted him with her life.

She wouldn't take the chance of delving into each one of those situations with Addison, only to allow him to misinterpret them, or to overlook the truth because Mick's character traits made him seem unreliable.

She went to the bathroom and splashed cold water on her face, hoping it could snap her out of this state she was in. But even as the cold drops of water ran down her face, she felt her life falling apart.

The telephone rang, the harsh sound cutting through the quiet and lacerating Erin's nerves. She ignored it for the moment and brought a towel to her face, wiping away the water. Pale gold eyes sought out their twin reflections, searching for the peace that would settle the turmoil in her heart. The phone kept ringing until the answering machine picked it up.

"Erin?" The familiar voice broke into Erin's gloomy thoughts. "This is Lois. Just calling to see how you're doing . . ."

Erin ran to her bedroom and picked up the receiver. "Hello?"

"Erin?" Lois asked again, hesitation and worry packed into the single word.

Erin sighed in relief. She needed Lois now, and her presence by phone was better than the chilling silence that surrounded her in the big house. "Hi."

"Are you okay?"

"Fine," Erin lied. "Where are you?"

"Pittsburgh. I had a couple of hours between flights. I've been worried about you, Erin."

Erin pulled her feet onto the bed and leaned back on the headboard, closing her eyes. The warmth of having someone care filled her. "So you decided to check on your lunatic friend to see if she's still holding herself together?"

"Okay," Lois said, undaunted. "If that's how you want to look at it. But I could tell you were pretty upset last night, and when you're upset, I'm upset."

Erin smiled sadly. Either Madeline or Lois would easily take her burden if they could, even share a few tears. But Erin couldn't transfer the weight. "I know, Lois. But I'll get through this, really. You'd be proud of me. I even went out for breakfast this morning and drove over to the lake." There, she thought. That should make Lois feel better.

"You did?" Lois asked, a hint of surprise in her voice. "Really?"

"Yes, I just got back, and —"

"Wait a minute," Lois cut in. "Are you being straight with me? I know you, Erin. You were upset. I'm having trouble picturing you doing either of those things alone, unless you were planning to throw yourself over a bridge or choke on your eggs, and frankly, you aren't the suicidal type."

Erin sighed and dropped her face in her hand. What was the point of skirting the truth when she wanted more than anything to talk about it? "All right," she whispered. "I didn't go because I wanted to, and I didn't go alone. I was with the NTSB investigator who's trying to pin the crash on Mick. He's trying to get me to help him do it, and he threatened to subpoena me if I didn't talk to him."

"So you did?"

"I talked to him, but I drew the line on certain things. He might still have me subpoenaed."

"Oh, Erin . . ." Lois's voice trailed off in sympathetic despair. "It just keeps getting worse and worse, doesn't it?"

"Seems to." Erin clutched the phone harder with her cold hand. "I'm at rock bottom."

A moment of silence lingered between them before Lois spoke again. "Do you remember when we were in training," she asked, "and that Bozo . . . Randy or Remus or Rowland . . ."

"Richard." Erin provided the name with a smile, knowing what Lois was leading up to.

"Yeah. Remember when he asked us why two cute little things like us had chosen piloting over stewardessing?"

Genuine amusement battled with Erin's tears. "And you sarcastically told him we chose it to meet guys."

"Only he was too stupid to know I was being sarcastic and made it his duty to

70

'weed' us out. Do you remember how he tried to undermine us at every opportunity, trying to prove that we didn't belong there?"

"Sure I remember. He was especially out to get you."

"To the point of tampering with the instruments in my simulator! I'll never forget the day I crashed repeatedly, never understanding why. The instructors started thinking I was stupid, and before I knew it, I was at the bottom of the class. I thought it was the end of the world. Do you remember what you told me, Erin?"

"That I'd chip in if you wanted to hire a hit man?"

"Besides that."

Erin reflected back to the day she'd found Lois in bed, despondent, ready to concede defeat and throw away her career plans. She recalled the feeling of helplessness she'd had, and the way she'd struggled for the right words to bring Lois back to herself. The words had come of their own accord, the way they often did when a friend was in need, but for the life of her, she couldn't recall them now. "No, what did I say?"

"First you prayed for me, and then you said that when you're on the bottom, there's no place to go but up. And you dragged me out of bed and informed me that if I didn't pull myself together and go back there to face that guy and show him that I could be a better pilot than he ever dreamed, then I didn't deserve to fly for Southeast."

Erin's heart lightened with the memory. "And you did, and he ended up being the one who flunked the program."

"Right," Lois said. "My point is that your advice was sound. You're at the bottom now, Erin, so the only place you can go is up. You'll fly again, when you're ready, and meanwhile, you don't have to let anyone bully you. Not even if he's with the NTSB."

"Sounds simple, doesn't it?" Erin asked. "When all I want to do is crawl under the covers and hide there, just like you tried to do back then."

"Don't hide," Lois told her. "Keep busy. You've got church, and the youth center, and the health club. They can keep your mind off things until I get back. And don't forget, Erin. Lean."

"Lean?"

"Yes. On Christ, remember? You told me back then that I needed to learn how to lean. I've been doing it ever since, but you, friend, need to learn how to practice what you preach."

"Yeah," Erin said, already feeling better. "I know you're right."

"Well, I'd better go. You'll be okay, won't you?"

"Sure," Erin whispered. "Listen, thanks for being there for me."

"Don't thank me," Lois said. "Thank Ma Bell. I'm gonna be praying for you. See you tomorrow."

"Bye." Erin held the phone to her ear for a moment after Lois had hung up, savoring the feeling of connection to someone who understood. Finally, she hung up, letting the abysmal quiet settle over her.

Unwilling to be defeated by despondency again, she pulled two unfinished canvases out from under her bed. She laid them on the four half-gallon cans of bright paint that sat in the corner waiting to be taken to the Christian youth center, where she worked as a volunteer two days a week. Then she went to the closet for the seven-foot-wide roll of paper leaning against the wall. It wasn't the day of the week she usually went to the center, but Lois was right. She needed something to do, something that was removed from death and flying and crashing and questions. She needed to hear the kids there laugh as they painted, needed to dodge the globs of paint flying across the room, needed to see their untamed creativity unfold on the wall murals they painted. Maybe then she'd feel useful instead of alone.

She packed the smaller canvases and paint cans into a box, tucked the larger roll under her arm, and started out to her car, forbidding herself to look toward the sky or at the dent on her fender that had altered her fate . . .

And she forbade herself to think about Addison Lowe.

CHAPTER FIVE

By the time Addison drove home, his anger had settled in the chamber of his heart where other smoldering injustices lay. And there were plenty of them. He was always the bad guy, the one ready to lay blame on someone or some *thing* that had caused a disaster. Always the villain, and he was getting tired of it.

He gathered his papers off the seat of his car and got out, shuffling them into order while he walked to the condominium the NTSB had rented for him. He reached into his pocket for his keys and pulled them out, jabbing one into the lock. But it wasn't locked.

Puzzled, Addison pushed open the door. His bewilderment was quickly resolved when he encountered the older man sitting cross-legged on his couch, smoking a cigarette and reading some of Addison's notes on the recent crash.

"Sid, I didn't know you were coming," he said, a trace of irritation in his tight voice, though he tried to conceal it. "You should have called."

"It was a spur-of-the-moment thing," the older man said, rising to his feet and dusting stray ashes off his gray trousers. "Thought I'd see how things were going."

Addison dropped his keys on the table, set down his things, and tried to control the tension rising to his head. He'd learned years ago that it was better to voice his feelings to Sid, or the man would run right over him. "Father-in-law or not," he said, "you don't have any business walking into my apartment anytime you please."

"I'm not here as your father-in-law," Sid said, stroking his gray mustache with the tip of a callused finger. "I'm here as your boss."

Addison turned back to him, bracing himself for whatever was about to come. The NTSB didn't send his superiors to check on him unless they weren't happy with his job. He'd heard it all before, but the lecture never failed to scathe him. "And what am I getting my hand slapped for this time?"

Sid chuckled under his breath and came toward him, his small build complemented by the silk tie and long-sleeved dress shirt that shouted authority. "Come on now, Addison. Where'd all that hostility come from? Can't we even take a minute to say hello?"

As usual when dealing with his father-in-law/boss, Addison felt his defenses lowering a bit. It was difficult to forget the pain Sid had suffered when his only child, Addison's wife, had been snatched from life before her time. After losing his own wife just years earlier, Sid had been the portrait of loneliness, and following the death of his daughter he had clung to Addison as if he were his last living friend. When the double-edged sword of working with a relative sometimes put him unnecessarily on edge, Addison reminded himself of his dead wife's adoration of the man, and the good relationship he'd had with him during the twelve years of his marriage to Amanda.

He smiled. "You're right. I've just had a trying day, and I guess I expect the worse. It's good to see you, Sid."

The men shook hands, and then, as he often did, Sid pulled him into an awkward male embrace. "Louisiana's treating you well," Sid said in a paternal tone, stepping back. "Looks like you've gotten some sun."

Addison disengaged himself from the embrace and went into the kitchen to search for something to offer his guest. "Yeah, well. We spent a good many days outside sifting through the wreckage. It was a little hard to tell one piece from another at first. Debris was scattered for a mile or so."

"But you've had it all tagged and stored

for at least a week now, am I right?"

Addison felt his defenses rising again. Sid was fishing, leading up to something. Already he could feel his anger pushing to the surface again, bracing itself for the boss-lecture that inevitably followed. He pulled out a pitcher of iced tea and poured Sid a glass. "More or less."

Sid's smile defined the age lines on his forehead and ridges down his jaw, and Addison wasn't fooled. He knew that smile — the kind a cartoon feline offered to a cornered mouse.

"So where'd you get that sunburn?" Sid asked, as if he still made idle conversation. "Looks pretty fresh to me."

"I didn't know I was sunburnt," Addison said, his tone growing less cordial. "I don't usually burn."

"Sure," Sid said. "Right here on your nose, a little across the cheeks. Take a little time off today?"

So that was it. Sid was trying to make a case for his not working hard enough, not getting the facts down as fast as they wanted. "As a matter of fact, no. I was interviewing the captain's first officer. It was difficult for her. The crash was only two weeks ago, and I had to question her on her terms. She wanted to talk at the lake, and since I wanted her cooperation, I obliged her."

Sid took his tea, chuckling in his maddening, friend-foe kind of way. "The job should have been so cushy when I was in the field. Questioning beside a lake. Not bad. Must be why it's taking you so long."

Addison exhaled loudly and went back to the living room. Wearily, he sank down into a chair and regarded the man who had never quite stopped grieving over Amanda's death. She was the one unifying factor between them, but sometimes their mutual love of her wasn't quite enough of a bond. "So is that why you're here, Sid? To badger me about how long the investigation is taking? Because it won't do any good. You know that by now."

Sid pulled the knees of his slacks and sat down, holding the tea on his knee. The condensation formed a wet ring on his pants. "There's been some concern," he began, "that you move too slowly. You know that crash that happened in Omaha two days after this one? It's already wrapped up. That investigator is free to move on to his next assignment. Meanwhile, we keeping waiting . . ."

"That crash didn't have any fatalities," Addison pointed out. "It was different. All they had to do there was question the pilot and passengers. The answers were clear."

"Some believe the answers are clear in this case," Sid said. "Some of your own team members, as a matter of fact."

Addison sprang to his feet, ire rising to color his face. He could tolerate criticism from his superiors, but the disloyalty of his team members was too much to accept. "Are you telling me that some of my team members have been complaining about my diligence in my job?"

Sid chuckled again, waving a hand to stem Addison's anger. "No, no, of course not. Settle down. It's just that it's become our impression that they feel they've come to a conclusion . . ."

"How can you even think that?" Addison asked, appalled. "I haven't even got all the test results back. I haven't even heard the whole tape yet."

"Mere formalities," Sid said, waving the details off with his hand. "In a case where things are so cut-and-dried, those are nothing more than formalities."

Addison couldn't believe they were discussing the same crash. "Cut-and-dried? How can you say that?"

"It was a matter of pilot error, obviously," Sid said.

"And I'm just trying to substantiate that,"

Addison argued. "What do you want from me?"

"We want you to follow procedure. We want you to finish his profile and his seventy-two-hour history, then make an announcement."

"What do you think I've been doing?" Addison shouted. "I spent the whole day doing that, and I have an appointment tonight at the health club to meet with another pilot who seems to have some more of the facts I need."

Sid's feigned pleasantness disappeared. "Don't raise your voice to me, Addison. I'm not above losing my patience with you."

Addison's jaw went rigid, and he clenched his fist and turned his back to the man who had driven him to the edge of fury more than once. Amanda had loved him, he reminded himself again. For that, he at least owed the man his respect.

"We want you to move this along. The press is waiting for an announcement, and the public is holding their breath. The longer you take on this investigation, the worse the airline industry looks. It doesn't take all day to question a first officer who wasn't even on the plane. Maybe if you did it in a more professional environment than the lake, you'd get somewhere a lot faster. Presuming that information is what you want, and not something else!"

Addison caught the innuendo and struggled not to swing at the man. "I don't work the way you did," he said in an explosively calm voice. "I try to make the person I'm questioning comfortable. I try to take into consideration that they're working through their own grief."

"Grief in a health club? Are you going to question the pilot during an aerobics class?"

"Racquetball, as a matter of fact," Addison admitted defiantly. "It works, Sid. If I can meet people on their own terms, they're a lot more willing to cooperate."

Sid set down his glass and crossed his knees. Silently, he shook his head, the way a father does when he can't believe the naiveté in his son.

"What do you guys want?" Addison asked, finally. "Bottom line. Just get to the point."

"We want you to go after the questions where you'll get answers. Go to the family. Question the wife about that seventy-two-hour history. Stop pampering and start drilling. Start at the core, and you'll cut weeks off the investigation. There isn't time to waste with lakes and health clubs. You have a job to do."

Addison crossed his arms rigidly, his compressed lips revealing his distaste. "So, does the NTSB plan to throw in some bright lights to put the subjects under, a few torture devices? That might save a little time, too. Maybe we could *make* those people talk. Show them we mean business."

"Come on, Addison, you know what I'm saying."

Addison leaned forward, waving his finger in the man's face. "And you knew before you came here what my reaction would be. Either I do my job the way that I see best, or you give this assignment to someone else."

Sid lurched up and grabbed Addison's hand. Their eyes locked. "You're walking on thin ice, son. I don't like it."

"Fine," Addison said. "Then let up. Let me do my job. If you can't do that, maybe I don't belong with the NTSB anymore."

"How can you say that?" Sid's question was an astonished whisper. "How *dare* you say that? After your wife — my little girl — died in one of those planes. How dare you act as if your responsibility was a chore? It's a privilege and an obligation! You used to see it that way!"

"I used to see a lot of things differently," Addison confessed. "When you promoted me to this position, I went into it with a fever, ready to change the world. I was angry and driven, just like you were. But that was a year and a half ago, Sid."

"She was your wife! Can you forget that easily?" Sid shouted.

"No, I can't forget!" Addison returned. "But I can stop being ready to convict the world over it. I can stop seeing every crash as a way to get retribution! I can show a little compassion now, and as God is my witness, I'm going to do it."

Electric silence enveloped them as they stood locked in each other's angry gaze.

Finally, Sid set his lips and spoke in a frosty voice. "You have to interview that family sooner or later, whether you like it or not, Addison. I suggest you do it sooner."

"I'll do it when I'm good and ready," Addison said. "But if I had my way, I wouldn't do it at all."

Sid lifted his chin with the sternness of an executioner and started for the door. Addison watched him open it, then linger in the threshold. Slowly Sid turned back, his expression unreadable, as though he might be about to beseech — or to threaten. "Don't push me, son," he finally said. "You're the best field investigator we've got. But if you throw that away, not even I can protect you."

"When I want your protection," Addison said, "I'll ask for it."

The door slammed, echoing through the small apartment, and jolting Addison as a guilty mixture of pain and resentment blended in his heart.

CHAPTER SIX

The youth center contained its usual sounds of young voices striving to rise above the din, music blaring a bit too loudly on contrasting stations of rock and rap, the echo of basketballs bouncing and sinking.

Clint Jessup, who helped run the center, in addition to being youth director at Erin's church, greeted her with an armload of basketballs. "Erin, what are you doing here? I wasn't expecting you today."

"Just had some spare time and thought I'd work on the mural," she said.

She could see from the look on his face that he had heard the rumors. "Wanna talk?" he asked.

She tried to smile. "Not really."

"I did take a few counseling courses at seminary, you know."

Counseling. She remembered her promise to Frank to get counseling, but something — pride? stubbornness? — stopped her. "I'm okay, Clint. Really."

"Well, Sherry's in the art room doing ceramics with the girls," he said, referring to his new wife, Madeline's former roommate.

"If you'd rather talk to her . . ."

"Clint, *please,*" she said. "I'm fine."

"Okay." He reached the supply closet and managed to get the door open, then let the balls fall in. "You know where we are if you need us."

Erin watched him disappear into the gym, then she set her paint cans down in the hall, next to the mural she and the kids had been working on. The project had been her idea a year ago when the center was first built, and the freshly painted walls had soon become covered with obscene graffiti. If the kids wanted to paint the walls, she thought, she'd give them something worthwhile to paint. Maybe they'd take more pride in facilities that bore their signatures.

It had worked. On her days to come here, a crowd of kids — aged eight to eighteen, and from backgrounds as diverse as flavors of candy — waited eagerly in the colorful corridors for her.

But today no one waited, because she wasn't expected. She knelt and unfolded the drop cloths she kept rolled beside the wall. After opening the paint cans, she headed upstairs to the supply closet where she kept all her brushes.

The heavy doors leading to the stairwell creaked as they opened, and she reached inside to flick on the light. The door shut behind her, and she started up the stairs.

"This isn't your day to come."

The young male voice startled her, and she glanced up the staircase, to the tawny-haired boy sitting on the landing between two twisting levels of stairs. His eyes squinted as they adjusted to the light. "Jason? What are you doing here?"

Mick Hammon's son gave a shrug that belied the drawn lines on his nine-year-old face. "Nothin'."

Erin finished the climb to where he sat, his arms hugging his knees. She lowered herself to the step beside him, unconsciously imitating his position. "Why aren't you playing ball with the guys?"

"Not in the mood," Jason said.

"Yeah," Erin whispered. "I know."

They sat quietly for a moment, neither venturing to broach the subject of the crash or the lies that circulated as a result of it or the pain that wouldn't die. Finally, Erin patted his knee, where his Levis had worn to a thin blue-gray. "Feel like painting?"

"I guess," he said.

Erin got to her feet, dusted off her pants, and held out a hand to the boy. Reluctantly, he took it and allowed her to pull him up.

"You're gonna be all right, Jason," she

whispered, holding his gray gaze.

Trust gleamed like the toughest metal in his eyes — eyes that looked much older than nine — but she knew the doubt that plagued him, as it did her. He dropped his focus to his dirty Reeboks, his shoulders rising and falling with a painful sigh. "I'll help you get the brushes," he said.

Jason was quiet as they painted, and he hung conspicuously apart from the ten other kids, who dove into the project at hand. As much as Erin tried to draw him in, he clung to his distance, working with a diligent hand on the section of the mural she had assigned him.

But that distance called attention to him, and some of the other boys — the rougher ones who would have been in street gangs or juvenile delinquent centers if not for the distraction of the youth center — couldn't stand leaving him alone. He had never quite clicked with many of the boys here, but his athletic nature, his creativity, and his friendship with Erin kept him coming anyway. The other boys were from poorer families, mostly fatherless, with little if any supervision from their mothers. Those were the boys who made trouble as easily as withdrawing the switchblades they often carried, the ones who chided and terrorized anyone who didn't fit. Jason was different from them. It was obvious by his behavior, his clothes, his silence . . . He was an open target for anyone who needed one.

Erin's muscles tensed in dread when three of the boys ambled toward Jason. There were looks of suspicious amusement in their hardened eyes, as if they planned to have "some fun" with the boy. She stopped painting and grabbed a rag to wipe her hands, preparing to intervene if it became necessary. She'd worked with these kids long enough to know that defending Jason too soon would humiliate him and make matters much worse than they were. Jason kept his eyes on his painting, never missing a brush stroke.

"Hey, Hammon," one of the boys, who went by the name of T.J., said, strutting toward Jason. The belligerent newcomer's thumbs were lodged in the front pockets of jeans that had been in good shape three or four hand-me-downs ago. "Guess your dad ain't such a big shot now, huh?"

Erin saw Jason's jaw twitch, but he set his mouth in a rigid line and kept painting.

"Mr. Airline Pilot," T.J. mocked. "Guess he won't be blowin' his horn off on career day anymore at school. You'll be just like the rest of us now."

Jason's hand froze and his face flushed, but he didn't offer the boys the satisfaction of turning around.

Erin held her breath, aching to step in. Instead, she followed her judgment and hung back, giving Jason the chance to stop the bullying himself.

T.J. stepped closer to Jason, trying harder to provoke a reaction. "Hey, boys. Did ya hear how Hammon's ole man zapped all those people? Freaked out and forgot which way was up."

"Wait a min—," Erin started to shout, but suddenly Jason snapped, and he swung around, crashing his small fist into the larger boy's face. In seconds they were on the floor, tangled in a violent embrace, hands grabbing and scratching and tearing as the crowd of kids surrounded them, cheering.

Horrified, Erin pushed through the growing throng of kids and dove for the two thrashing bodies.

"Stop it!" she screamed, pulling on the boy closest to her. At this juncture they were faceless creatures eagerly inflicting pain on one another. "Stop it!"

"What's going on here?" Clint bolted up the hall, pushed through the melee, and grabbed the scruff of T.J.'s shirt. Erin wrapped herself around Jason's thrashing arms and pulled him away. As tightly as she held him, he continued trying to reach toward T.J., dead set on making the boy pay for his words.

T.J.'s nose and mouth were smeared with blood, and each raging breath he took made him seem more animalistic.

"Get him out of here!" Erin told Clint. Clint wrestled T.J. up the hall. "T.J., you aren't welcome back until you can respect the place and the people who come here! I won't tolerate that kind of behavior!"

"*He* started it!" T.J. shouted back. "I was just *talking* to him! Why don't you throw *him* out, too?"

"I'll deal with him," Erin said, casting an annoyed glance down at Jason, who still thrashed in her arms. "Don't you worry."

T.J. jerked out of Clint's grip and, calling his friends to his side, left the center in a cloud of rage.

When Erin was certain the danger was past, she turned her attention to the troubled boy. He pulled from her grasp and dashed to the stairwell. She followed, closing them off so they could escape the crowd's scrutiny.

"Jason," she said, panting, "what got into you? You can't pull a Hulk Hogan every time someone says something stupid."

"What did you want me to do?" he cried. "You heard what he said about my dad!"

"He didn't know what he was talking about. He's jealous of you, Jason. You're everything he wants to be, so he tries to belittle you, hurt you, make you seem more like him so he won't have to envy you."

"That's bull!" Jason leaned into the corner of the stairwell, letting the shadows hide his bruised face. "He's not the first one to say what he did, Erin."

She wilted against the opposite wall, racking her brain for words that would make some sense of it all. "I know, Jason. But you're going to have to ignore it. You can't let it get to you. Your dad wouldn't have wanted you getting in fights over him."

"Well, my dad isn't here, is he?" Jason shouted defiantly, his young voice cracking with fury. "*Is* he?"

Speechless, Erin tried to hold back her own tears. She stepped closer to the boy, her mouth twisted with pain, and reached out for him.

Jason pushed past her out the doors.

Erin couldn't maintain her interest in painting after Jason left, so she instructed the kids to wash their brushes and put them away.

Wearily, she loaded the paint back into her car and drove home. The emptiness of the house mocked her. Over and over, she saw Jason's raging, tearless face, confused and haunted by a crash that no one understood. Out of necessity, she forced herself to eat a sandwich. By the time she was finished, she was ready to leave again, to go anywhere, to tackle anything except the memories that plagued her.

She changed into a pair of shorts and gathered her racquetball racquet and sped like a woman possessed to Marty's, the health club frequented by most of the airline employees because of its proximity to the airport.

Once she'd arrived, Erin sat staring vacantly in the dark crowded parking lot. There would be pilots inside who'd already heard how she'd abandoned the flight yesterday. Flight attendants would treat her with sympathy. Even people who had nothing to do with the airline but who'd heard the gossip would probably be watching her, clicking their tongues and shaking their heads and declaring what a shame it was that the usually vivacious Erin was losing it.

The roaring sound of a plane overhead drew her eyes upward. Through the window, she followed the progress of tiny lights ascending into the dark sky. That sick feeling gripped her again. Determined not to surrender to it, Erin grabbed her racquet and duffel bag and hurriedly left the car.

Marty, the hulking proprietor for whom the club was named, was sitting behind the front desk when Erin bolted in. "How's it going, Erin?" he asked when he saw her.

"Pretty good," she lied. "Is there a court open?"

"Sure is. You want me to line up an opponent?"

Erin shook her head. "Just want to hit some balls. Practice my strokes."

He handed her the clipboard to sign in. "If you get tired of it," he said, "you ought to try our new aerobics class. Get some of those endorphins pumping. It's real good for depression."

Erin gave him a not-you-too look. "Maybe later. Thanks, Marty."

The door to the empty court banged shut behind her, sending off an echo. Erin dropped her duffel bag on the floor and bent over it for her glove and wristbands. She glanced out the glass wall behind her, almost certain that someone was sitting on the spectators' bleachers, watching her. But no one was there.

Pull yourself together, Erin, she ordered herself. *Don't let this thing beat you.*

Slowly, she started her routine warm-up. But neither the exercise nor the solitude helped her to escape the tension that had her wound tighter than a propeller spinning out of control.

Addison Lowe saw Erin through the glass wall a few moments later, warming up with the grace of a professional athlete. He told himself that this wasn't the time to see her again, that he should leave and let her work through her problems in her own way. He'd gotten the information he needed from the pilot he'd come here to meet, and he really had no business hanging around. But the sight of Erin compelled him to stand at the glass and watch.

He'd had her figured wrong, he told himself as she picked up her racquet and served the ball, then backhanded it against the right wall to ricochet back to her again. When he'd seen her that morning, she'd seemed too fragile, too broken, and he would have bet she was at home, wrapped in some sort of refuge, unable to cope in any way. But now he saw the aggressive side of her as she ran back and forth across the court, slamming her racquet into that ball with the anger and fury of someone with a debt to collect. Did that energy come from her anger?

She hit the ball too low, and he watched, breath held, as she recovered it, never missing a beat. Her hair swayed into her face and back. The muscles in her legs twisted and stretched as she leaped into the air and then crouched near the floor, always hitting the ball before it bounced a second time. Great *whacks* sounded with each stroke. Despite what he'd seen of her, Erin Russell was not a loser, he decided, neither on the court nor in the cockpit. Right now, she just needed a little help coping.

Drawing his heavy dark brows together, Addison leaned against the glass, watching more intently. After a rally of five or more minutes, Erin finally let the ball pass her, and set her hands on her hips while she caught her breath. She turned around and wiped her face on her wristband, and he saw that her eyes were red and wet. Her shoulders heaved, and the tormented expression on her face broke his heart.

Their eyes met through the glass before he had the presence of mind to step away from it, and he didn't miss her look of shock and accusation. Quickly, she turned away from him and wiped her face again. Erin found the ball, picked it up, and prepared to serve it once more.

Addison didn't know if it was ego or a feeling of kinship that forced him to finally knock on the glass. Before he realized what he had done, he had caught her attention again. Erin turned around quickly, stared at him for a moment, annoyed, then reluctantly came to the door. She unlocked it and held it slightly ajar. "I have this court," she said.

Addison slipped inside and dropped his bag next to hers, swinging his racquet in his hand. "It was the last one," he said. "I thought I might talk you into a game."

Erin let the door swing shut and stepped toward him, her red eyes summoning an unyielding strength as she confronted him. "I think we covered just about everything today, Mr. Lowe. I want to play alone."

"You were killing yourself," he observed. He tossed his own ball into the air, then caught it in one hand. "Come on, I'll go easy on you."

"Don't do me any favors."

"You're awfully tough on yourself," he muttered.

She set her hands on her hips, letting her racquet dangle from its wrist thong. "Mr. Lowe, you have no right to intrude on my private time. I may have no choice but to cooperate with you to some extent in the investigation, but I don't have to let you bully me in my personal life."

"It's a game, Erin," he said in a tone that exaggerated her overreaction. "Just a game. No questions, no arguments. Just a friendly game."

Her stiff lips moved to speak again, but instead, Erin dropped her hands and moved onto backcourt, a purposeful expression on her face. "Serve," she said, riveting her angry eyes on the front wall.

Addison couldn't help smiling as he hit the ball. The spirit of competition welled inside him, and he liked it. He hadn't felt it this intensely in a very long time.

When they had each won once, Addison breathlessly tried to convince Erin to call it a draw. He wanted to talk to her, to tap some of the emotion brimming in her eyes, swinging in her fists, kicking in her step. He wanted to be her friend, because she seemed to need one.

But Erin hadn't come here to talk, least of all to him. She was here to vent her grief, and she wouldn't stop until she was too exhausted to feel the pain anymore. Addison realized with sagging spirits that he was a mere instrument to keep the ball coming. He could have been anybody with a racquet.

He saw her tears again during the third

and deciding game, the grinding of her teeth as she swung, the ruthless way she dove for the ball and skidded across the court on bare knees, never acknowledging the pain. Her only goal, it seemed, was to fire that ball into the wall and hope it came back harder and faster the next time.

Slow down! he wanted to shout. *This ball won't numb the pain! I know! I've been there.* But instead, he kept smashing the ball with all his might, his heart aching like his weary muscles the harder she fought to keep the rally going.

The final point was hers, partly because she'd fought harder for it, and partly because Addison was too exhausted to rival her vengeance. He slumped against the wall, gasping for breath, thankful that, at last, they could talk.

But Erin had nothing to say. She merely wiped her face and neck on a towel she had brought, dropped her gloves and wristbands into her bag, and slipped the duffel bag's strap over her shoulder. "Good game," she muttered. "Thanks."

And before he could catch his breath to reply, Erin was out the door.

CHAPTER SEVEN

The laugh tracks of Nick at Night provided little comfort to Erin as she lay limp on the bed. Even though she felt exhausted, her mind was fully alert. Lucille Ball bumbled through a scene, trying to pull something over on Ricky, but none of it seemed the slightest bit funny. She didn't usually watch television to fall asleep; instead, she mentally grumbled when she heard it playing in Madeline's room at night. Now she needed the company, the noise, the distraction . . .

The day played through her mind like old film clips: Addison's vivid eyes studying her with concern . . . then with regret . . . then with delight . . . then with authority . . . Addison's eyes, piercing, alert. Addison's eyes, competitive. Addison's eyes, disappointed.

Addison's eyes.

What was it about him that she couldn't get out of her mind? She closed her own eyes and tried to see him in a more rational light. Who was he, really, besides an NTSB investigator? Who was he inside? She thought of the sad note in his voice when he'd confessed that he had lost someone close to him in a plane crash. Four years ago, and he still looked freshly torn when he spoke of it. Was it a lover? A close friend? A family member? A wife?

The last thought jarred her heart inexplicably, and a frown stole across her forehead. *Not a wife,* she thought. A friend was bad enough. What if Mick *had* been her lover or her husband? Would she have ever recovered? Probably not, when the chances looked so remote now. She wouldn't wish such pain on anyone. Despite how angry he had made her this morning, she was quite sure that not even Addison Lowe deserved that kind of pain.

You don't forget. Ever.

Would Erin still be this strongly affected by the crash four years from now? Would she have abandoned her flying and found some other occupation that was nice and safe, without responsibility? It would be so easy now to just give up, run away, forget who she was and what was important to her. But easy wasn't always best. A life worth living, she'd always said, is one worth taking risks for. If she overcame her fear now, went back up again, someday she could be captain of the largest planes Southeast had to offer, flying the most exciting routes in the world.

No, she would never forget Mick or the crash that threatened to destroy her. But wouldn't she still have the things she had worked so hard for?

I've got to fly. The unspoken words incited cold chills, yet covered her in a thin sheen of perspiration. *I've got to make myself do it.*

Tears filled her eyes, rolled down her cheeks. "But I can't," she whispered aloud.

The bitter memory of yesterday's ordeal came back to her, harassing her like a plaguing spirit that only she could set free. She had tried to feign control, had tried to pretend — for her captain's sake — that she was fine and ready to fly. She had tried desperately not to let him know that her confidence in herself was deflating like a balloon flying on its own air until the moment it ran out and hit the ground.

Maybe if it hadn't been raining, like the night of the crash, or if she hadn't thought about it so much before boarding, building on her dread, she could have coped. Silence had precluded all the usual cockpit conversation as Erin had watched the jet in front of her taxi down the runway and launch into flight. Her mouth had gone dry. Her muscles had become rigid. Tears had gathered in the crescents of her lashes. Unexplored options flitted through her mind like images of doors through which she could still escape. She could have asked Jack to fly this leg of the trip, since the two would alternate for the length of the flight. But what if she couldn't manage to take over when her turn came? If she panicked, Jack would be forced to fly for too long, and his fatigue and her nerves would make for a hazardous combination.

"Southeast 34 taxi into position and hold. Be ready for an immediate."

The controller's words had constricted her chest and rendered her trembling hands useless. She had riveted her eyes on another aircraft — an L-1011 — descending toward the runway. She'd jumped slightly when the airplane touched down.

"Erin? You okay?"

Trying to breathe, she had assured Jack she was fine and forced herself to taxi into position, but already perspiration was gathering on her temples. She had sat rigidly, contemplating the runway waiting for her to conquer it, as she listened to Operations' calm orders to other aircraft. She'd watched the order of the smooth takeoffs, the precision of the uneventful landings, and for a moment, she'd started to believe in herself again. She was a good pilot. Her record was spotless. There was no reason she couldn't make herself fly again.

But then the order came that brought life down to a choice. "Southeast 34 cleared for takeoff."

Erin had closed her eyes and struggled to answer, but the words wouldn't come. It wasn't too late, she'd told herself. It wouldn't be too late until she was airborne.

"I can't do it, Jack . . . I can't."

"It's okay, Erin."

Calmly, without judgment, Jack had taken over the plane and radioed back to the tower that they needed to have a wing checked and would have to pull out of the lineup. But Erin knew that everyone who'd heard the transmission was shaking their heads, aware that Erin was bailing out again.

How could she go through that again? How?

The tears came harder now, bits of her soul mingled in each one. She'd pull herself together, she told herself. She'd make herself do it. She was too strong to let this defeat her. Too strong.

Sleep came on cat's feet, sneaking up on her, dragging her under. In her dream she relived the night of the crash over and over, and this time she was in the cockpit, next to Mick, where she should have been. Flying the plane, going down, down, down . . . But in her fear, no scream escaped her . . . only the mute, rustling sound of a bird's broken wings . . .

It was late morning when Erin awoke, feeling physically more rested than she had since the crash, but mentally as fatigued as she had at any other time. She was reading the paper and nibbling on a cold piece of toast when Lois bolted through the door.

"I'm home."

Erin's eyes brightened instantly. "Lois! I didn't expect you this early."

Lois set down her bags and regarded her friend seriously. "I came as soon as we landed. Wanted to make sure you weren't hiding under those covers."

Erin dropped her toast on her plate. "No, I actually crawled out to feed myself," she teased. She stood up and gave Lois a hug. "I'm glad you're back. I can use a mother hen to lash me with an occasional lecture."

"Pep talk," Lois corrected, returning the embrace. "Not lecture, pep talk."

"Whatever," Erin said, pulling back. "So how'd it go? Did you have a nice trip?"

"Nice?" Lois asked, her you've-got-to-be-kidding look answering the question. "Let me tell you how 'nice' it was. We had a pregnant woman on the way to Atlanta who went into labor during flight. Her contractions were three minutes apart when we landed."

Erin followed Lois into the den, watching her kick off her shoes and collapse on the sofa. "At least you didn't have to deliver it."

"No, but I wasn't so sure about that for a while there. Good heavens, could you *imagine?*"

Erin laughed aloud, forgetting how seldom she'd done that lately.

"That's not all. We had to go into a two-hour holding pattern over Atlanta because the traffic was so bad. We literally had to go back to Mobile to fuel up just to keep holding. I've got a whopping headache, and I'm wrung out."

Erin went back into the kitchen and poured her roommate a glass of tea. "Go change clothes and relax. Have you slept?"

"I can use a couple more hours," Lois said. "But I can't." Lois threw her wrist over her eyes and moaned dramatically. "I have to go back to the airport. So do you."

"Me? Why?" The apprehension in Erin's voice forced Lois to look up at her.

"It seems that the takeover is complete. We no longer work for Southeast. We're Trans Western employees now, but I don't know if they're going to change our name. Rumor has it that a lot of changes are about to take place — big ones. They've called a meeting of all pilots who are in town at one

107

o'clock, so they can break the news to us."

The thought of being in a room full of her peers, all of them cognizant of her state of mind, sent a new rush of panic roiling through Erin's stomach. "But I'm on leave of absence. I —"

"Redlo said to tell you to be there. It was an order, Erin. And you're going if I have to take you at gunpoint."

"But you could tell me what they say. I don't have to —"

"You *do* have to, Erin. You're still one of our pilots. I won't let you miss this. There are going to be some cuts, I've heard. I don't know if that means the number of pilots, the routes, or what. You at least have to act like you're interested, so they won't cut you."

Erin set the glass of tea on the coffee table and tried not to be so transparent. It was a meeting. Just a meeting. No one was going to pressure her into flying. No one was going to throw stones. "All right," she said. "I'll go. You don't have to get so excited."

Lois smiled and reached for the glass. "I'll go change and try to forget holding patterns and birthing mothers, and work myself into my submissive mode. I have a feeling we're all going to be that way a lot for a while."

108

Submission wasn't the word for what Trans Western seemed to want from them. *Blood* seemed more accurate. The pilots seethed as the new owner, Collin Zarkoff, a tyrant whose expression told them either his shoes were too tight or he had a strong aversion to the human race, stood before them outlining the changes about to be made. He announced twelve percent cuts in pay for all flight attendants and machinists; twenty-five percent cuts for all pilots; longer working hours; fewer sick days; cuts in time off and sleep time between flights, barely keeping the minimums the FAA demanded. And, he added, "his people" would be doing careful studies on each of the Southeast pilots, to determine if their records indicated any of them could be cut and replaced with Trans Western employees.

The cons of the merger made the pros seem minimal, though there were a few. Trans Western's motive for the takeover was to include more of the East Coast in their flight routes. Southeast, in turn, would have more western routes. And Trans Western had bigger and better airplanes to offer, so pilots like Erin, who'd expected never to go farther than a 727 as long as they stayed with Southeast, now would have the opportunity to fly L-1011s and 747s some day. But those benefits didn't override the sacrifices demanded.

Before the wave of protests could rise high enough to reach Zarkoff, the owner warned the president of the pilots' union that he should advise his members to take what he offered or lose their jobs. He wasn't in the mood for union games, he said. He had an airline to run — one which, he pointed out, was losing money hand over fist, and he had to cut back to survive.

It didn't take long for the president to call a union meeting, and Erin felt herself getting caught up in the spirit of her coworkers. No one seemed to be interested in her aborted flight, or her panic, or her refusal to fly again. This was too immediate, too personal.

"As far as I'm concerned," Ray Carter, the president, began, "this is war. If that man thinks he can cut our salary by one-fourth, he's nuts!"

The crowd roared approval, but Erin and Lois were cautiously quiet.

"Over the past five years, I've willingly taken pay cuts that amounted to forty percent of what I was making," someone shouted. "Now he wants to cut out another fourth of that? What am I supposed to do? Sell my house? Stop eating?"

Most of the members voiced agreement.

"What about those longer work hours?" a pilot from across the room demanded. "In the wake of a major crash at this airline, he wants to put the pilots under more stress?"

Erin couldn't sit quietly for that. She sprang up, raising her voice above the others. "Wait a minute! That crash had nothing to do with pilot stress, and until the investigation is over, I think comments like that should be avoided."

The pilots grew quiet, the reminder of Erin's association with Mick settling their anger and making them consider their words before they spoke. Erin began to feel decidedly uncomfortable at the newfound quiet, and she sank slowly back into her seat.

Sensitive to Erin's discomfort, Lois took the opportunity to stand up and offer her views. "Look, I'm as upset as you guys, believe me. I have bills to pay, too, and I agree that we can't tolerate his version of our working conditions. But we've got to face the reality of this industry, and the reality is that the airlines — all of them — are suffering. Without the takeover, Southeast was on the way to bankruptcy. If we want to keep our jobs, we have to play the game his way, at least to some extent."

The pilots began shouting disagreement

or approval, but the president's voice was singled out. "*His* way?" Ray Carter yelled. "I say we play *our* way. We can strike!"

To Erin's relief, half of the members shouted their rejection of the suggestion, but the other half gave equal decibels of support.

"What about the air traffic controllers during the Reagan administration?" Lois shouted. "They all lost their jobs. What about the TWA flight attendants a few years ago? Forty-five hundred people are still out of work. And if any of you had done the least bit of research into this, you'd know that Zarkoff has taken over companies before. He *likes* it when the employees strike, because he can replace them immediately with people who are willing to take half of what he's offering us."

"She's right," an ally piped up. "Zarkoff has a reputation for never backing down from his first offer. I know a guy who flies for Trans Western, and he said Zarkoff's first offer is usually his best. If we dicker, we might wind up with less."

A new rise of shouting occurred, but Ray Carter banged his gavel. "We aren't getting anywhere," he said. "We need a committee to hash this out. I recommend a committee of twenty representatives chosen by the membership."

The members opened a round of applause, finally agreeing on something. The rest of the meeting was taken up by nominations for the committee and a secret-ballot vote.

As the meeting broke up, Erin felt a sense of relief that she was no longer the source of whispering and gossip among them, though she couldn't help worrying at the state of the pilots' union and where their tempers would lead them.

She was on her way back to her car when Frank, her boss and assistant chief pilot, intercepted her in the corridor. "Erin!" he called in a no-nonsense tone that told her he wasn't having a good day. "My office."

"But I —"

"Now!" he ordered and hurried back to the terminal.

That familiar strangling feeling rose inside her as she followed him into his office, bracing herself for another lecture. He plopped into his chair, set his elbow on the armrest, and spread his fingers over his chin.

"I'm worried, Erin. Real worried. About this takeover, the pay cuts, the stress it'll put on my pilots, the threat of Trans Western cutting down my payroll . . . all of it. But I'm especially worried about you. You're deliberately staying away, and I'm warning you, you're going to get lost in the shuffle.

And when you do, there won't be a single thing I can do about it."

Erin shifted uncomfortably in her chair. "Frank, we've been all through this."

"Not to my satisfaction, we haven't. You were upset the other day. I let you off the hook so you could go home and pull yourself together. I'm not going to do that today."

"Frank!"

Frank leaned forward, clasping his hands on his desk. "Erin, I want you to look me in the eye and tell me that you honestly don't ever want to fly again. That you don't ever intend to."

Erin met his gray eyes, so crisp, so aware, and she knew he could see right through her. "It isn't a question of wanting to, Frank. You know that."

"What is it a question of, then?"

"Fear," she said. Moisture welled in her throat.

"Fear," he repeated. "Do you know how normal that is after a crash? *I'll* probably be a little scared the next time I fly, because of that crash. But Erin, fear can be a good thing. It makes us more careful. Keeps us alert. It doesn't debilitate us for the rest of our lives. Do you really want to do that to yourself?"

"No," she whispered.

"What?" he asked, forcing her to say it louder, to hear it herself.

"I said, *no.*"

"And do you think Mick would have quit if it had been you in the crash? Would you have wanted him to?"

She fought the tears welling in her eyes. "Of course not."

"Then fly, Erin. Give me one less thing to worry about. I swear to you, as soon as you're airborne, it'll all fall into place. You'll feel a lot better, and you'll get over that fear."

"And what if I don't?"

"You will. I know you, Erin. I'm willing to take that chance. This block you have against flying is your way of grieving over Mick, of doing some sort of penance for not going down with that plane."

Red heat warmed her cheeks. "Since when have you been practicing psychology?"

"I'm not practicing it," he admitted. "I've talked to the staff psychologist about you. That's his theory."

Erin's mouth dropped open, and her eyes caught fire. "You what? How could you do that?"

"It's my job, Erin. I care about my pilots. I put my rear end on the line for you with the chief. You said you'd go for counseling, but you haven't."

"I haven't had a chance! I've been busy. Nobody asked you to have someone psycho-analyze me secondhand. I resent that."

"Resent it all you want," Frank said, leaning back in his chair. "But I think he was right, and I think you can fly if you have to. And you do have to. I don't want you to lose your job. I don't want you to throw it away. Can you try again for me, Erin? For the guy who won't give up on you?"

Erin stood up and raked her hand through her ruffled hair. Her mouth compressed as she paced across the room, but the turmoil inside her escalated. What choice did she have? Trans Western would see that she refused to fly when they read her file, and she would be the first to go. Frank was right. She didn't want to throw away everything, but she wasn't sure she could hold on to it with such terror inside her. Still, she had to try. She stopped in front of his desk, focusing on a paperweight of a DC-9. She'd have to fly with a new captain, probably one who would see his assignment with her as some sort of punishment. No one would be as patient — as tolerant of her — as Jack had been two days ago. And Jack would certainly avoid her in the future. Still, she couldn't help embracing the hope that was the only light in this miserable tunnel she'd dug for herself.

"Can . . . can I fly with Jack? That is, if he'll still have me after the last time?"

Frank's stern expression collapsed and softened. "He's requested you for his next flight, Erin. Tomorrow to St. Louis. Can I schedule you?"

She stared at him for a long moment, weighing one action against another, groping for the courage to say yes and mean it. When she didn't find it, she went forward without it. "Schedule me," she said without inflection, "but I can't make any promises."

"That's good enough for me," Frank said, and smiled for the first time that day.

CHAPTER EIGHT

Lois was already home when Erin got there, and Madeline, who had gotten back in while they were at the meeting, sat and watched as she wore a path in the rug pacing from one corner of the living room to the other. "You won't believe this," Lois said anxiously to Erin. "You just won't believe this!"

Erin dropped her purse and leaned over to give Madeline a welcome-home hug, then regarded her agitated friend, thankful to be distracted from her flying by whatever catastrophe Lois was experiencing now. "Believe what?"

Lois stopped her pacing and punched her fists into her hips. "You know that committee of twenty the union voted on to hammer out grievances?"

"What about it?"

"They voted *me* on it," Lois cried. "*Me!* Can you believe that?"

Erin tried not to smile. "Actually, I can, since I voted for you."

Erin might as well have admitted to electing Lois for a suicide mission.

"How could you?" Lois asked, astounded.

"Erin, I can't be on that committee with nineteen angry men who think a woman's opinion means nothing unless it has to do with recipes or needlework! What were you thinking?"

Erin went to the kitchen and retrieved a bottle of soda from the refrigerator. "The same thing as everyone else who voted for you, I guess. All I know is that if I have to let someone else do the fighting for me or my job, I'd want it to be you."

"But George Vanderwall is on that committee, Erin! The most belligerent captain in the company. He treats women like pestering mosquitoes!"

"He is opinionated," Erin agreed. "Which is why we need you to balance things."

"Don't sweat it," Madeline said. "Lois, you'll do great."

Lois sat on the kitchen table, pleading with them both to understand, as though they could relieve her of her new responsibility. "Look, most of those committee members are dead set on striking. How am I going to convince them to compromise, when there isn't a chance in the world of their listening to me! I'll be like an invisible force who talks until I'm blue in the face, but no one will ever listen!"

"Madeline, did you check the answering

machine?" Erin asked absently.

"See?" Lois shouted. "Right now, you aren't listening to me."

"I am," Erin argued. "I just wanted Madeline to hear her messages before they're erased. Lois, none of what you said is true. You underestimate yourself."

"Underestimate?" Lois asked. "What about you?" Her eyes followed Madeline as she headed toward the answering machine, whose lights had been blinking since she'd been home. "I've told you the same thing."

"About what?"

"About flying. About getting back up there where you belong. About not throwing everything away."

Erin dropped her teasing, and her expression suddenly became serious. "I went to the meeting, didn't I?"

"Yeah, after my threat to lead you there at gunpoint."

Madeline chuckled as she began rewinding the messages on the tape.

"Well, you'll be happy to know that I'm flying to St. Louis tomorrow."

Madeline snapped around, and Lois's mouth fell open, her eyes brightening at once. "Really, Erin? You're not just trying to appease me?"

Erin dropped her gaze to the soda that

suddenly seemed tasteless. Her hand was already trembling. "Really. And if it's all right with you, I'd rather not talk about it."

"All right," Lois said, her tone softening. "Not a word." She joined Madeline at the machine as she flicked the play button, then grinned over her shoulder in silent congratulations to her friend.

The beep sounded on the machine, followed by a distinctly masculine voice. "Erin, this is Addison. I'd like to see you later today, if it's okay. That is, if you're not mad at me for letting you win last night. Call me here at 555-3213."

Both women spun around, wearing flabbergasted, but pleasantly surprised, expressions. "Addison? Last night? Is there something you've forgotten to mention?"

Erin avoided their eyes and pulled out a small canvas she'd stored under a cabinet. Ignoring Lois and Madeline's unyielding scrutiny, she sat down at the table and began sketching. "Let me win," she mumbled under her breath. "That'll be the day."

"Erin!" Madeline shouted. "Who is he?"

Erin finally looked up, and briefly considered telling them both that he was the NTSB investigator who had come to town to make her life miserable. But then they'd be on the subject of the crash again, and of her flying, and of her terror and grief. And she didn't want to talk about any of it anymore. Not thinking about it was the only way she could cope until she had to fly. "He's a guy I played racquetball with last night. No big deal."

"What's he look like?"

"What difference does it make?"

Lois turned off the machine and stooped down next to her friend. The grin on her face was tinged with delight. "Erin, you're hedging."

Erin's lips curved at Lois's curiosity. "No, I'm not. I suppose he's nice-looking."

"You suppose?" Lois stood up again and crossed her arms. "Erin, are you going to call him back or not?"

"Nope."

"And why not?"

"Because I have plans this afternoon. It's my day to work at the youth center. I promised I'd help the kids with the skyscraper mural today. They're counting on me."

"Well, you won't be there forever. You could at least call him and set something up for later."

Erin tried not to smile at her friend's naiveté. "Lois, if I wanted to call him back, I would. Please stop mothering me."

Lois clapped her hands on her sides. "See?

Just like I said, you never listen to me. How can I expect to influence nineteen opinionated pilots, much less hundreds of our union members? Maybe I ought to just resign from the committee right now."

Erin dropped her charcoal and shook her head in disbelief. "How can you see any similarity between your being on a committee and your advising me about men? It's emotional blackmail, that's what it is. You think I'll feel guilty enough to call this guy back, just to prove that I do listen to you."

"Did it work?" Lois asked, one eyebrow hiked expectantly.

"No."

Lois sighed and Madeline grinned across the room at her. "Well, it never hurts to try, does it, Lois?"

"That's right," Erin said. "Lois, remember that when you meet with the committee."

If there was one thing that Addison Lowe hated, it was waiting. And waiting for a woman to return his call just about made him crazy. *She's not going to call,* he thought as he paced the hangar where he and his crew had stored the tagged wreckage. Maybe he should have made the call sound more authoritative. *Erin, this is Mr. Lowe, NTSB.*

I need to ask you a few more questions. Call me before three so we can set up an appointment.

Not that it would have done any good. And it wouldn't have really been the truth. Oh, sure, he had scores of questions yet to ask her, but not until he'd done a little more homework first. The plain, simple truth today was that he couldn't get her out of his mind since she'd walked out on him at the health club last night. He wanted to see her, heaven help him. And it was quite clear that she didn't want to see him.

He checked his watch, saw that it was approaching five. Almost time for dinner. If he could just catch her before she ate, maybe he could talk her into having dinner with him. But then he was faced with the dilemma of whether to tell her the truth about why he wanted to see her, or pretend it was business. He wasn't a good liar, never had been. The truth would be written all over his face. Besides, he didn't like the idea of exploiting his work on the crash to get a date. That wasn't his style.

"Hey, Addison, you want me to order us some sandwiches?" Hank, his flight-control specialist, asked across the building. Already, the rest of his team had left for dinner, since they had worked through lunch, but Hank had been too engrossed in the pieces of wreckage he was analyzing.

"No, not for me," Addison said, walking around the pieces to reach him. "I'm going out. Don't you need a break?"

"I'll take one later," Hank said. "I just don't get this."

"Get what?" Addison asked.

"Well, this whole crash. It looks like Hammon followed all the proper procedures before takeoff. Even if Hammon had passed out cold on his approach, there were a first officer and a flight engineer on the plane who could have taken over. Someone could have kept that plane from flying into the ground. It makes more sense that something went wrong with the plane's computer system . . . maybe it was on automatic pilot and the system went haywire, but I can't find any evidence of that. I'm trying to piece it all back together, but there isn't a lot left of it."

"Even if that was the case," Addison said, "Hammon could have overridden the computer and straightened it out manually. A plane doesn't nosedive without everyone on board knowing it. And the control tower has records that there were no problems before the final approach."

"Still," Hank said, "there's got to be an explanation that makes sense."

"Look, I don't want it to be pilot error, either. If you have any hunches, we'll follow them. And I don't care what Sid or any of the brass in Washington say. We're going to dig until we get to the truth — no matter what it is."

Hank leaned back in his folding chair and looked at his friend. "So what has that woman said about his pilot skills? You know, the first officer who missed the flight?"

Addison wondered if Hank could read his feelings. "I haven't been able to get much out of her. I'm hoping to catch up with her tonight. But generally, she seems convinced that it wasn't pilot error."

"They always are."

Addison looked pensively down at the pieces of wreckage, wondering what they were missing. "Tell you what. When the guys get back, start piecing together the elevator system all the way from the controls in the cockpit, through the cables, to the hydraulic actuators. If the plane malfunctioned, we should see something wrong there."

"Will do," Hank said.

The phone rang, startling Addison, and he dove for it. "Addison Lowe."

But it wasn't Erin. It was someone in Washington with some information Hank had requested. He surrendered the phone, then ambled to the front window of the hangar, wondering if he should wait any longer for her call.

Okay, he thought finally. This didn't have to be a big deal. He would drive over to her house. Ask her to dinner. Explain that it was pleasure, not business. Beg a little. Use the I-hate-to-eat-alone line that bore more truth than he liked to admit.

And if that didn't work, he'd kidnap her and hold her captive until she liked him.

He chuckled lightly. Maybe that would be the only way with Erin.

The drive to Erin's house was short, and as he got out of the car and walked to her door, he found himself tensing up like a teenager asking for his first date. This was ridiculous. He was thirty-nine years old. She was just a woman. A woman with sad hazel eyes and hair that never did what it was told and a soul so deep a man could drown in it . . .

He knocked, and Madeline opened the door quickly, her arms full of sketches. Her eyes brightened at the sight of him.

"Yes?"

"Uh . . . I was looking for Erin . . ." He extended his hand, then withdrew it, realizing that shaking hands would make her drop her armload. "Are you her roommate?"

"Yes . . . one of them." Madeline gave him a quick once-over, then grinned as if she approved. "You must be Addison."

He hesitated for a moment, and his heart accelerated. Had Erin mentioned him? "Yes. How did you . . . ?"

"I heard your message," she explained, nodding her head back toward the machine. "Erin's not here." She glanced down at the stack in her arms, decided to set them down, and realized she had ink on her blouse. "Oh, great," she said. "Look at me. I'll have to go change. Come on in."

"No, I can see you're on your way out. I'll just call Erin later."

Madeline looked up at him. "I'll tell you where you can find her. She's at the youth center, painting those murals." With a wry grin, she added, "I'm sure she'd love to see you."

Addison's heart rate climbed again. "Youth center, huh? Okay. Give me directions, and I'll go try to find her."

Madeline jotted down the directions, and Addison headed out to find her.

Addison saw her before he'd even come through the glass doors — Erin on a ladder, painting a mural of skyscrapers in primary colors. She turned to the side, shouted something to one of the teenagers working on the street at the bottom of the wall, and laughed like she hadn't a care in the world. He watched as a dollop of red paint dropped from her brush onto her bare knee, and she pulled at her paint-smudged sweatshirt and wiped at it, smearing it across her leg. Stretching back up to reach the top of the building she painted, she revealed the baggy denim cutoff shorts, also smeared with paint, tucked beneath the baggy sweatshirt.

He pushed through the doors and heard the babbling sound of busy teenagers and children, all painting at various levels on the wall. Erin babbled right along with them. "How's that look?" she asked anyone who would answer as she gave the red skyscraper a final touch.

"You ain't finished, are ya?" a tough-looking kid asked.

"Well, yeah . . . I thought so."

"What about the antennas? How can the people who live there get cable TV if there ain't no antennas?"

"We aren't going for reality here, Zeke. I don't want antennas cluttering up this building."

"Well, what good is art if it ain't like the real thing?"

Erin laughed and climbed down from the ladder. "If it bothers you, go up there and paint antennas."

"You got it."

Erin wiped her hands on the back of her shorts and checked out the progress of a child of nine or ten diligently working on a car traveling down the mural's street. The girl looked up and laughed at her. "You have red paint on your nose."

Erin laughed again, setting Addison's heart dancing. "That's the only place you *don't* have it. We're a mess, aren't we?"

Addison couldn't help answering the question that wasn't addressed to him. "That's a matter of opinion," he said. "If you want to know mine, I think red paint becomes you."

Erin turned around, and her smile instantly faded. "How did you know I was here?"

"I went by your apartment. Your roommate told me."

She grabbed a rag draped over the ladder and began wiping her hands self-consciously. Her formerly open expression hardened into a defensive mask. "Well . . . I can't answer any more questions now. I'm busy. It isn't the time."

"I'm not here to ask you questions," he

said, stepping closer and lowering his voice to keep from arousing too much curiosity. "I came to see if I could con you into having dinner with me."

"Dinner?" she asked.

"Yeah. You do plan to eat tonight, don't you?"

"Well . . ." She looked around her, at the work yet to be done before the children would start home. "Not until I'm finished here. Besides, I'm not dressed. I —"

"Do you have an extra brush?" Addison asked.

"What?"

"An extra brush. For me."

"But . . . you'll ruin your clothes. You'll —"

"Come on, let me help. I'm not too bad with a paintbrush, you know. My specialty is model airplanes, but I think I can handle this. And afterwards we'll go get a hamburger where no one will care if we're covered in paint or not."

Erin glanced self-consciously around her, picked up a dry brush, and reluctantly handed it to him. "I don't know. I really don't want to talk about the crash tonight . . ."

"I told you. It's strictly pleasure. I just hate to eat alone." There, he thought. Short

131

of begging, he'd used every argument he had.

She glanced at him in his khaki slacks and his yellow shirt and thought how she'd love to see them covered in paint smears. It would serve Addison right. "Okay," she said with a sigh. "But remember, you asked for it."

CHAPTER NINE

Lois grinned all the way to her meeting at the way Madeline had sent Addison to find Erin. But that smug feeling disappeared like a blue sky overtaken by storm clouds as soon as she found herself among the committee of angry pilots more than ready to scream "strike."

"He has to know we mean business," Ray Carter, the committee chairman and union president, said as he paced the floor. "Without a strike, he isn't going to listen."

"It's blackmail, that's what it is! We shouldn't strike, we should sue!" someone else said.

"Let's strike *and* sue!"

Lois sat mutely with a stack of photocopied articles on her lap, very much aware that these other pilots — older, wiser, more aggressive, more experienced in the industry — would scoff at her arguments. She hadn't been joking when she'd told Erin that no one ever listened. It was true, and now she wondered why she'd agreed to serve on the committee, when the decisions were all but made. It didn't matter if she disagreed. She would simply be one of those responsible for any consequences the union suffered because of their decisions.

"Lois," Ray asked suddenly, pivoting around in midstep and pinning her with his eyes. "You're the only one here we haven't heard from. Are you with us or not?"

"On suing, striking, or both?" she asked, her mouth going dry.

"Any of it."

"Well, I think we should consider our options first."

"If you have any, let's hear them. You came in here with an armload of *something*."

"Well . . ." Lois looked down at the stack of articles, and wished she'd never brought them. This crowd would snuff her out before she even began to speak. "These aren't options, really. They're more like consequences."

"Consequences? Like what?"

Lois stood up, hoping her height of five feet ten inches would lend her courage. It had always served her well before. "They're articles about the TWA flight attendants' strike," she said, passing them out to the others. "We're all aware of the fact that forty-five hundred flight attendants lost their jobs and still haven't gotten them back. The owner considered them expendable, and they were replaced."

"True," a man named Degall agreed. "But the circumstances were different. Flight attendants don't require years of training and experience. Besides, in their case negotiations weren't handled well, and their demands were too high."

Ray Carter stepped closer to her, his eyes full of disbelief. "Are you saying we shouldn't act? We should accept what they threw out to us and not do anything?"

Lois shrank slowly back into her seat, trying to avoid the fire that had an excellent chance of spreading wildly. "No, of course not. I'm just saying that we should learn from history. Not make the same mistakes."

"Just what *do* you suggest?"

"I don't know," Lois said. She cleared her throat. Her voice was rasping, as it always did when she felt backed into a corner, but she forced herself to go on. "It just seems to me that we need to agree on exactly what kind of cuts we *will* accept, because we know we have to accept something. The flight attendants and machinists have. And we'll have to negotiate. That's obvious. I just think we should avoid talking strike for a while."

"Well, if we don't talk strike, what threat can we hang over Zarkoff's head? What motivation will he have to give us what we want?" Ray asked.

Another relatively quiet member of the committee, Larry Miller, piped up. "If Zarkoff doesn't care whether we go on strike or not, then a strike threat isn't motivation."

"Right," Lois added, her courage building now that she had an ally. "Look at it from his point of view. Some of you, the ones in this room with seniority, are making a lot of money. If he can get us to walk out and can hire all new pilots at starting pay, he'll save millions."

"But if we all refuse to fly, he can't run the airline," someone said. "And then he'll *lose* millions."

Voices of approval added to that sentiment all over the room, and Lois sank back into her seat.

"We have to give him a threat," Ray said. "And to do that, we have to call a strike vote. We have to get the members behind us."

"All right," Larry, Lois's ally, said. "But if we're going to make that recommendation, I move that we also allow Lois to point out her side of the argument to the members, so that they can make an informed decision. And these articles need to be distributed first to each member."

Silence reigned, and Lois felt her throat

constricting. Not her. Not a planned presentation in front of hundreds of pilots. Sure, she could stand up spontaneously, utter an argument or two, but to be one of the scheduled speakers? Oh, her mouth would glue itself shut and she wouldn't be able to get a word out. Besides, they'd never listen . . . never . . .

"I . . . I think someone else could really do a better job . . . ," she began.

"All right," Ray conceded grudgingly, ignoring Lois's objection. "It couldn't hurt to present both sides. Lois, have your argument ready for the Friday meeting. I'll see that each member gets the articles well in advance."

They're not listening to me now, Lois thought on a wave of panic. *I'm trying to tell them I can't do this, and they just . . . won't . . . listen!*

"Now let's talk about recommendations for negotiations. What *will* we accept? Bottom line," Ray demanded.

Lois felt dazed, and suddenly she knew the panic Erin spoke of in the cockpit. Hers always came on a podium . . . the dry palms . . . the cotton throat . . . the stuttering . . . the palpitations . . . the dizziness . . . It was terrible to have strong convictions that needed voicing, yet to be as anxiety-ridden as she was when she had to plan to speak.

The rest of the meeting seemed a blur as she tried not to think about her presentation. Briefly, she wondered if Erin would consider swapping skins for a while. She'd feel much more comfortable copiloting in Erin's place than standing up in front of hundreds of pilots and presenting the unpopular side of this argument!

The sky in the mural took on a special life of its own as Addison worked with his paintbrush. He didn't make fun of Erin's amateur sketching on the canvas, or of the smaller children's attempts at helping. He seemed to realize without being told that the mural was for the kids, by the kids, and about the kids.

"So," he asked, when he climbed off his ladder to change colors. "Did you do all these murals around here?"

"We sure did," replied ten-year-old Zeke. He'd been one of the first kids they'd reached at the center, and had since become a little preacher to the other kids. They'd even held his baptism in the youth center's swimming pool.

Erin glanced at Addison, knowing he'd been addressing her. They exchanged pursed smiles.

"They're good. It sure beats the heck out of graffiti scrawled all over the walls."

"Why do you think we started it?" the kid asked before Erin could answer again. He took his arm and pulled him toward the edge of the mural. "See right there? I painted that. It's downtown Shreveport, and I painted that cross in, and all them people prayin' and stuff. It's about hope, this whole mural is. Prayer gives you hope. Did you know that?"

Addison's grin slowly faded as he began to take the boy more seriously. He stooped down and examined the area of the mural Zeke was showing him. "Yeah, I know it," Addison said. "Prayer does give hope. It's gotten me through some tough, tough times."

"Me, too, man. My big brother was shot down on Jackard Street last year. Man, talk about prayin'. I didn't think I'd ever get over it."

Addison looked up at the rough kid. "Who taught you about prayer, Zeke? Your mama?"

Zeke laughed. "No, man. I taught *her*. She didn't know where to turn when my brother died. But I knew, 'cause Erin told me."

Addison's eyes gravitated up to Erin's, and she smiled self-consciously and turned back to the mural. "Zeke's been a real blessing around here," she said.

"I can see that." When Zeke went back to painting, Addison climbed back up the ladder. Erin couldn't help watching him. His pants were ruined, with paint smudges everywhere. Green paint was smeared across his shirt. And a decidedly attractive blot of red decorated one jaw. For the most fleeting of moments, she allowed herself to make the mental note that red paint flattered him, too. But just as quickly, she shoved the thought away. She couldn't be attracted to the man who would nail Mick. She wouldn't allow it.

"So . . . are you going to have dinner with me to keep me from having to eat alone?" he asked, as he painted in a bird flying overhead.

"Well, I —"

"Can't," Zeke cut in before Erin could get out the words. "Mama's making spaghetti. But you can come if you want."

Addison dropped his brush and tried to maintain a straight face. "Thanks, Zeke. No, I'll have to take a rain check."

"Sure?" the kid asked. "Since you hate to eat alone and all?"

In spite of herself, Erin couldn't help being moved by Addison's efforts not to embarrass the boy. "Tell you what, Zeke. Since you can't make it, how about I keep Addison company while he eats?"

"Okay by me," Zeke said, with an indifferent shrug. "If it's all right with him. You two'll have to work that out yourselves."

"What a good idea," Addison said, eyes dancing with laughter. "But I don't know, I'll have to think about it. I kinda had my heart set on spaghetti."

Erin tried in vain to suppress her grin. He was good at this, she thought. Melting her carefully constructed ice barriers was too easy for him. "I'm sure Zeke'll give you a rain check. And by the way, I'm not changing my clothes," she informed him. "If I go, I'm going just like this."

"That's okay," he said, going back to his painting. "I like to go out with colorful people."

Although she had threatened to dine dressed — and painted — as she was, Erin had really expected to go in and change when she took her car home. But Addison, who had followed her in his car, had other plans.

"How's this?" he asked, driving up to the Sonic Drive-in.

"Wow," she deadpanned. "You really

141

know how to impress a girl, don't you?"

He laughed. "There's a price for getting me covered in paint. You'll have to eat in the car."

"No problem," she said, lifting her chin like a trooper. "I happen to like the food here."

"Then you aren't insulted?"

Erin turned her painted palms up. "Hey, who am I to criticize, when you gave up Zeke's mom's spaghetti for a burger with me?"

"It was a sacrifice, you know."

"I know."

Their eyes met in the dusk of the car, and they both smiled. A moment of understanding passed between them, without thoughts of the crash or the airline or the investigation to intrude.

Then, just as quickly, came the unbidden defensiveness she clung to like a shield, reminding her that, in many ways, he was the enemy.

"You know," she said, deliberately shattering the moment, "I may be wrong, but I think you're supposed to push that button to order."

"I know." He smiled but didn't take his gaze from her. "Listen, I was thinking. Why don't we go over to those picnic tables to eat? It's a nice night . . ."

"You won't be ashamed to be seen with a painted lady?"

"Don't forget, we match. It'll give everyone who sees us something to talk about."

Erin shrugged. "I'm used to that."

He pressed the button, and a voice asked for their order. "What'll you have?" he asked her.

"Whatever you're having," she said.

His eyebrows went up a notch. "We'll have a couple of burgers, no onions . . . two fries, large . . . two large cokes, and a Butterfinger Blizzard with two spoons."

"Will that be all?" the voice asked.

"We'll start with that and see how it goes," he said.

The order taken, they left the car and wandered over to a picnic table. The wind was brisk but still held the warmth of a tropical fall. A subtle dusk fell over the picnic area, the twilight sky clinging to daylight while inviting the night. Addison leaned against the table and smiled down at Erin as she slipped onto a bench. Confused, she looked up at him, amused at the paint smudge on his chin, amused at his choice of restaurants, amused at the glimmer of delight in his eyes. Again, she told herself not to enjoy him, and her smile faded as her gaze drifted away.

"I liked seeing how at home you were with those kids," he said. "They treated you like you were family, and you had them so interested in the project."

"Kids love to paint," she said matter-of-factly. "Those murals are their own personal touches to the center. We all like to be around something that's a little bit our own. It keeps them off the streets, using their time constructively."

"But it's more than that. You're sharing your faith with them, aren't you?"

"That's what it's all about."

He gazed at her for a moment. "How'd you get started doing that?"

Good, she thought. A safe topic that didn't involve intimacy of any kind. "A few years ago the local youth council came to the company in a big promotion for Big Brothers volunteers. It sounded like a good idea to me, so I asked if they could use a Big Sister. I started out with a thirteen-year-old girl who had a lot of problems, and I really got hooked on her." She chuckled and propped her chin on her hand. At another table, several yards away, a baby cried. The mother picked it up, and the child hushed. "It was amazing to see how a little caring could change someone," she went on. "When my church was involved in building the youth center last year, I thought working there a couple of days a week might be rewarding."

"Has it been?"

"Are you kidding? Some days it's my life-line. I don't have to take my problems there. The kids don't judge or pry . . . at least not intentionally, and heaven knows some of them have problems much worse than mine. Of course, it isn't all a picnic. Some of those kids are rough . . . troublemakers, always bucking authority, starting fights . . ." The thought of Jason and T.J.'s fight flitted through her mind.

"But you don't give up on even those, do you?"

She paused for a long time, contemplating the disgust she'd had for T.J. after his cruelty to Jason. Would she turn him away if he came back to the center? No, probably not. "I'm tempted sometimes. You don't know how tempted. But if they're willing to at least meet me halfway, I'll try . . ."

"I wonder if they know how lucky they are to have you," Addison asked in a quiet voice.

"I'm not the only one. There are lots of other volunteers." She swallowed and met his dark emerald eyes, holding her with a touch of awe . . . and more than a touch of intention.

Footsteps on the gravel behind them startled them both, shattering the moment.

"Two burgers, no onions, two large fries, two large Cokes, and a Butterfinger Blizzard?" the girl asked in a nasal twang, while she popped her gum.

"That's us," Addison answered.

When the girl was on her way and the food was laid out in an awe-inspiring spread, Erin and Addison ate and teased about each other's appetites. After the food was gone, they cleared the table and sat back down, neither anxious to end the closeness that seemed to exist apart from time, the closeness that had no context in their lives or their problems.

Darkness had fallen without warning, and the breeze rustled the palm trees skirting the picnic area as they sat on the tabletop. The other scattered diners had left.

And they were alone.

Something about that was comforting to Erin, and those objections that tried to surface in her heart grew vague . . . distant.

Their shoulders brushed as they sat side by side, speaking in softer tones, comfortable yet maddeningly tense. Addison seemed to get closer each moment . . . his voice grew softer.

He's going to kiss me, she thought, her heart

setting a sprint-rate rhythm.

But he didn't. Not yet.

"I probably shouldn't say this," Addison said in a low voice, watching her lips as he spoke, "because I realize that it isn't entirely professional . . . or sophisticated . . . or even particularly smooth."

"Say it," she whispered.

"I just . . . I like being with you, Erin. You make me feel good, and . . . well, I just hope you won't let my investigation keep me from seeing you . . . like this . . . again."

She gazed at him in the darkness and watched him slowly wet his lips. Her fingers gripped the edge of the table. Slowly, he moved his head toward her, watching her mouth with enchantment. His lips grazed hers lightly, then withdrew. Her knuckles ached as she squeezed the table harder.

Their lips touched again, lingering longer this time, and he shifted slightly and slid one rough, shaky hand up her arm. The touch sent her heart careening, and her hand released its hold on the table and rose tentatively to feather through his soft black hair.

He moved both arms around her, crushing her against him as he deepened the kiss. Birds tittered in the trees and Erin's heart. Wind whistled through the leaves and Addison's head. Crickets sang, toads called, and Erin and Addison fell a little bit in love.

The kiss broke after a small eternity, but it was too soon for either of them. They gazed at each other, stricken, without breaking their embrace.

Addison stroked her cheek with his knuckles. "You're beautiful, Erin."

She felt more heat warming her cheeks and opened her mouth to speak, but no words emerged. Instead, Erin dropped her head. He pressed his lips against her forehead.

"Come on," he whispered. "I'll take you home."

The drive home was as quiet as it had been the day before, but this time their thoughts were far from airlines or flying or the tragic specters that plagued them both.

He pulled into the driveway outside her house, turned off the engine, and sat quietly for a moment.

Erin saw the light on in her window and noticed Lois's car parked in the carport. "Lois is home," she said quietly.

"Come on," Addison said. "I'll walk you to the door."

He held his arm around her as they walked, then suddenly stopped. Before she could say good night, he cupped her paint-smudged chin and lifted her face to his. "Hate me when I'm questioning you," he whispered, "and fight me if you want. But when I ask to see you . . . apart from the investigation . . . don't say no."

She didn't have to answer, for the way she met his lips halfway and responded to his embrace and reacted to his kiss, told him she would be there.

She didn't invite him in, which was just as well, he thought. It would be excruciating to make small talk with Lois when all he could think of was the way he was beginning to feel about Erin.

Someday she might feel the same, he thought . . . if he didn't make her hate him in the process.

CHAPTER TEN

His eyes are darker than Grandpa's pond, but lighter than the weeping willow that droops all over his lawn.

Southeast 34 cleared for takeoff.

You'll be fine, Erin. You're doing fine.

Eyes like summer. Like warmth. Like peace.

What if I can't do it? What if I can't?

Erin, don't say no . . . You're beautiful . . . beautiful . . .

The tape . . . I need to know what happened . . .

Southeast 34 cleared for takeoff.

His kiss is as soft and restless as the wind before a storm.

I can't breathe . . . I can't fly . . .

Erin, you're doing fine . . . Erin . . . Erin . . .

"Erin? Erin, are you all right?"

The words, both real and dreamed, merged together in Erin's mind, cutting her senses with sharp edges.

"Erin, wake up! You're dreaming! Wake up!"

Erin struggled to the surface of her sleep and sat up, disoriented. Perspiration had gathered on her upper lip and in her hair, and her body trembled as if she'd lived the nightmare.

"Erin, calm down. It was just a dream." Madeline sat beside her on the bed, a cool glass of water in her hand. "Here," she whispered. "Drink this."

Erin tried to catch her breath and grabbed the glass with both hands, struggling not to spill it as she drank. "Thank you," she said. She lay back down and shoved her bangs back from her damp forehead. "I'm sorry I woke you."

"You knocked over this vase," Madeline said, referring to the ornament on Erin's bedside table. "I came to see what happened, and you were thrashing around and crying . . ." Madeline's voice trailed off, and she touched Erin's arm. Her face held that maternal, best-friend-in-the-world look. "Do you want to talk about it, Erin?"

Erin didn't answer. She wasn't sure.

"Was it about your flight this morning? Are you still scared?" she asked quietly.

Erin's eyes filled with hot tears, and her mouth contorted in pain. She covered her eyes with her hand and nodded silently.

"Then don't do it," Madeline said.

Erin wiped her eyes and looked at her friend. More tears rolled down her face. "I thought you were all for it."

"What do I know?" Madeline asked.

"I have to do it," Erin whispered, the weight of her fear flattening her words. "I have to get over this, and I don't know any other way than just to do it."

Madeline took Erin's hand and nested it in both her own. "Things have a way of working out, Erin. They always do."

"For you, maybe."

"Oh, right. That's why I got abducted and held captive a few months ago. Don't forget how we met."

Erin hadn't forgotten. She had been hired to fly Madeline, her friend Sherry, and their captors to safety. It seemed like so long ago. "Even then, it all worked out, Madeline."

"Even now, it's going to work out for you, too," Madeline returned. "Take last night, for instance. That major hunk fell out of the sky and landed at the youth center. I mean, is that coincidence or what?"

Erin offered her friend a knowing smile, recognizing her attempt to change the subject. "I wouldn't use that word, exactly."

"Well, whatever works," Madeline said without regret. "I took one look at that guy and decided I couldn't send him on his way. He's almost as good-looking as Sam. Does he sing?"

Erin grinned. Sam was known for his

crazy, off-key singing during most of his waking moments. "I don't know," she said, slowly forgetting the terror in the dream, only to remember the soft, peace-invoking thoughts of Addison. "But I'll find out."

Madeline grinned her approval, and Erin reached for the glass again. "By the way," she whispered before she drank. "Did you notice the color of his eyes?"

That morning, Erin tried to keep thinking of the color of Addison's eyes as she prepared for her flight. She donned the uniform with the wings she had worked so hard to earn years ago when female pilots weren't common, especially at Southeast Airlines. She tied the white bow around her collar and set the black hat upon her head, never once letting herself dwell on the fear that lurked behind every shady corner in her heart.

For Mick, she thought. *I'll do this for Mick. He wouldn't want me to quit flying . . .*

Her hands began to tremble again, and she felt slightly faint. *Perfect love drives out fear.* Addison had reminded her of that. *Addison,* she thought. *He said I was beautiful. He wants to see me again. Addison, with the jade green eyes . . .*

The turn of thoughts calmed Erin's fears and made the task before her more approachable. She'd get through it, and when it was over, she wouldn't be afraid. She'd have her confidence back . . .

She drove to the airport, reminding herself that there was no rain and it was daylight and the sky was clear. It was a perfect day to fly . . . a perfect day . . .

Wary faces watched her as she approached her gate at the airport, and she knew what the crew was thinking. Would she make it this time? Would she be able to go through with it?

Jack, her captain, waited by the door to the ramp. His smile lacked apprehension, and she wondered where he found his faith in her. "You okay, Erin?"

Fine! I'm fine! she wanted to scream. Instead, she nodded and smiled tightly. "Yes. Great."

"Good," he said. "It's a beautiful day."

"Beautiful," she agreed absently.

She stepped to the window and watched the luggage being loaded onto her aircraft. It *was* a beautiful day, she thought. So why did she feel only the invisible forces somewhere in that sky, the forces that had foiled Mick's flight and sent 151 people to their deaths?

Addison saw Erin the moment he rounded

the curve that led to Southeast Gate 14, and mutely he nodded at whatever the chief pilot was telling him. She was dressed in the pilot's uniform she'd had on the first time he saw her, and again she was staring out that window, hugging her arms, with suppressed terror in her eyes.

"We'll get you a representative for your board, to answer questions about policy . . . ," Jackson, Erin's chief pilot, who was even superior to Frank, was saying.

Without meaning to ignore him, Addison stopped and gaped at Erin. Surely she wasn't flying. Not when she'd already expressed her fear to go up, not when she was shaking so badly now.

"I think that should make your job . . ."

Addison raised a hand to stop Jackson's rambling, without taking his eyes off Erin's back. "Excuse me, Bill. I was just . . ." He turned back to the chief pilot, frown lines distorting his expression. "Is Erin Russell scheduled to fly today?"

Jackson lifted his shoulders. "I don't know. I suppose she is, or she wouldn't be here."

Addison's frown alerted Jackson that there was a problem. "Are you aware of her condition?"

"She's been under some stress since the

crash," Jackson acknowledged without concern, "but Frank assured me that she just needed some time. Why? Is there something I don't know?"

"Yeah," Addison said. But, before he was asked to expound, he left the chief pilot and wove through the waiting area toward Erin.

Erin jumped slightly when Addison touched her back. She turned around, and her first instinct upon seeing him was to smile.

But Addison's authoritative look stopped her. "You're not going up today, are you?"

"Well . . . yes. I feel fine," she said. "I'm ready now."

His expression disputed her words. Roughly, he took her hand, raised it, revealing its trembling. "A pilot with complete confidence doesn't shake like a terrified child."

Anger flashed in her eyes, and she jerked her hand away. She saw Jackson coming up behind him and shot Addison a warning look. "You're out of line, Addison. This is none of your business."

"It's my business when I see a pilot putting an airplane full of passengers in danger."

"I'm not putting them in danger! I'm a good pilot!"

"Then how can you even consider going up today?"

"I have to, Addison. It's my job. You do yours, I'll do mine."

"Mine happens to be making sure that crashes don't recur."

"You don't have the authority to ground me!" she bit out. She turned to her boss, her feelings wavering between hysteria and terror. "Does he, Bill?"

Bill Jackson stepped between them, a frown graphing his usually preoccupied features. "Wait a minute, Addison. What's going on here?"

"She isn't ready to fly yet," Addison said. "She's terrified. She hasn't come to terms with things yet."

"You don't know *what* I've come to terms with! You don't know anything about me!"

"She's being pressured to fly, because of the takeover," Addison continued. "Three days ago I *heard* her telling Frank that making her go up now would be — and this is an exact quote — dangerous and irresponsible. Is that what happened, Erin? Are they *making* you go up?"

Flames of rage colored her eyes. "How dare you!" she seethed. "You have no right —"

"*Is* someone pressuring you to fly, Erin?"

Jackson cut in quietly.

"No! I'm ready. I am."

Addison shook his head slowly and regarded the chief pilot. "She's right, Bill, about my not having the authority to ground her. But you do. And I have to strongly recommend that you ground her until she can prove to one of us that she's capable of being responsible for that airplane."

She looked beseechingly at her boss. Surely, he wouldn't listen to Addison. He would let her go ahead with the flight, wouldn't he? And if he did, would she let him down as soon as she got in the cockpit?

"I'm sorry, Erin," the chief pilot said. "Addison has good instincts. I have to trust them."

"But —"

"See me in my office in an hour," Jackson continued. "We'll work something out to keep you on the payroll in spite of this."

The chief pilot left them alone, Erin gaping at Addison, Addison looking regretfully at her. The color of his eyes had changed, she thought bitterly. They were cold now, like the sharp edges of emeralds, full of purpose and reason and the intention to cut right through her if she got in his way.

Her cheeks blazed even hotter than before. "You jerk," she whispered. "You made me trust you. You made me drop my guard. I should have known that you'd use that against me the first chance you had."

"Erin, this has nothing to do with —"

"Save it," she snapped. "Go find somebody else's life to ruin."

Before Addison could find a response, Erin had vanished from his sight.

Addison tried to get Erin out of his mind for the next few hours as he sat in the hangar, studying the computerized reports of instrument readings he'd gotten back from Washington that day. His team was still working, examining pieces of the plane that hadn't been sent to headquarters. So many conclusions could be drawn from the angles of damage on the turbine blades, or whether the engines had been running, or the impact with which metal was torn. That was why they'd spent the first week and a half of the investigation with the wreckage right where it had crashed, surveying different pieces in relation to landscape and buildings, to decide exactly how the plane had hit. But there was no getting around the hard evidence he'd found. The plane had flown straight into the ground, with no apparent attempt to pull the nose up to save it.

Find somebody else's life to ruin!

Was that what he was doing? he asked himself. Was he ruining the life that Mick had left as a memory? Was he ruining the lives of Mick's family? And most importantly, was he ruining Erin's?

The noon heat beat down on the metal hangar, warming him unbearably, and making his shirt stick to his body. He walked across the hangar to the table where copies of the other reports lay. He picked up the printed copy of what had been found on the flight data recorder, the metal tape that recorded statistics but no sound. When the cockpit tape was repaired, they'd match the vocal transmissions to this data, and he would know the speed, heading, altitude, vertical velocity, and elapsed time when each radio transmission was made. Until he had the tape, he couldn't really be sure what had gone wrong. But how could he ignore the evidence until then? And how could he manage the conflict of his feelings for Erin and his feeling about his report? Sid would have a field day with the confusion he was feeling.

You made me trust you.

"Blazes," he whispered, staring at the date before him. Why had he gotten her grounded the way he had? Why hadn't he been more gentle? More understanding?

Because he had been so shaken up to see

her even attempt it, after what she'd said in Redlo's office, that was why. Because there hadn't been time. Because she was under his skin, and when he thought about her, he lost his head.

Saddam Hussein will become a missionary before she'll speak to you again, he told himself. Erin hated him now, and he couldn't blame her. If he hadn't been so stricken with that sense of responsibility . . .

He stopped himself from wallowing in misery. The investigation was all that mattered, he told himself. He'd forget her and just do his job the best way he could. He made a difference, and if she couldn't see that, then it wasn't meant to be . . .

The other men on his team eyed him cautiously, each starting to speak in turn, then letting the subject of the day's events drop. It was hard keeping secrets from them, when they often worked together around the clock. They had all heard Bill Jackson a little while ago, when he'd come to assure Addison that Erin was "taken care of."

Only Hank, his closest friend on the team, dared to broach the subject. "You did what you had to do, Addison. Don't sweat it. It's her problem, not yours."

The declaration bore no comfort. "Yeah, well," he said, knowing his depression over the matter spoke volumes about his feelings for Erin, "I'm not so sure about that."

And before any more discussion on the topic could be aired, he found himself loading his briefcase, buttoning his shirt, and leaving the hangar. He'd find her, he told himself, and explain. He'd make her understand. Not because he cared, but so that he could finally concentrate on his work.

Erin pulled into the Hammon's driveway and saw Jason in front of the garage, bouncing a basketball listlessly on the concrete. He glanced up and smiled slightly, waved, then hooked the ball into the basket. It bounced back down and rolled off into the ditch beside the drive. Jason didn't go after it. Instead, he stuffed his hands into his pockets and waited for Erin to get out of the car.

As she got out and smoothed out the jeans she'd changed into, Erin wondered why she'd come here. Jason didn't need her misery heaped atop his own. He didn't need to know of her fears or her anger. For all she knew, he didn't want to face her after the fight with T.J. But she had been worried about him. Somehow, just helping him cope helped *her* to cope. "Hi, Jase," she said, unable to work up much of a smile. "How's it going?"

"Pretty good," he said with no inflection in his voice. He frowned then inclined his head, as if he'd found a major, suspicious flaw in her. "What are you doing here?"

"I came to see you," she said. She went to the side of the verandah Mick had built to surround the house, and sat down. "Any crime against that?"

"No, but I mean . . . well, I just saw you a couple of days ago, and the day before that, and the day before that."

"Are you saying you're getting sick of me?" she teased.

"No. I mean your schedule. Four days on, three days off. Shouldn't you be working today?"

Erin lowered her face and studied her shoes. The kid was too smart for his own good. She should have known he could see right through her. "No, I've decided to take some time off of flying for a while."

"Why?" he asked, as if the decision affected him directly.

"No reason. I'm just tired of the schedule. I need a break."

The look on Jason's young face told her he wasn't buying her story. "It's because of Dad, isn't it?"

Erin's eyes flashed, her gaze meeting his head-on, and she knew she should never have come here today. "No, Jason. Really."

Jason ambled toward her, scuffing his Reeboks on the pavement. Slowly, he sat down on the deck beside her. "It's okay," he said quietly, in a voice that made her forget he was only nine. "You can tell me."

She smiled sadly and took his hand. "It's nothing, really," she said, trying to keep all emotion from her voice. "I've just kind of lost my interest in flying. Bill Jackson is putting me in scheduling for a while, until I decide what I want to do. It'll be a nice break." *A nice break.* Those were Bill's exact words, as he'd officialized her temporary grounding. He trusted Addison, he said, and had to believe him when he said she wasn't ready. Besides, Southeast couldn't afford not to cooperate with the NTSB.

"What's scheduling?" Jason asked.

"Oh, I'll be working the month-to-month schedules for the crews, working their bids for flights. Finding replacements when someone's sick, filling open time, reserves, that sort of thing. Apparently the scheduling department is shorthanded since the takeover, because Trans Western has given us some new routes."

Jason's twisted face told her he wasn't impressed. "And you won't be flying *at all?*"

She swallowed and tried to reinforce her

164

smile. "Not for a while."

Jason exhaled deeply. "Why? Dad used to say that flying got in your blood. That a true pilot couldn't ever really give it up."

"It isn't always that simple," she said.

"It is for me," Jason argued. "I'm gonna learn to fly as soon as my mom lets me. I'm gonna be a pilot like Dad." He paused and focused on the sky, his young, pale eyes filling with conviction. "I'll show everybody that Hammons don't screw up."

Erin laced her fingers together, studying them to keep her emotions at bay. She hadn't expected such a direct proclamation from Jason. Until now, he'd been evasive about his feelings. "You don't have to prove anything to anybody, Jason."

"But the things they're saying about him . . ." Jason looked at Erin and held her eyes, searching them for honesty. "He didn't screw up, did he, Erin? Dad was too good a pilot to do that, wasn't he?"

Erin pulled the stiff child against her, fighting the tears in her eyes. "You better believe he was," she said. "And anybody who says different better have some hard evidence, 'cause they're going to get the fight of their life from me."

By the time Erin was back home, her

anger had reached a fever pitch again. Anger for what Addison had done to her, anger for what Addison was doing to Mick, anger for what Addison was doing to Jason.

She tore into her apartment and pulled out a blank canvas, quaking at the thought of Jason's eyes as he'd asked her about the crash, of Addison's eyes as they'd controlled her. He had betrayed her after she trusted him, and that hurt more than anything else that had happened that day.

She got her charcoal out of a drawer where she kept it and began marring the white canvas with heavy, vicious marks. If it weren't for him, she'd be flying now . . .

The thought stopped her cold, and she stilled her hand and caught her breath. Would she be, or had he saved her from another instance of humiliation? Had he kept her from freezing again?

It didn't matter. He still had no right. No right at all.

The doorbell rang. Annoyed at the intrusion, she dropped the charcoal and canvas, then went to answer the door. Addison stood there, a look of reluctant regret on his face. His hand shot out to brace the door when she started to close it on him.

"I have nothing to say to you," she said.

Addison pushed his way inside, his eyes

as insistent as hers. "No. We have to talk, Erin. You've got me all wrong."

She crossed her arms and cocked her head up at him. "Then you don't think I'm unstable and a hazard to the airways, as you told my boss?"

"You weren't ready, Erin. You know you weren't ready. Redlo admitted he pressured you into flying."

"I could have done it," she said. "I could have."

"Maybe so. Maybe you would have forced yourself." He slumped against the back of the sofa. "Erin, I did it because I care about you. I didn't want to see you go up there, putting yourself in that kind of danger. My job is preventing crashes!"

He stopped and drove a hand through his hair, turned his back to her, then turned around again. "Can you honestly stand there and tell me that you were looking forward to flying, that you could have just hopped back into the cockpit and dashed over to St. Louis without consequence? You were shaking, Erin, and I saw the fear in your eyes. You hadn't resolved it yet."

"All right," she admitted through gritted teeth. "So I was nervous. I've been nervous before, but no one ever grounded me for it. I'm a responsible pilot. If I hadn't thought

I could do it, I wouldn't have."

"Then you would have taxied down the runway and frozen, like the other night?"

"No!"

"How can you be sure?"

"How can I *ever* be sure," she blared, "if I don't try? How can I resolve it if I'm grounded?"

"It won't be forever, Erin," Addison said in a half whisper. "Please, trust me. As soon as you can prove to me that you've come to terms with the crash and that you aren't terrified, I'll recommend that you fly again."

"That's it, isn't it? The crash. This is your leverage to get me to tell you whatever you want to know. If you have this hanging over my head, I have to please you, don't I? I have to cooperate, just to keep you from getting me fired altogether. What else do you want from me, Addison? What's next? A little physical cooperation?"

He opened his mouth to fling a retort, but stopped short. His face seemed to pale as she glared at him. Then, quietly, he turned and walked out the door.

Erin stood frozen, more shaken and frightened by her own feelings than she'd ever been by the prospect of flying.

CHAPTER ELEVEN

Erin stood paralyzed beneath the hard, hot jets of spray showering down upon her. The heat made reality seem sharper, more painful. Tears of self-condemnation streamed down her face, mingling with the cleansing water. For the first time in her life, Erin had to admit that she didn't like herself very much.

What had she been thinking? How could she have thrown sex up at Addison that way, when that hadn't been the issue at all? It was stress, she justified. People did crazy things under stress.

She shut off the water and stepped out of the shower, drying herself roughly with a thick towel. Along with her self-condemnation — perhaps because of it — rose a fresh, blossoming anger. He had tampered with her life and left her without a career. How would she ever fly again?

She heard the front door closing, then the sound of Lois's soft, tentative voice through the bathroom door. "Erin, I'm sorry," she said hesitantly. "I heard about what happened at the airport."

Erin dried harder with her towel and told

herself she was done with tears. She wrapped herself in the towel and opened the door, letting the steam escape and the fresh air rush in to relieve the mirrors of their fog. Lois stood at the door, peering in. "Erin, are you okay?"

"Remember the NTSB investigator I told you about?" Erin asked as she headed for her room.

"Yeah."

"Well, he's the same guy Madeline sent to find me yesterday. The same one I went out with last night."

Lois followed, her eyes wide. "The same one who got you grounded?" she gasped. "He seemed like such a nice guy. Just this morning you were saying what nice eyes he has."

Erin retrieved the towel and went to the mirror, rubbing the wetness from her hair. "Yeah, well, just this morning I didn't know he was going to turn on me. He overheard me talking to Frank, and he used my own words against me."

Lois went to the bed and sat down. "I should have known he was too good to be true. The most attractive ones usually turn out to be jerks. I guess I just thought if I couldn't find a real prince, then maybe you could."

Erin began jerking the brush through her wet hair, her freshly scrubbed face glowing anew as she recalled the scene when he'd come here. Tears welled in her eyes again, but she forced them back. She wasn't able to stop the trembling of her lips, however. "The thing is . . . he's probably right. Part of me was enraged at his audacity . . . but the other part was . . ." Her voice trailed off into a shamed whisper. ". . . so relieved. Lois, how will I ever get over this fear if they won't let me fly?"

Lois smiled suddenly. "Like I told you, there's nowhere to go but up. And I was talking to Jack right before takeoff, and he offered to let you use his Cessna to get your confidence back. So see? You can fly. Addison Lowe can't take that from you."

Erin took a barefoot step closer to her friend, all anger draining from her face and leaving in its wake the beginnings of hope. "Jack offered that? Really?"

Relief danced in Lois's pastel blue eyes. "Really. We agreed that if you take it up a few times, you can prove your confidence is back, and they'll *have* to lift your suspension."

Erin took a long breath and gazed thankfully at her friend. "Lo, you just might be a lifesaver."

Lois sprang off the bed. "Jack said he was calling his wife before he left, to tell her. You can touch base with her about the details. The Cessna is yours as often as you want it."

Something close to a smile brightened Erin's face. "It'll work," she whispered. "I know it will. Thanks, Lo. You're the greatest —"

Lois waved off the compliment. "Save it," she said. "I need something more tangible than mush and gratitude. Help me get my presentation for the union members ready. I traded my next two trips, since the meeting's tomorrow, and if you think you've lived with fear, you haven't seen my knees shake when I address a roomful of people."

"Anything," Erin agreed. "We'll start right now. And tomorrow you'll knock 'em dead."

"We both will," Lois said.

Addison pulled the massive hangar door shut with all his might, letting the roar and thud reverberate throughout the big building. He flicked on the light, and grinding his teeth, marched to the tagged wreckage assembled on various tables and on the concrete at his feet. His crew had probably gone for a late lunch, so he was all alone in the bland building. Furious, he cursed the crash and this thankless job of his and his burdensome sense of responsibility.

But most of all, he cursed his passion and the anger Erin Russell had ignited in him . . .

Without thinking, he slammed his fist into a battered file cabinet, but the act did not help him to vent his anger. Instead, it merely heightened it. He bent double, clutching his bruised fingers.

She hated him now. And no matter what he did from this point on, he would always remember the day he robbed her of her career and made her despise him. The day he smothered out a little of himself.

He sat on the floor, leaning back against the corrugated wall, the rumble of aircraft outside vibrating in his heart and stomach. He hated himself. Not since Amanda's death had he felt so low.

He ran his fingers through his hair, propped his elbows on bent knees, and looked up at the ceiling, as if he could see his wife's pale, pretty face there now. *I miss her, Lord,* he prayed. *I miss her so much. But there has to be more than quiet and loneliness. Isn't there more, Lord? Isn't there? Or am I too big a fool to find it?*

The engines outside seemed to become still, the walls ceased to vibrate, and Addison, for a fraction of a moment, thought he felt a peaceful reply. *There is more, Addison. There is more . . .*

For the first time in several years, Addison knew the sting of tears.

Addison saw Erin the next day before she saw him. She was with Lois, standing in the coffee shop line behind her friend, wearing a trim blue dress that followed the lines of her waist, then tapered out to midcalf. She looked more lovely than he'd ever seen her.

He wasn't sure what propelled him toward her, when he knew he was the last person she wanted to see. But before he knew it he was in line behind her, reaching for the same salad as she.

Erin looked up at him and drew back her hand. Eyes the color of the setting sun glared at him, then darted away. "Sorry," she said stiffly. "You take it."

"No, you had it first." He set it on her tray.

She turned away and looked toward the cash register.

"Listen," he said quietly, "could we sit down . . . talk . . . ?"

"I'm busy," she said.

"Maybe later?" he asked.

"Later I'll be working."

"Is it working out all right? Scheduling?" he asked for want of anything better to say.

Erin turned her head slowly back to him, her cold eyes making him pale and sending a shiver curling down his spine. "I'm a pilot," she said through her teeth. "How do you think it's working out?"

Addison dropped his eyes, stepped back, and let her follow her friend to a table. His appetite lost, he left the cafeteria and headed back to the hangar.

"No strike, no strike, no strike!" Lois called from the lectern at the center of the stage in the airport auditorium. "Not until all else has failed!"

Applause rose from the room where hundreds of Southeast pilots were gathered, and stunned, Lois watched the ovation. In the audience, she saw Erin cheering, and wondered if she looked as pale as she felt. Her knees were shaking as she gathered her papers, and she ran one moist palm down her skirt and cleared her throat. Besides the speech, Lois had survived Ray Carter's evil eye, which could have murdered her if those daggers in his gaze had been real instead of illusory. Moments before Lois had stood up to speak, Ray had had the entire union spitfire angry and ready to strike. She'd had only

175

passion and prayer — both of which proved invaluable.

Ray stepped up to the podium, dismissing Lois by turning his back to her. "All right, all right," he called out impatiently. "Quiet, please." He waited until the applause died down, then cleared his throat authoritatively. Taking his dismissive cue, Lois went back to her seat beside Erin.

"You've obviously just heard two very different sides to this issue," he said. "Since most of you seem to have been persuaded by Lois's tactics to . . . what was the word she used . . . compromise? Well, since most of you seem to believe that's the path we should take, I'd like to make a recommendation that we hold off the strike vote temporarily — just long enough to meet with Mr. Zarkoff firsthand, so that he can prove to us that he isn't going to budge an inch. This is open to discussion."

One of the first officers near the front stood up. "Ray, I agree that we should hold off on the strike vote, but I wonder if it isn't a bad idea to try to negotiate with Zarkoff ourselves. Maybe we should hire a professional negotiator."

A round of mumbled agreement followed, before someone else stood up. "A professional negotiator has nothing at stake. He wouldn't know us. I think we should have our own people there."

Lois stood up, waiting to be recognized, but Ray flatly ignored her. Anger compelled her to speak anyway. "Excuse me," she shouted. "But I'd like to speak. I think I have a compromise."

"Another one?" Ray said in a patronizing tone. "Well, heaven forbid we should overlook another little compromise. Please. The floor is yours."

Lois ignored his condescension and reminded herself of the success she'd had moments earlier. "I recommend that we hire a professional negotiator and elect a small bargaining committee of four or five to go to the table with him. That way, we'd have professional advice and expertise, while still keeping our own hands in and being able to speak for ourselves if the need arises."

Another round of approving applause followed, and Lois sat back down, feeling a rush of dizziness. There, she'd said it, and they hadn't ignored her or thrown tomatoes. At least, not yet, though she expected Ray to find something to launch across the room any minute.

"I move that we call a vote," someone said. "Seconded!"

Compressing his lips tightly, Ray Carter

called for the inevitable vote to accept Lois's recommendation. It would have been unanimous, except for the few diehards who were anxious to go on strike and "show Zarkoff who he was messing with."

Lois felt relief and a moment of ecstasy at the progress she'd made . . . until she heard herself being nominated for the bargaining committee. When the vote was final, she found that she'd been elected . . . along with Ray and three others who were hostile, at best, to her cause. They would meet with the original committee of twenty for recommendations, they were told, then take their grievances and demands to their negotiator. And when the time came, they would each have to speak to Zarkoff on behalf of the other members.

Terror smothered out relief as Lois sat, paralyzed, imagining herself shaking like a marionette as she addressed Attila the Hun and "his people." And if she lost everything for the pilots because of a paralyzing case of nerves, it would be her fault. Ray Carter wouldn't hesitate to blame her, and she'd be tarred and feathered in one way or another.

The members buzzed out of the room when the meeting was over, but Lois stayed still in her chair.

"Lois? What's the matter?" Erin asked. "You were great. You changed their minds."

"They did accept all of my recommendations," Lois muttered, staring vacantly ahead.

"So why do you look like you've been punched in the stomach?"

"Because I don't want to be one of the five to go up against Zarkoff. This has gotten way out of hand, and I think I'm gonna be sick."

Erin took her friend's hand and stared into her face. "Lois, calm down. It'll be fine. You're the best person for the job, and you know it."

Lois raised herself out of the chair. "Excuse me, Erin. I have to find some place to lie down. I don't feel very well."

Erin smiled sympathetically as Lois, dazed and still shaking, rushed out of the room to come to terms with her own version of terror.

CHAPTER TWELVE

Terror wasn't something Erin expected later that afternoon when she was off work and hurried over to the private Pioneer Airport to fly Jack's Cessna. She'd expected to feel good about flying such a light aircraft, to conquer her fear as she took it into the sky . . .

Instead, that familiar, smothering panic cycled up inside her as she stood outside the plane, regarding it as if it were the enemy waiting to swallow her up and take her to her death.

Wind whipped her hair around her face as she stood on the small runway, glancing from side to side to see if anyone was watching her. A machinist strolled across the pavement, but he seemed oblivious to her fears. She swallowed the knot in her throat, held her breath, and took a few steps closer to the plane.

Slowly, she climbed in, closed the door, and leaned back against the seat. Why, her mind railed, did it feel like she was offering herself up as a sacrifice to a cruel, ominous sky?

Her breath came in shallow gasps, and her

hands trembled as she went through the short checklist that all pilots knew like their names or addresses or Social Security numbers. Controls, instruments, fuel were all as they should be. With trembling hands, she started the engine to check the ignition system, then sat still, listening to it rumble beneath her. It was simple, she told herself. So simple. She'd flown one of these as a teenager. It had been as easy as riding a bike. Why couldn't she do it now?

I can do it, she told herself. *I can. I'm not going to let it beat me.*

She tried to pull herself together and checked the interior to make sure the doors and windows were closed and latched, then set her props into takeoff position.

The plane was ready. All she had to do was radio the small tower, to make sure she was clear for takeoff. All she had to do was go down that runway, launch into the sky, and use those wings that seemed to be mercilessly clipped.

I'm a pilot. A good one.

But the affirmation didn't help. She was paralyzed with the engine running beneath her, the fumes rising in blurs from the concrete, the oxygen seeming to thin out in the cockpit. Terrorized, she hadn't even moved an inch.

"Oh, God, I know you didn't give me a spirit of fear!" she cried aloud as tears filled her eyes. "So where did this come from?"

She would have given everything she owned for a portion of the peace she knew was her inheritance. But it seemed so far out of reach that she feared she'd never know it again.

Erin got out of the plane when she felt she could walk back into the small terminal without calling too much attention to her tear-stained face. She wiped her eyes, locked the plane, and gave it one last look. Sun glinted off the metallic surface and shimmered over the red stripe running from nose to tail. What was there to fear from this small plane? she asked herself. *Nothing,* her mind answered, but her heart concocted endless lists of irrational worries. "I'll get you yet," she told it, as if it were some animate force to be reckoned with. "I won't be beaten."

Sniffing back her misery, she walked to the terminal door, went inside, and stood frozen, suddenly realizing that Addison had been right when he'd had her grounded. He had saved her from more humiliation, or worse. If she had forced herself to go up, she might have frozen in the cockpit. He had known it. And he had done the right thing.

Wanting suddenly to talk to him and absorb some of the peace he had given her the other night, she looked around for a pay phone. Her hands shook as she searched her wallet for the phone number that Madeline had transcribed from the answering machine and stuck in her purse. Trying to control her breath to lessen the panicky waver in her voice, she inserted a coin and dialed.

Addison answered on the third ring. "Hello?"

His voice was quiet, his tone downbeat, and Erin almost hung up. But she was getting much too weary of running.

"Addison?"

His pause was eloquent, and finally he said, "Erin?"

"It's me," she said, swallowing hard. "Um, Addison, I owe you an apology. You did the right thing yesterday by not letting me fly. I wouldn't have made it."

She heard something rustling, as if he had shifted the phone to his other ear. "Erin, are you all right?" he asked.

"No . . ." She cleared her throat. "Yes. I just . . . wanted to apologize for all the things I said."

His voice dropped to a more intimate pitch. "I owe you an apology, too. For losing my temper the way I did."

The mention of what had happened between them twisted her heart, and she dropped her head against the phone. Her voice rose to a squeaky pitch. "Listen, are you busy? I mean, if you are . . ."

"No, not at all," he said quickly. "I could come over if you want —"

"I'm not at home," she cut in. "I'm . . . out. I thought maybe we could meet at Marty's. Play a game of racquetball . . . or something."

"I'll be there," he said without hesitation. "Twenty minutes all right?"

"Fine," she said. "I'll see you then, Addison."

She hung up the phone and rubbed her face with a hand that hadn't been steady in days. But Addison was coming, and somehow things didn't seem quite as dismal as they had a few minutes ago.

CHAPTER THIRTEEN

Addison Lowe wasn't sure how it had happened, but somehow he felt he'd been given a second chance. Erin didn't hate him. Wasn't avoiding him. Had even apologized!

He pulled his car into the parking lot at Marty's and sat still for a moment before getting out. The thought of her weepy voice when she'd called twisted his heart. Had something happened?

Soberly, he got out of the car, pulling his duffel bag with him, and started inside. She was waiting beside the door for him, for he couldn't come in unless he was accompanied by a member.

"Hi," she said when he pushed through the glass doors.

He stopped and swept his gaze over her, over the windblown hair that he'd grown to love the way he loved her eyes and her smile. He saw the red stains beneath her eyes, evidence that she'd shed more than a few tears. Still, she looked more beautiful than he'd ever seen her. But then, he thought that every time he saw her.

"Hi," he returned with a tentative smile.

"I'm really glad you called."

She dropped her eyes, reminding him of a wide-eyed, innocent doe, and he saw that she didn't want to talk about their earlier conversation. He stood quietly as she signed him in, then led him to the court they'd been assigned.

Still quiet, they each warmed up in their own way, and finally Erin tossed him the ball. "You serve," she suggested in a soft voice.

There was a change in her playing tonight, Addison thought, after the game had started. He was winning, for one thing, because there was no vengeance in her swings, only weariness and lethargy. It was as if she didn't really want to play, but needed something to do because she didn't want to talk, either.

When he'd defeated her, he decided that the game wasn't a good idea, after all. It was a pretense for something much more important. "What's the matter, Erin?" he asked. "I thought you wanted to play."

"I did." Her breath was shallow and rapid. She leaned back against the wall, letting her racquet hang from the band around her wrist. "I'm just a little tired, I guess." She slid down the wall, put down her racquet, and hugged her knees to her chest.

Addison sat down beside her. "Talk to

186

me, Erin," he said, the room's acoustics amplifying his voice. "This morning you hated me. Couldn't even look me in the eye. What happened?"

He saw the tears in her eyes even as he asked the question. Her hands came up to shield her face, and her cheeks and neck went crimson as she attempted to control herself. Though he had vowed to keep his hands to himself, Addison couldn't help pulling her against him. "Erin?" he asked, a little frightened at the strength of her emotions . . . and the ones they evoked in him.

"I probably shouldn't have called you," she said, the words coming out in a slow, shaken strain. "I don't really know why I did."

"I'm glad you did," he whispered. Addison touched her hair gently, and when she moved her hands away from her face, he met her eyes.

"It's just that I knew I'd been unfair yesterday. All the things I said . . . when you were right . . ." The words faded. "You *were* right, Addison. I would have gotten in that cockpit, maybe taxied down the runway, and frozen again. I would have, and you could see it."

"I wasn't being brutal, Erin. I care about you. I didn't want to see you hurt."

She stifled a sob and wiped at her red-blotched eyes. "Addison, what's wrong with me? Why can't I do it?"

"Because the crash turned your life and everything you believed about your profession and your friends, upside down. It's shaken you up, and it seems like the nightmare will never end, but it will. I know, Erin. When it happened to me, I didn't fly for six months."

"But it's my whole life," she said in a squeaky voice. "I don't have a purpose without it. I'm not cut out for a desk job. It's the first time in my life that I have absolutely no control, and it scares me, Addison. I'm scared to death."

Addison cupped her wet chin, letting her tears slip through his fingers, and brought her face to his. His heart twisted with every new tear that dropped from her lashes, and at that moment he would have given her anything he possessed to make her stop crying. "I know that you're a woman of faith, Erin. It's strong enough that you give it to others. You should know that sometimes, when we have no control, that's when we should let God have control."

"I know that," she whispered. "And I'm trying. I just don't understand."

"I'll help you, Erin," he whispered. "Let

me help. Tell me what to do."

"If I just knew . . . ," she said again, clenching her hand into a fist. "If I could just know what went on in that cockpit that day. Why did that plane fly straight into the ground? He had flown that approach a thousand times. Why this time? What happened?"

"That's what I'm trying to find out," Addison assured her. "And when I do, I'll tell you, Erin. I promise you, I'll do my best to get to the truth."

He could see that the promise wasn't good enough, and he knew she feared that the truth wouldn't be what she wanted to hear. She covered her face again, and Addison pulled her head against his chest.

"Promise me you'll be fair, Addison," she murmured. "Promise me you'll give him a chance."

"If you promise that whatever I find won't make you hate me," he whispered. "I don't think I can stand that again."

Erin gave a tentative nod, but Addison doubted it was a promise she could keep. If the truth didn't give her peace, he hoped that he could heal her heart in some other way.

She brought her wide, glossy eyes to his. He stroked her face with his hands, making a half frame of that exposed expression that he never wanted to forget. Slowly, he bent over and closed his lips over the wet web of her lashes, allowing the dampness to paint his mouth. His breath left a warm, invisible mark of possession on her forehead, a mark that he hoped her heart read and approved.

She lifted her face and searched his eyes, poignantly touching some lonely place in his heart. When he bent to kiss her, she seemed to melt. He felt the world realigning, as if God was giving him a sign that he had not forsaken either of them. It felt so right, so good . . .

He broke the kiss and looked into her eyes. "It's funny how one bright moment with you can make all the moments alone seem so dim. I've felt that gray loneliness a lot, Erin. I've gotten used to it. But it's been a long time since I've known this brightness. I didn't even know to pray for it. I thought it was gone to me forever."

And as he let the words sink into the depths of her heart, Addison kissed her again.

CHAPTER FOURTEEN

Addison pushed the key into the lock of his front door and stepped inside, turning on the dim light that illuminated the small foyer.

He sank onto the sofa and leaned back, letting the feelings of peace and love linger in his heart. But unbidden, Amanda's serene face formed in his mind, and his heart twisted. The love for her was still there, and along with that long-lingering love came murmurs of regret. There would never be another, he'd thought after her death. Never.

So he had clung to that love, that memory, for four long, empty years, and it had served him well enough. But now there was Erin.

The telephone rang, startling him from his reverie, and he picked it up, hoping it was Erin. She could lay his guilty thoughts to rest and remind him how good it felt to have someone in his life.

"Hello?"

"Don't tell me," his father-in-law barked out, his voice filled with blatant irritation. "You've been out questioning some friend of a friend of a cousin of the captain on a boat on the Gulf and couldn't get back to shore until the middle of the night."

Addison closed his eyes and told himself not to get his ire up. He could handle this. "I take it you've been trying to call."

"For hours," Sid said. "And don't give me that song and dance about how you were out doing your job."

"As a matter of fact," Addison said through his teeth, "I wasn't. Tonight was pleasure instead of business. I am allowed a little pleasure, aren't I? Or has the NTSB added an amendment to my job description?"

A moment of thick quiet stretched over the line, and he could almost hear Sid seething. "You were with a woman, weren't you?"

Addison breathed a half groan, but reminded himself that Sid felt, wrongly or not, that he had a stake in Addison's love life. After all, he had been married to his only daughter. Gentling his tone, he answered the volatile question. "Yes, Sid. I was with a woman. I know that doesn't sit well with you, and as much as I care for and respect you, I don't think I owe you explanations about every detail of my private life."

Without meaning to, Addison held his breath as the line went silent again. Finally, the inevitable question came. "Who is she?" Sid asked. "Did you just pick her up in a bar, or did you know her before?"

The flames of wrath began to climb up Addison's cheeks, and he stood, clutching the phone to his ear. "I don't pick women up in bars!"

"I see." The words were barely audible, and Addison sensed at once that Sid would have preferred that he did. Such an encounter might have been considered a one-night stand, written off to restlessness, and then forgotten. "Then you're serious about this person?"

Addison began pacing in an arc across his floor. He had only kissed her, for pete's sake! Why did he feel as if he'd been caught doing something disgraceful? Wasn't this between him and his wife's memory? Wasn't it something that only he should deal with? "Sid, it doesn't concern you. It has nothing to do with my job."

Instantly, he hated himself for reducing Sid's judgment to professional interest. Never would he forget the way he'd found Sid a few days after the funeral. He'd been sitting alone in a dark house, cluttered with half-eaten meals left to spoil on tables and windowsills, his television blaring mindless garbage. Sid himself had been staring into space, unchanged and unbathed since he'd buried his daughter. Ever since that day Addison had bonded with him in their common loss, and Sid had clung to him like he was his only living relative. Except for a few distant cousins across the country somewhere, he *was* the only family Sid had left. "It's time I joined life again, Sid. It's time you did, too."

"Who is she?" Sid asked again, biting out the words.

Addison hesitated, then decided it was best to get it out, so that Sid could get used to the idea. "Her name is Erin Russell. She was Hammon's first officer . . ."

"Then she *is* connected with the crash," Sid cut in, as if he'd found the loophole he needed to convict him.

"Yes, to some extent."

"Then there's an obvious conflict of interest," Sid went on, a note of relief softening his tone.

"How do you figure that?"

"Well, it's obvious. Friends protect friends. She probably figures if she gets to you, she can change your mind about the cause of the crash. Is that what's holding things up?"

Addison sank back into his chair, rubbing his face. "Sid, you've known me for years. You know how stubborn I am. I'm not easily influenced. Things are going slowly for the same reason they were the last time I spoke to you. I don't have the tape, and I don't have all of the test results —"

"If you'd been home or at the hangar instead of warming up to some woman, maybe you'd know that the tape was flown to you today!" Sid cut in.

"I didn't get it," Addison said. "Who'd you send it to?"

"You, who else? You *are* the senior member of this team, aren't you? It came in a flight bag with some other mail from headquarters. I take it you haven't looked at any of that yet, either."

Addison glanced at the flight bag lying on the table. "Oh, that. I just got it tonight, right before I went out. I figured whatever it was, it could wait a few hours."

"Well, it *won't* wait!" Sid shouted. "I'm warning you, I'm getting sick and tired of you dragging your feet!"

"I'm not dragging my feet," Addison stated, his ire rising again. "And let's be honest. You're not half as upset with my job performance as you are with my love life."

Sid didn't respond for a moment, and Addison could feel the turmoil he'd set in the man's heart. It reached out to him in a strangling grip. "I thought you loved Amanda."

The grip tightened, making him ache. "You know I did," Addison said, the timbre of his voice raspy. "But Sid, it's time I went on with my life."

"And that means falling in love with every distraught lady pilot who comes along?"

"No," Addison said through clenched teeth. "Just one."

Addison felt little satisfaction at his frankness when Sid slammed the phone down. He heard a loud click, and fresh guilt surged through his heart.

Replacing the phone in its cradle, Addison went to a large window that looked out over the bay and pulled back the drapes. Blackness peppered with occasional clusters of light assaulted him, reminding him of the blackness he'd felt in the first months after Amanda's death.

Is that what you want, Sid? he wondered. *For me to live the rest of my life without loving again? Because I don't think Amanda would have wanted that for me. She loved me.*

The picture of his wife came into his mind, but it was faded and dim now, like an old photograph that couldn't capture the spirit of the subject. Next to it, he saw Erin's face, vivid and bright, forging a lighted path through the dim corridors of his heart.

I thought you loved Amanda. His father-in-law's words rang through his head, but not loudly enough to blur his image of Erin, or bring Amanda's back to life.

Still, he couldn't escape the guilt Sid had provoked. Betrayal, delay, neglect. He looked at the flight bag of mail lying on the table. In a way, Sid was right. Maybe he had neglected things tonight. He'd had every intention of opening the bag and seeing what headquarters had sent him, but Erin's call had destroyed any thoughts of work that night. Now he had to open the mail, listen to the tape, and determine if it would be just another piece of a growing puzzle or the vital link he needed.

Trying to stop thinking of Erin and his wife, he tore into the large envelope. Addison pulled out a computer printout and the tape wrapped safely in a plastic box. Some answers would be there, answers that could set Erin's mind to rest or send it into even more turbulent winds. Was Sid right about that, too? Was he letting her feelings sway him, even to the point of slowing him down?

Unable to find the answer, Addison opened the tape, stuck it into the small tape deck on his television, and sat down with a pencil and the computer printout that was a transcript of the cockpit conversation, coupled with the data from the flight data recorder. The tape began, and he strained to make out the normal conversation that wasn't unusual in the cockpit. The uneventful takeoff on the return flight from Dallas International Airport, the checklists, the transmissions from the tower. Time passed slowly as he studied each line of dialogue for some hint that things were not as they should be . . . some mention of an instrument malfunction . . . a yawn from a fatigued captain . . . a report of bad weather, something he might have missed from approach control. But the flight was as ordinary as any he'd ever heard recorded.

Until the final approach.

He listened, fatigued, head aching with strain, as the first officer — who might have been Erin if not for the accident that Addison counted as a miracle — spoke to the approach controller about descending to the glide path, or the angle at which they could approach the runway. Nothing strange occurred, nothing unusual. Everything was as it should be.

He got up and turned the tape up, then went back to his seat and rubbed his eyes, straining to hear the first officer calling out the altitudes and airspeeds as they descended.

And suddenly came the words he'd been anticipating and dreading at the same time, their volume escalating with urgency. "You're getting low on the glide path, Mick. Too low. Pull it up, pull it up!"

And then there was the sound of impact and silence, which Addison interpreted as a crash that still couldn't be explained, and 151 deaths that affected hundreds more lives. All he knew for certain was that the tragedy was Mick's fault. Neither the first officer nor the flight engineer had any indication earlier that anything was wrong. When the first officer warned Mick about the glide path, it wasn't too late to correct their approach. Why hadn't Mick righted the plane? Why had he let the nose drop that way?

There was only one answer that came to Addison's mind. Mick had panicked. Maybe something had diverted his attention for a second — it wasn't unusual to drop a little below the glide path — but when he'd realized he was low, he'd lost his head. And the panic that could have lasted a fraction of a second had driven the plane down and ended the lives of all those people.

Addison shut off the tape and went to the couch and lay down, massaging his temples. *God, why couldn't there have been a better reason? Why couldn't it have been instrument malfunction or a wind surge or lightning, or any number of things that could purge Mick of this blame? For Erin's sake, why couldn't you have let me find some other conclusion?*

Because there was none, he thought dismally. And as much as he knew it would hurt Erin, he couldn't compromise his report. He could, however, listen over and over until he made sure that he wasn't missing something, and Sid and the rest of the Board didn't have to like it. Then he would prepare Erin, and hope that she didn't blame him for drawing the conclusions he must.

Wearily, he went back to the tape deck to rewind the tape and started playing it again. It would be a long night, he thought. But if he had to come up with a report he didn't like, he was going to be as sure as feasibly possible that he wasn't making a mistake.

CHAPTER FIFTEEN

Erin sat at her desk in the scheduling office the next morning, desperately trying to sort out a whirlwind of emotions. Terror — the kind that turned her heart inside out and kept her from functioning logically. Grief — the kind that lingered somewhere dark, even when there was brightness. Anger — the kind that turned her from a rational woman into someone who almost couldn't cope. Love — the kind that Addison had drawn out of her last night when she had been certain that misery wouldn't surrender to any other emotion.

She closed her eyes and thought of the Cessna she hadn't been able to fly and the fact that she'd turned to Addison. She should be angry with herself, and yet she wasn't. She was frightened by the illogical nature of her feelings. She didn't like running on pure emotion. Not when she knew that the investigation was still being conducted and that Jason and Maureen were still victims of gossip and speculation and that Addison had the power to change their situation. How could she simply follow her feelings and forget all that? But more importantly, how could she blame Addison, when he'd already demonstrated his enormous sense of responsibility to her?

The door opened to the office, and she glanced up, over the dozens of others who worked diligently on their computers and phone lines. She saw Addison scanning the room for her. His eyes met hers, and he smiled — a tentative, tired smile, and then he started toward her.

"Hi," he whispered when he reached her desk.

A self-conscious smile spread from her eyes to the corners of her lips. "Hi."

"Erin, do you have time for a break? I need to talk to you."

She felt a flicker of alarm and glanced down at the work on her desk, then checked her watch. Was he going to call their relationship quits, just as it had gotten started? Erin wondered, studying his face. Would this be a let's-not-take-this-too-seriously lecture? Swallowing, she got up from her desk. "I guess." She looked at him with tender appraisal and noted the shadows beneath his eyes and the weary slump to his posture. "Is something wrong?"

"I just want to talk to you," he said softly.

The gentleness in Addison's voice sent a

fresh surge of worry coiling through her as Erin followed him out into the terminal and up the stairs that led to the lounge where Southeast pilots and flight attendants usually rested between flights. No one was there this time of morning, so Erin followed him in and sat down. "What is it, Addison?" she asked.

Addison sat down across from her and rested his elbows on his knees. "I got the tape back yesterday," he said. "When I got home from your place last night, I was up all night listening to it over and over."

"Oh," she said, suddenly numb. She leaned back in her chair and laced her hands together in her lap, waiting. There was no time to feel relief that she had been wrong, that the bad news wasn't about them. It was still bad news. She could sense it. Barriers began to rise around her, and she felt her muscles tightening. He had heard the truth, the fear, the death. He had experienced Mick's end.

Silence held its tight breath between them, and Erin struggled to find the most pertinent questions in her mind. *Was Mick afraid? Did he know he was crashing? What went wrong? What broke down? What proved to you that it wasn't Mick's fault, because it wasn't, you know, it wasn't his fault. It couldn't have been . . .*

Instead of voicing the myriad questions, she cleared her throat. "Could . . . could I hear?"

"No, Erin," he whispered. "Not until I file the report."

"When will that be?" she asked.

"Soon," he said.

"Soon . . . meaning you've come to your conclusion? Meaning you've almost finished the investigation?"

"I still have some legwork to do," he said quietly. "I haven't finished Mick's seventy-two-hour history before the crash or his profile . . . but I'm pretty sure of what happened."

She didn't want to ask . . . couldn't ask. The words just wouldn't come. Instead, Erin stood up, her red dress rustling against her legs. She crossed her arms, hugging herself for comfort, and went to the window to gaze outside.

"Erin, I wanted to talk to you before I filed the report. You deserve to know. You need to know."

Still, she didn't answer.

"It's my opinion, based on the facts and the data, and now the tape, that Mick was, indeed, at fault. That he got slightly below the glide path of his final approach and pan-icked when he realized it, wasting valuable seconds that could have been utilized to correct the problem."

"Mick didn't panic." Erin bit out the words, her eyes turning as hard as marble, focusing on a spot below the window. "Mick never panicked."

"Everybody panics sometime," Addison said.

"Not Mick!" She turned back to Addison, her flushed cheeks rivaling the color of her dress. "Addison, there's another reason. Mick had flown that approach too many times. You know it, and I know it. He had over five thousand hours of flying time under his belt. For heaven's sake, he always told the story of the time in the Air Force when his plane caught on fire. He still landed it and got out safely. He wasn't the type to panic."

Addison couldn't be swayed. His mind was made up. "Erin, I listened to the tape over and over. I've gone over the facts a hundred times. He made a mistake, panicked, and flew the airplane into the ground."

"Did you hear that on the tapes?" she asked. "The panic? Did he say, 'Oh no, I'm below the glide path! What am I going to do?' "

"No."

"Then *how do you know?*" she shouted.

"What other explanation is there?" he demanded. "His first officer warned him he was too low. He *told* him to pull up. Erin, he didn't!"

Familiar tears rushed to cloud Erin's vision again. She covered her mouth and shook her head. "There was some reason," she said. "You've just got to look harder. Something happened in that airplane that you couldn't hear on the tape, Addison."

Addison dropped his weary head into his hands. "Erin, you've got to accept it. I've done the best I can."

"Have you?" she asked, and he didn't miss the note of accusation in her voice. "Have you talked to others who could tell you that there was no way on earth that Mick Hammon panicked in the cockpit? Have you talked to his wife? His son?"

"I plan to," he said. "It just isn't something I'm looking forward to."

"Why?" she asked. "Because you feel guilty? Because you're afraid they'll see you as the enemy?"

Addison rose to his feet. "I'm *not* the enemy, Erin. I interpret data and facts. That's all I can do."

"We're talking about human beings, Addison. Not a bunch of numbers. You can measure impacts and angles and altitudes all you want, and you can listen to all the tapes in the world, but that still won't tell you a thing about Mick Hammon's fortitude. *People* will. You won't take my word for it. Take theirs!"

"It won't change things, Erin."

She heaved a loud sigh and turned back to the window. She wiped her eyes. "I have to get back to work," she said. "Your mind's made up. There's nothing I can do to change it."

She started to cross the room, but Addison grabbed her arm, forcing her to stop. "Erin, you said that you wouldn't hate me for this. That you wouldn't blame me."

Erin swallowed and pulled her arm out of his grasp. Coldly, wordlessly, she opened the door.

"But you *are* blaming me, aren't you?"

She stepped over the threshold and looked down at her shoes, so delicate and far removed from those she wore with her uniform. "No, Addison," she said quietly, knowing it was a lie. "I don't blame you."

"Then when can I see you again?" he asked. The question was a test, and they both knew it.

Lifting her chin, she leveled her cold eyes on him. "Saturday," she said. "Three o'clock, at the youth center. You can help with the airplanes we're trying to paint."

Surprise, relief, and the slightest hint of apprehension colored his eyes. "Okay," he said, with a reluctant smile. "Saturday it is."

Erin didn't answer his smile. Stiffly, she went through the door and let it close behind her.

On the way back to her office, Erin thought about her plan. Jason Hammon would be at the youth center Saturday, and it was high time Addison met him.

Maybe then he'd see her point, she thought. Maybe then he would back off and see that all the "facts" in the world weren't worth the devastation his report would inflict on a little boy and his grieving mother. Maybe then he'd find some other conclusion to his report.

Because until he did, Erin feared there was no future for them at all.

CHAPTER SIXTEEN

The youth center was abuzz with excitement Saturday, because the mural the kids had been working on was finished and they were about to begin a new one. Twenty kids showed up, including Jason Hammon, whom Erin had persuaded to attend, and each was clamoring to make the first mark on the new wall. The new mural would be a tribute to the nearby airport. Several of the kids had suggested the idea because of the number of airline employees who had volunteered their time and support to help get Shreveport kids off the streets. Madeline and Sam, also regular volunteers, were there to help. Sam, as usual, had a cluster of boys around him. She was grateful that he gave of his time, because he was a wonderful witness to kids who needed someone to look up to.

He sang "Ba-ba-ba, Ba-ba-ber Ann," as he shook up the cans of paint, and Madeline sang right along with him — as some of the kids did.

His silliness boosted the spirits of everyone, but Erin couldn't pump hers to the point of the others'. She knelt on the floor, preparing drop cloths, charcoal, and paints, while the kids studied the sketches she'd done and argued over which parts they'd paint. Jason hung back quietly from the rest, still not ready to take part in the light bantering that went on among the kids. He saw them all as T.J.s, she realized, as threats to his name and his memories . . . as enemies to be reckoned with. What he didn't know was that few of these kids knew who his father had been, and most of them hadn't been around for the fight with T.J. Erin looked up at him, offered a smile, then glanced toward the glass doors, wondering when Addison would arrive.

"I get to do the 747," Zeke shouted above the din, pointing at the largest plane in the sketches. "It's bigger, and it'll take a lot more talent. See, I been thinkin' about sorta showin' the inside, like cuttin' it in half or somethin' . . ."

"That's an L-1011," Jason cut in, his voice toneless, standing back with his hands buried in his denim pockets.

"What is?" Zeke asked, pivoting toward the nine-year-old and squinting his eyes in a way that might seem threatening to someone who didn't know better.

Jason's shoulders squared. "It's not a

747," he repeated. "It's a Lockheed 1011."

"So who made you an authority?" another kid asked.

Jason lifted his shoulder with feigned indifference. "I know airplanes."

Zeke regarded Erin, still kneeling on the floor. "Hey, Erin. Tell this kid that this is a 747."

Erin couldn't help smiling. "He's right, Zeke. It's an L-1011. And if I were you, I'd listen to this kid, because he *does* know airplanes."

Zeke assessed Jason curiously. "Well, it's still mine," he said after a moment. "Just because you know what it is, don't mean you get to paint it."

Jason shrugged again, the gesture as close as he could venture to revealing his feelings. "That's okay. I didn't want it. I want that one there. The 727."

Zeke was satisfied. As though he were the self-proclaimed leader, he got the sketch of the 727 and thrust it into Jason's hands. "Sure thing. It's all yours."

Erin stopped sorting her equipment and sat back on her heels, gauging Jason's reaction as Zeke extended a hand that unmistakably said, "Gimme five." For a moment Jason only stared at it. When Zeke didn't withdraw it, Jason reluctantly gave it the friendly slap he was waiting for.

"Why d'ya want that one, anyway?" Zeke asked, analyzing the sketched airplane that Jason held.

Jason swallowed and looked down at Erin, barely masking his surprise that this smart-talking kid from the poor side of town didn't know that Mick was Jason's father, and hadn't heard the rumors. Her eyes were tender, understanding, and worried. Would he tell Zeke now, possibly refresh his memory of what he may have seen on TV, give him the opportunity to whiplash Jason with careless words? But Jason didn't let her down. "I want this one because that's what Erin flies," he explained quietly.

"That true?" Zeke asked, giving Erin a chance to refute Jason's word.

Erin studied the charcoal pencils lined on the floor, considering her answer. *It was true once,* she felt compelled to say. *Now I can't even cut it in a Cessna.* Instead, she decided to stand behind Jason. "I told you," she said. "Jason knows his stuff."

The general buzz began again as she passed out charcoal and assigned places on the large mural, hurrying back and forth from one child to another, offering help. She didn't notice when Addison at last stepped through the glass doors.

He came up beside her and tapped her shoulder. His eyes were guarded, as she was sure hers were.

"Hi," he said.

Something in her heart tripped and stumbled forward. But the coldness wouldn't go away, and she couldn't forget her purpose for inviting him here today. It was too important.

She forced a false smile all the way to her eyes. "Addison."

Something in his own expression flickered, almost as if he sensed that her smile wasn't genuine. He glanced around. "Lot more kids here today than there were the other night."

She nodded. "Yeah. They always show up in droves when we start a new mural. Everyone wants to get his mark on it. Later, when we're painting, they kind of come in cycles."

"Hey, Addison," Zeke called from his station down the wall.

Addison gave Zeke an amused grin. "How's it goin', Zeke?"

"Not bad. You know anything about airplanes?"

Addison chuckled and winked at Erin. "Oh, maybe a little."

Still angry about the report, she turned away without responding to his quip. He took her arm and made her look up at him. "Look," he said softly, "I can see that neither of us has really gotten over our anger after the other night, but I came, didn't I?"

"Yes," she said. "You came."

"I came because something's happening between us, and I think we can work through the problems."

She turned her guilty eyes away.

"Addison? Addison? How 'bout comin' down here to help me out? I've got this 747 that needs —"

"It's an L-1011," Jason reminded him, grinning now.

Zeke laughed. "Oh, yeah. Well, whatever it is, man . . ."

"Besides," Jason flung, beginning to get comfortable with Zeke. "I thought you said it needed special talent, that only you . . ."

"I just *asked*," Zeke said, annoyed. "Me and Addison, we work real good together."

In spite of the serious moment between Erin and him, Addison couldn't help smiling at Zeke's antics, and he started making his way toward the boy. But Erin stopped him when she realized that he would miss talking to Jason if he started helping Zeke. "I wanted to help Zeke with that L-1011," she said. "I need you to work down here. Next to Jason." Zeke shrugged.

"I don't need help," Jason said, insulted. "I can do it."

"I know you can," Erin said, ushering Addison down toward Jason. "But I want a lot of detail on this one. Addison knows a lot about planes, and he can help you get it just right." She turned to Addison, her smile returning with reluctant glory as she set a possessive hand on Jason's shoulder. "Addison, this guy is one of my best friends in the world. I want you two to work together."

"No problem," Addison said, slightly confused. She watched as he regarded the work the boy had already begun. Erin hoped the detail in the drawing didn't clue him in to the fact that the boy had an unusual knowledge of planes. "Not bad," he commented. "Great start. This wing might be a little longer, though. Do you mind if I . . . ?"

Eyes narrow with concentration, Jason broke his charcoal in half and handed one piece to Addison, allowing him to correct the proportions of the wing. "That's a lot better than what I did," Jason said. "I knew something was off. Just didn't know what. Do you think I got the nose right? It looks a little too round to me."

Erin stepped back, watching with barely concealed emotion as the two worked together like old pals. She felt the sting of tears behind her eyes, but willed them back. It was just a matter of time — minutes? hours? — before Addison discovered that Jason was Mick's son, and that Erin had set him up. He'd be angry with her, and he would have reason. But this ploy was her last tool to change his mind about the conclusions in his report. If he could just get to know Jason, see how vulnerable he was, like the boy the way that she did . . . Erin knew he'd find some way around reporting that Mick had screwed up.

Sam changed his song to "Da doo ron ron ron," and some of the kids she would never have expected to sing a note began to sing, too. Addison, who had met Sam on the way in, joined in, and to her amazement, Jason began singing, too. Madeline winked at her, and she winked back. As they worked and sang, she supervised the rough sketching of the tarmac, the terminals, the baggage trucks, the other airplanes lined up, and the ones in the sky. As she answered questions and passed out compliments that made their little chests swell with pride, she couldn't help straining to hear Jason and Addison's conversation when they weren't singing. So far, neither had figured out who the other was. But they were becoming fast friends, and she could see that Addison was impressed with the boy.

Once she had everyone working on their own, she stepped back to pull her thoughts together and wondered where she would take things from here. If their identities didn't come out this afternoon, she'd tell Addison later. It would be the best way, she decided, for she'd be able to sit down with him and explain what she'd done. And why.

The pat little ending to her scheme didn't come about as planned. Addison and Jason had been working together for more than an hour when she could feel the truth pushing its way out. Addison had won Jason's trust. And, curious as he always was, Addison asked the obvious question.

"How does a nine-year-old boy like you know so much about airplanes? Especially a 727?"

Jason continued his fine sketching and lifted one small shoulder. Erin noted that Jason's throat bobbed. She held her breath and tried to look busy. "My dad was a pilot," he said, keeping his voice too low for the others to hear. "The captain of a 727. He and I did a lot of models together."

Addison didn't make the connection. "I see," he said, his voice dropping in pitch. "Is he retired?"

"Huh-uh," Jason said, not taking his eyes

from the drawing. Pink blotches colored his cheeks.

Addison didn't press, for it was obvious, then, that Jason wasn't volunteering anything. Quietly, he finished drawing the tail of the aircraft.

"He died." The words came on a hoarse whisper, and Addison stopped drawing and turned to the child.

"I'm sorry," he whispered. "I didn't know."

Jason sketched faster. "About three weeks ago. His plane crashed."

Erin went limp against the back wall as a look of stark realization dawned on Addison's stricken face. Slowly, his hand came down from the mural. The charcoal dropped from his hand and rolled off the drop cloth onto the cold Formica. "You're . . . you're Mick Hammon's son?"

Erin saw Jason's wide, trusting eyes settle on Addison. "You knew my dad?"

Addison turned around, his eyes on the edge of despair, but accusation was rampant as he gaped at Erin. *How could you?* those eyes asked. *You tricked me.*

"Did you?" Jason asked, clinging to the question that was so important. "Did you know him?"

Slowly, Addison turned his pale face back

to the boy. "No, son," Addison confessed. "I didn't know him. But I've heard a lot about him."

Jason's face flushed to red, and he abandoned the refuge of the sketch. "It's not true. None of what you've heard is true!"

Addison stepped back, dumbfounded. "I didn't hear anything bad about him, Jason. Just what a good man he was . . . what a good pilot . . ."

Jason started to speak, then glanced over Addison's shoulder at the other kids still chattering as they worked, and his voice became a whisper. "It wasn't his fault, you know. My dad was the best pilot Southeast ever had. It wasn't his fault the plane crashed."

Addison seemed to struggle with emotion, and he reached out a shaking hand and mussed the boy's hair. Erin could have sworn she saw the glisten of tears in his eyes as he tried to speak. But no words would come.

"Hey, Jason," Zeke called from down the wall, interrupting the poignant moment. "Come see what you think. I drew an American flag on the side, so it'd look patriotic and all. And look how I shaped these windows. Pretty spiffy, huh?"

Jason glanced at Addison softly, swallowed

his emotion, and went to Zeke, as if thankful for the distraction. "Oh, no," he moaned when he saw the sketching. "You can't just put an American flag on something because you feel like it! And you can't change windows. That's not how it really looks."

"Hey, man," Zeke said. "We aren't going for reality here."

Erin would have laughed at his use of her own words, if it hadn't been for the fissures cracking through her heart, exposing the white-hot core of regret. Addison didn't grace her with another look. Instead, he leaned against the wall, disregarding the damage his shoulder was doing to the drawing. He seemed to be trying to pull his emotions together before they flew out of control — in which direction, she wasn't sure. The small muscles in his face hardened. A vein in his temple throbbed.

Finally, just as she started to speak he looked at her with a look of condemnation, shook his head in disgust, and started toward the exit.

"Addison?" she asked. "Where are you going?"

Addison didn't answer. Instead, he pushed through the doors and headed out into daylight.

Quickly, Erin threw down the rag and

charcoal she was holding. "I'll be back in a minute," she called. She darted out of the center just as Addison screeched from the parking lot.

Erin ran to her own car and pulled out behind him. He drove too fast for her to catch him, but she stayed behind him, desperately trying to keep up. Her own anger welled inside her, spurring her on. Of course he was angry, but what did he expect her to do? Sit back and wait for him to ruin lives, now that he'd admitted what the conclusions of his report would be? Did he expect her to forget the results of the investigation and accept it?

A car pulled out between them, and she slammed on the brakes. The rubber on her tires skidded, reminding her of the morning of her fender bender and the concussion that had kept her from flying. Things would have been so different if the accident hadn't happened. Drastically different.

She swerved around the car and headed in the direction she'd seen Addison travel. He was blocks up ahead, but she changed lanes and wove between cars until she was close to him. He pulled into a condominium complex and parked his car. Erin drove in to double-park behind him, cut off her engine, and got out of the car.

"You're wasting your time, Erin," Addison shouted, slamming his own door. "I don't have time for your games."

"Games?" Erin shouted. "You think this is a game?"

Addison started up to his apartment. "Call it whatever you want. It was a dirty trick, and I would have expected you to be above something like that."

Erin followed behind him, taking three steps for every one of his. "I'm not above anything that will keep that little boy from having to defend his father and his name. I'm not above anything that'll keep Mick's memory from being dragged through the mud!"

"I don't drag people's memories through the mud," Addison said through his teeth. "I tell the truth! That's all!"

"No matter who it destroys? No matter what it means?"

Addison rammed his key into his lock, then swiveled to face Erin, his face flaming. "Don't you understand? I don't want to destroy anyone. Especially that little boy. I was going to meet him, talk to him. You had no right to set me up!"

"*When* were you going to? You still haven't even met his mother. You're afraid to, Addison. I saw your face when you realized

222

who he was. You were horrified! I don't think you would have done it voluntarily."

"I would have, Erin! It's my job! I just don't happen to enjoy seeing people's pain. I remember it, Erin. I was there myself, remember?" He started to pass through the door, then turned back as if to push it shut, but Erin burst through and closed it behind her.

She leaned back against the door, staring at him across the small foyer. "I don't know who you lost, Addison, or what happened. But that little boy lost his father, and Maureen lost her husband. I can go on, but the balance of their lives will never be the same again."

"That isn't my fault!" Addison rasped. "Did I make him crash? Did I kill him?"

"No, but you're killing his memory. You're taking away anything good Jason can be proud of about his dad!"

"I can't do that!" Addison said. "If Mick Hammon made an impression on his son, nobody — not you or I — can take that away from him."

"They can, Addison. You don't know what it's like. Mick was his father. His *father!* You don't know what he's going through already, *without* the rumors and smears."

Addison slammed his fist against the wall,

and Erin jumped. "I *do* know, Erin! I *do* know! Amanda was my *wife!* I lost my *wife* in a crash."

Erin caught her breath, and her bold resolve drained slowly out of her. She regarded Addison as he slumped against the wall opposite her, the admission draining him of his fight. His eyes glistened again, and his face seemed to lose all color.

"So don't tell me I don't know what those people are feeling," he said, his voice dropping to a waver. "Don't come in here and accuse me of bypassing them out of cruelty. I know what it's like to be questioned, when you have more questions yourself than you could ever answer. I know what it's like to be hassled by the press, when all you want is to be left alone with your grief. I know the pain a person experiences when he's slept in the same bed with someone every night for years and suddenly has to get used to that bed being empty. I was trying to spare them for as long as I could, Erin. I had hoped I'd be able to clear him of responsibility first, so my interview with him wouldn't be necessary!"

He choked on the last words, rubbed his jaw. His eyes focused on her with disgust. "But you had to play God and get me together with the innocent little boy, corner me so I'd learn my lesson."

Erin's gaze faltered. That was exactly what she'd done, and for the life of her she couldn't find any defense.

"Well, I learned a lesson, all right," Addison added. "About you. I never thought of you as a manipulator before today, Erin. But that's just what you are. And what about Jason? What will he think about either of us when he finds out who I am . . . when I really do have to talk to him? It'll just make it a thousand times harder for him, because he trusted me for a time."

Tears of shame and regret stung Erin's eyes, and she stepped toward him, hands outstretched. "Addison, I —"

"Go home, Erin," he said, his tone as dead as the look in his eyes. "Just go home."

What could she say? That she was sorry? In all fairness, she wasn't certain she was. But she didn't like the image he had of her now, or the determination he had to end what they had begun. Slowly, she went to the door, opened it, and stepped back into the sunshine.

She stood on the step for a moment, looking out toward the parking lot, then heard the door being pushed closed behind her. Her heart sank a dozen levels before she forced her legs to move back to her car.

CHAPTER SEVENTEEN

Addison pulled into the driveway of the Hammon's house and regarded the brick, split-level home that had been groomed and maintained with great care for years. The home lay nestled in an upper-middle-class Shreveport subdivision, complete with security at the gates that isolated it from the crime and violence of the city streets. He shut off his engine and sat in the dark car for a moment. His job stank, he decided. When he'd started it, he'd never expected to become a post-death agent whose inevitable knock on the door dredged up heartache and grief.

And what would Jason think when he saw that *he* was the one "nailing" his dad? Would Jason hate him? Curse him, in his nine-year-old way?

He rubbed a hand over his rough chin and thought of Maureen's grief — grief that would have to be set aside while he asked her what he needed to know. He hadn't forgotten the "official" visits he'd gotten after Amanda's death.

"We're terribly sorry about your loss, Mr. Lowe. We hate to bother you, but we need to

talk to you about a settlement . . ."

No one had blamed Amanda, a mere passenger, for the crash, though. No one had drilled him to support a theory that the person he loved was in the wrong . . . the way he would drill Maureen tonight.

Maybe Erin had been right. Maybe it had been his conscience that kept him from going to the family. Or maybe what he'd told her was true — that he dreaded making them relive the tragedy, and that he simply wanted to spare them for as long as he could. For the life of him, he didn't know if his procrastination had been noble or cowardly.

Regardless of the answer, he had no choice but to see them tonight. Erin's stunt this afternoon had cinched it. Now there was no putting the interviews off.

Like a man heading voluntarily into a lynching, Addison got out of his car and started up the walk. Mrs. Hammon had left the porch light on, probably for him, since he'd called to tell her he was coming. He couldn't help remembering the night that the airline official had called him to say *he* was coming to discuss the terms of their settlement to avoid a lawsuit. He had paced the small, empty living room in the dark before the man came, gnashing his teeth and asking himself how those idiots thought they could pay him any adequate compensation for his wife's life.

Was Maureen pacing now, wondering what this NTSB official would demand to know about her personal life with her husband and wondering if throwing him out would do Mick's cause more harm than good?

He reached the front door and rang the bell, then wiped his palms on his jacket. He hung his head and waited.

Maureen answered quickly, a tentative smile on her pale face. She looked smaller than he'd expected, more fragile, and there was a delicate beauty about her. Her red hair was pulled back in a chignon, and she wore little makeup. "Mr. Lowe?" she asked.

"Yes." He held out his hand in greeting, and she took it in her own. "Mrs. Hammon, I'm terribly sorry about your loss . . ."

The visit went well, much better than Addison had expected, for Maureen was unexpectedly honest in answering his questions. She never dangled the guilt over his head that Erin had, never mentioned the cruel phone calls she'd been getting, never referred to Jason's pain. She simply said that she wanted to get the investigation over as soon as possible so that she and her son could go on with their lives.

Addison was just closing up his clipboard of notes when Jason came downstairs. At the sight of Addison, he halted midstep.

Maureen stood up. "Honey, it's all right. You can come in. This is Mr. Lowe of the National Transportation Safety Board."

Jason's hands coiled into fists on top of the banister. His lips drew back into thin lines. "Why didn't you tell me?" he asked Addison in a voice full of loathing.

Thinking he was addressing her, Maureen frowned. "I told you he was coming," she said.

Addison held up his hand to her, silently conveying that this was between the two males. He took a few steps toward the boy. "I didn't tell you because I didn't know who you were until you told me who your dad was."

Jason contemplated the explanation, his small nostrils flaring. "But Erin knew, didn't she?"

Addison dropped his gaze to the floor. Jason needed Erin now. It wouldn't help to make him angry at her. "She . . . she thought if we met that I'd change the thrust of my report," he said, knowing his voice lacked the conviction needed to excuse her. "That knowing you would change my mind."

229

Maureen knitted her brows together, puzzled. "Wait a minute. You two have met? Through Erin?"

"She tricked me," Jason said, lips quivering. "She didn't tell me he was the one who's saying the crash was Dad's fault."

"Jason . . ." Addison reached for him, but the boy backed away, his eyes glossed with tears.

"Get away from me!" he demanded as he ran. When he slammed the front door, the impact shook the house.

Silence wove an explosive web between Addison and Maureen as they looked awkwardly at each other. "I'm so sorry," Addison said. "Erin meant well, but . . ." His voice faltered and he looked toward the door through which the angry child had disappeared. "Do you . . . do you mind if I go talk to him?"

Tears came to Maureen's eyes. "Please," she said. "I don't know what to say to him anymore."

Addison left her alone then, and went quietly out the front door, his eyes searching through the darkness for the boy. He followed the deck that surrounded the house until he found Jason sitting on the redwood floor, legs hanging over the side, feet scuffing the dirt below him. Gritting his teeth and fighting the searing emotion tugging at his face, Jason took a rock and launched it through the air. It landed some yards away with a thump.

Addison leaned against a post and gazed down at the boy. "You have a right to be mad," he said quietly.

"I don't want to talk to you anymore," Jason returned.

The words were like a cold hand squeezing his heart, but Addison wouldn't give up. "Then can you listen?"

Jason didn't answer. He only sent another rock barreling through the air. It plunged into a pile of leaves.

Addison sat down on the deck next to the boy, his shoulders slumped. It was a dark night, for the clouds hung low beneath the moon and stars, lending a dismal feeling to the already charged atmosphere. What could he say to the boy, when his world seemed to have ended? He racked his brain, his heart, for the needs he'd had when Amanda had died. He remembered that he'd wanted to know what had gone wrong, in grueling detail. He'd actually wanted to picture the crash so it would become real, something he could grasp. Only then could he begin to sort out the senselessness of it all. But Jason was just a child. Did he have that same need?

The haunted look in the boy's eyes told Addison that he did.

"I want to tell you what I know about the crash," Addison said finally. "Because I think you have a right to know. Has anyone told you how it happened?"

Jason's hand froze in midair just before launching another rock. "No," he said.

"Do you want to know? Because I'll only tell you if it's something you want . . . or need . . . to know."

Jason turned his hand and let the rocks slip to the ground, one at a time. A slow nod was Addison's answer.

Addison thought for a moment, choosing his words with painstaking care. "According to the tape and all the other information we have, nothing went wrong during flight," he began quietly. "It was on the final approach into Shreveport that something happened."

Addison picked up one of the rocks that Jason had dropped and rolled it in his palm, considering how to say what Jason most needed to hear, without taking the easy way out and lying. "Jason, do you know what a glide path is?"

"Yeah," Jason whispered. "I think so."

Addison wasn't convinced, so he explained to make sure, using hand gestures to illustrate what seemed vague. "It's the

232

angle of about two and a half degrees from the runway, one that the plane has to line up with on its approach. There's also the localizer, which lines you up with the runway. After you've centered up the localizer and are aligned with the runway, the glide path bar comes down on the instruments, and when it reaches the center, you're on the glide path. If the bar goes up a little, you pull the nose up a little . . . if the bar goes down a little, you push the nose forward a little. Staying on that path helps you make a smooth landing." Addison fingered the rock in his hand and pushed out the breath constricting his words. "Well, your dad got a little below the glide path."

Jason didn't say anything. He sat frozen, staring into the dirt beneath his feet.

"Sometimes things go wrong that distract a pilot," Addison continued, his voice blending with hushed night sounds. "Maybe he was thinking about getting home or was tired or maybe something important was on his mind. All we know is that the plane slipped below the glide path, and he didn't get it pulled up in time."

"That's not how it happened," Jason refuted, each word uttered with great emphasis. "Dad wouldn't have gotten distracted. He wouldn't have done it."

Addison set his gentle hand on the back of Jason's neck, trying to make the truth into less of a monster. "Jason, your dad was one of the best pilots I've ever profiled. He had an excellent record. People had the utmost faith in his ability. I know that he didn't let it fall on purpose."

"My dad didn't kill all those people." Tears burst from Jason's eyes, and even the dim hues of moonlight caught them rolling down his cheeks.

Addison stroked Jason's neck, not sure what to do to comfort the child. "Jason, we're not talking about him holding a gun to someone's head or snapping or doing anything malicious. It just happened. Even if the report says pilot error caused the crash, it doesn't mean that your father was any less of a pilot, or any less of a man."

"He didn't do it," Jason repeated. "You've got it all wrong. You need to look harder. You'll find something else. Something else went wrong."

"I've looked through everything, Jason. I've done everything I can to get to the truth."

"But it's not fair!" Jason shouted, launching himself off the deck and turning furiously back to Addison. "It's not fair!" He rubbed his fist across his face. "You aren't looking hard enough!"

The sting of rare tears ached in Addison's eyes, and he tried to swallow the emotion in his throat. "Jason, I've tried to be fair. And I'll keep trying. I wish I could tell you something else, but I thought you deserved to hear the truth . . . to try to understand."

"Well, I *can't* understand," Jason cried, wiping away his tears with his sleeve. "Can you?"

Helplessly, Addison shook his head. "No, I can't. And I wish to God that it wasn't my job to report it. But would it make it any easier if there *were* something else? If I found that the crash was out of his hands? That he had nothing to do with it? Would it really make any difference in the way you feel?"

An eternity passed between them as Jason wept against the post, his back turned to Addison while he pondered the question. Finally, he turned around, his sobbing gasps racking his small shoulders. "No, it wouldn't make a difference," Jason choked. "He'd still be gone. It still wouldn't bring my dad back. But it would make *them* shut up about it. All those people saying —"

A tear dropped onto Addison's cheek, and he tilted his head and arched his brows, grasping for some words of comfort to offer the boy. With only instincts to guide him, he opened his arms, and Jason came to him, clinging as he wept his heart out.

"It hurts," Addison whispered. "I know how it hurts. I lost my own wife in a crash. It's like somebody ripped out your heart and there's this great big hole there, empty . . . But your mom told me your dad was a Christian, Jason. And we don't have to grieve as non-Christians do, because we'll see them again. To God, it's only a few minutes until we're with them again. But it still hurts, and no one can understand unless they've been there. I've been there, Jason. I've hurt like you hurt."

He held the boy as Jason sobbed out great chunks of his misery, soaking Addison's shirt, never letting go of his neck until the agony was spent.

That night, Addison lay on his bedcovers, staring at the ceiling, feeling more alone than he'd felt in the last four years. The feeling was so similar to the one he'd experienced during the days after he'd first learned of Amanda's crash. Then, he couldn't believe that she wasn't going to walk in through the front door. The loneliness had been suffocating, painting his life in dead, gray colors.

Erin, his heart called in the night. *Why did you have to set me up? Why couldn't you have trusted me to do the right thing?*

He threw a wrist over his eyes and thought of the red welts around Jason's eyes when he'd cried himself dry tonight. Then he thought of Erin's angry, guarded eyes yesterday after he'd warned her of the conclusions in his report. Usually, her eyes shone like rays of sunlight into his empty heart. But they had been cold today, and Addison Lowe had caught enough of that chill to last a lifetime.

We were a fairy tale, Addison thought. *My fairy tale.* But fairy tales, like life, shouldn't always be played out. Their relationship simply wasn't meant to be. They were two opposing forces, neither willing to give in.

Maybe some men were only meant to know love once in a lifetime, he thought with a heartrending sigh. Maybe he'd already had his share.

So now why did he see Erin, instead of Amanda, when he closed his eyes? And why had her pain penetrated his professional numbness and become his own pain?

And why had he let an angry, frightened pilot and a troubled child make him feel like a heel for doing his job?

Why had the crash even happened?

Why had he ever met Erin . . . ?

CHAPTER EIGHTEEN

The scent of just-brewed coffee drifted up from the pot and filled the Hammon kitchen the following Monday. Erin leaned on the bar, watching Maureen pour. Her fragile hands shook, and some of the coffee sloshed onto the counter. The trembling was all too familiar to Erin. "Are you all right, Maureen?" she asked.

"Fine," she said. "It's just a little spill."

Erin studied the woman's pale face as she wiped up the liquid. She was pounds thinner than she'd been before the crash, and she hadn't had a lot of weight to lose. The smudges of weariness under her eyes provided a stark contrast to the whiteness of her cheeks. She looked old and tired enough to sleep for a year.

Erin let her finish fixing the cups, then took hers before Maureen could spill it again.

"So," Maureen asked, feigning higher spirits than Erin believed she really felt. "How long have you got?"

"About an hour," Erin said. "It's strange having a set lunch hour when I've been so used to a pilot's schedule. How does the saying go? You don't know what you've got till it's gone?"

The potent cliché hung in the air, and Erin was instantly sorry she'd said it. They'd all lost . . . and Maureen's loss was much deeper than her own.

"You know, I've been meaning to call you since Saturday," Maureen said, taking a seat across from Erin. "But I can't seem to keep my mind on anything."

"Call me?" Erin asked, bringing the cup to her lips. "What for?"

"About last weekend," Maureen said. "About Addison Lowe."

Erin almost choked on her coffee. "Addison? You met him?"

Maureen nodded. "He was here."

The torment in Maureen's expression made Erin want to die. "Oh, Maureen, I'm so sorry."

"Why?" she asked, meeting Erin's eyes directly. "He couldn't have been kinder, despite the things he had to ask."

Erin listened, dumbfounded, as Maureen described the visit to her. The portrait Maureen painted of Addison as a kind and sensitive man shouldn't fit into her idea of him after the fight they'd had last Saturday . . . yet strangely, somehow, it did.

"It was the first time Jason cried since the crash," Maureen said. "And Addison was there for him."

"But didn't he break down *because* of Addison?" Erin argued. "I mean, if he'd never come up with this pilot error business in the first place, Jason wouldn't have been so upset. And to sit there and tell a child so blatantly, so cruelly, that his father made a mistake . . ."

Maureen took Erin's hand. "He needed to have it explained to him," she said quietly. "God knows, I couldn't do it. I don't understand it myself. Addison was the only one who ever tried to make Jason understand."

"But he's just a little boy! That's so cruel."

"He didn't just drop the facts in his lap and leave, Erin. Addison followed it up with the kind of masculine tenderness that Jason misses so much."

Erin's gaze fell to her cup as the images whirled through her mind. Addison confronting Maureen. Addison talking to Jason. Addison comforting the distraught boy.

The telephone rang, startling her out of her reverie, and she waited for Maureen to answer it. Maureen's spine stiffened, and her hands began trembling more as they smoothed back her hair. She looked distracted.

"Aren't you going to answer it?" Erin asked.

Maureen shook her head quickly. "I can't," she said. "Would . . . would you do it for me?"

Confused, Erin picked up on the fourth ring, noting the fear in Maureen's face as she did. "Hello?"

"He murdered my daughter," a voice said. "Murdered her. Because of his lousy addiction to whatever he was on, my little girl is dead."

Erin's eyes flashed protectively to Maureen. Was this what she'd been experiencing day and night? "Who is this?" Erin asked helplessly.

"It doesn't matter," the voice answered. "I just hope your husband rots in hell for what he did."

Erin felt her face turning a pallid shade of white, like Maureen's, as she hung up the phone.

"It was one of them, wasn't it?" Maureen asked, her tears beginning to trickle over her lashes.

"You mean there are more?"

Maureen took her cup to the sink and dropped it with a crash. "All hours, day and night. They all say the same things. I've thought of getting an unlisted number, but then I'd feel so cut off from friends and

241

family, and I don't have the energy to call them all with the new number."

"I knew there were *some* phone calls, but I had no idea . . ." Erin's voice broke off, distraught, and she pulled the crying woman into her arms. "I'm so sorry, Maureen," she whispered, squeezing her eyes shut. "So sorry."

The two women held each other and wept for a patch of time before anger dulled the grief in Erin's heart. "If we could just get Addison to change his report. If they would just quit saying it was pilot error."

Maureen pulled herself together as much as she was able and stepped back, holding Erin at arm's length. "You listen to me," she said. "Addison Lowe may not say what we want him to in his report. And we may have to defend Mick against the cruel people out there who use his information against us. But he's a good man, Erin, and he's doing the best he can."

The words drifted into the dark void in Erin's heart, the part she'd tried to keep empty of anything but anger where Addison was concerned. The need to believe Maureen burned through the icy walls, and the warmth she suddenly encountered there left her confused and more miserable than she'd ever been in her life.

CHAPTER NINETEEN

Addison looked like he'd spent the night in a combat zone of some Schwarzenegger movie. And he felt like he'd been dragged by the bumper of an army jeep. Standing weary and haggard before the men who'd been working on his team since the crash, he tried to straighten his slumped posture and look authoritative. But he and insomnia did not do good things for each other.

"We've got to start over," he told them in his no-nonsense voice, beginning to pace like a sergeant before a unit of new recruits.

"Start over?" one of his investigative engineers asked, astounded. "What do you mean, start over?"

"With the wreckage," Addison clarified, as if the men didn't know. "Man, it's hot in here!"

Knowing his men wondered if he'd snapped at some point during the dismal weekend — and not caring much — he yanked off his jacket and tossed it over a gray folding chair. "We're going to go back through every last piece of that plane . . . every nut, every bolt, every instrument . . .

and we're going to make absolutely sure that the crash happened the way we think it happened."

"But, Addison, we've already done that," Hank ventured. "Nothing's going to change just by going over it all again. And headquarters is waiting —"

"Don't tell me what headquarters wants!" Addison shouted belligerently, his voice echoing from the metal roof and reverberating off the walls. "This investigation is *my* responsibility. I call the shots! It's all on my head!"

"But, Addison," another team member, Horace, protested. "I promised my girl I'd be back in D.C. in time for —"

"You shouldn't have made any promises!" he cut in, startling them all. "We're staying here until the job is done. And anybody I see half doing it because he wants to get home can find alternate employment."

The men grew quiet. Except for the rumbling engines of the airliners outside, there was no sound in the hangar. Eyes were averted. Arms were crossed. Impatience ticked away like a time bomb.

"So . . . are we going to just keep looking until we find the answers you want?" Hank asked. "The answers that'll please your lady friend?"

Addison turned his head around to face the man he'd worked with the longest. The one who'd been the most faithful. The most diligent. His anger subsided, for he knew the men had a right to question his motives, when they'd watched him run the gamut of his emotions, all over Erin. He hadn't made his relationship with her a secret, after all. He shook his head slowly. "Just like you guys, I think we'll find exactly the same conclusions that we have now. But we won't have any doubts. And we'll — *I'll* — be able to live with my report." His voice faltered, then he met the man's eyes directly. "And to answer your question, no, I'm not waiting until Erin Russell approves of my findings. Chances are, she'll be miserable with the results no matter what we come up with."

He clenched his hand into a fist at the sharp thought of her and felt his face reddening. "I just want to know that I didn't make too many assumptions. That I didn't stop just short of finding something important. We're all too good at what we do for that."

The men nodded grudgingly, and the anger and defensiveness in their eyes faded a few degrees. He had gotten through to them and made himself sound less like a beast hanging on the edge of sanity than an investigator determined to find the truth.

"Hank, I want you to finish piecing together the elevator system while the others work elsewhere. How close are you to finishing it?"

"Pretty close," Hank said. "But I figured there was no point now that we've heard the tapes. If it's clear the pilot was in error —"

Addison cut him off. "I want to make sure that when the first officer told Hammon to pull up, there wasn't some reason he couldn't."

"That's a long shot."

"Do it anyway," Addison said. "And hurry."

Trouble was, he was pretty sure that the truth wouldn't change. They couldn't dissect the crash, any more than he could dissect his miserable heart. But he could give it a try.

Erin tried to ignore the smell of airplane exhaust and gaseous fumes and the deafening sound of engines that made her heart vibrate as she stepped up to the hangar where the wreckage was stored during the investigation. She saw an open door on the corner of the metal structure, but stopped before she reached it and wrapped her arms around herself.

After she'd left Maureen, Erin had spent the afternoon watching for Addison, waiting to see him in the lounge or the coffee shop, waiting to see his jade, aching eyes, waiting to tell him she'd been wrong. If Maureen could handle the conclusion of his report, surely she could, too. But the day had unfurled like an old piece of tape that was hopelessly stuck to its roll. It had taken all the coaxing and peeling and tearing she could manage just to get to the end. When she was finally off work for the day, she decided that she'd find Addison if she had to turn Shreveport upside down. So she had come to the most obvious place first. This hangar. The hangar that stored the final moments of Mick's life. The proof that he wasn't coming back.

She wanted to see Addison, to tell him that she'd been wrong about him, that she appreciated what he'd done last weekend for Jason, that she'd like another chance, that she missed him, that she couldn't explain the dull ache that had dogged her all week. But somehow, now that she was here, she was afraid to go inside. Afraid to face the end of Mick's life in pieces of aircraft, all disassembled and tagged.

She started to turn back to the terminal, but the thought of another lonely night seemed worse than the fear that sent her heart careening. She had to see Addison. Even if it meant going inside.

Slowly, she stepped into the doorway.

She saw him immediately, crouched down on the concrete floor, examining the pieces of the wing lying before him, as if some crumb of evidence might fall out of the metal and proclaim that they'd had it all wrong. His shirt was soaked with perspiration, its tail hanging out, as if he'd thrown it on as an afterthought.

Deep lines of fatigue and concentration were etched in the hard angles of his face. Shadows occupied the normally crinkled lines of laughter beneath his eyes. To any passerby, he might look awful. To Erin, he was light to a dismally dark heart.

She looked around, saw that no one else seemed to be here with him, that he was working alone. Tentatively, she moved toward him.

The sound of her heels on the concrete summoned Addison's attention, and he snapped his head up. His eyes meshed with hers across the large room . . . questioning, welcoming . . . and yet condemning.

"Are . . . are you alone?" she asked.

He glanced around him, as if he hadn't given the fact a thought until she brought it up. "Looks like it," he said coldly. "Even NTSB people have to eat."

"Not all of them," she said quietly.

Her voice was lost beneath the sound of a passing plane, and Addison stood up, hands riding his hips, a screwdriver dangling from his fingers. "What?"

"Nothing," she said.

He nodded in frustration and wiped at his face with the back of his hand. "Look, I don't know why you came here, but this is not the best place for you . . ."

"I came here to see you," she said, feeling the wrenching of emotion in her heart. "I've been looking for you all afternoon."

He shrugged, the indifferent gesture punctuating the uncracking facade he wore. "You would have found me here."

"I did," she pointed out.

He nodded. "Yeah. Guess you did."

"I talked to Maureen today," she said quickly, before they got into another round of meaningless banter that would rob the moment of its significance. "I wish I'd called her earlier. She told me about Saturday night. About how you were with Jason."

He uttered a mirthless laugh and went to the table to toss down the screwdriver. "And don't tell me. You came here to thank me for not coming on like the Hitler you had me figured for . . ."

"No," she said. "I came here to tell you that I was wrong to manipulate you into meeting them."

"You sure were."

She felt familiar tears springing to her eyes, and turned away. Her hand swept through her hair. "Addison, I'm trying to apologize."

"For what?" he asked. "For thinking I don't have feelings? That I *like* it when my reports hurt people? For setting me up?"

A tear rolled down her cheek, but she quickly wiped it away. "Addison, I'm sorry. I was wrong."

Shaking his head, he ambled toward the corrugated wall and leaned into it, bracing himself on an elbow. She started to go toward him, but suddenly he ground his teeth and kicked the rippling metal, sending a loud clang echoing throughout the hangar. She jumped and muffled her sobs.

Addison turned back toward her. "Don't be sorry, Erin," he shouted, "because I'm not the big hero. I'm human. And as much as I want to, I can't let that little boy's pain, or yours, change my report."

He stepped toward her, biting out each word. "I have . . . to tell . . . the truth. Can you understand that? Because as much as I felt for Jason Hammon and his mother, as much as I may even feel for you, *I* don't have the power to change the facts. They are what they are!"

Erin set one hand across her stomach and covered her eyes with the other. Her nose was a shiny shade of crimson. "I know you can't change them. Just like I can't change the feelings I have . . . about the crash . . . and Mick's dying . . . and my flying again . . ." Her voice broke off before she could list even half the things plaguing her.

As if he couldn't bear to face her pain, Addison turned his back to her and leaned over a table, his head dropping down. She could see his own pain, his own despair, and though she ached — though he had *made* her ache — she wanted to heal him. Did it mean she was in love, she wondered dismally, that she could stand there and let him hurt her and still not want to see him hurt?

She went toward him, the sound of her clicking heels incongruous in the palpable tension of the room. "Tell me about her," she whispered when she was close behind him. "Tell me about your wife."

A moment of startled silence passed between them, but Addison didn't move. A machinist's jeep sped by outside, a voice in another hangar shouted to someone on the runway, a plane's engine shook the building. Finally, Addison spoke. "I loved her," he whispered. "Probably as much as Maureen loved Mick. As much as Jason loved his dad."

More tears rivered paths down Erin's cheeks, and her lips twisted, but she didn't answer.

"She was going to New Jersey to visit her old college roommate," he went on. "I was supposed to go with her, but I couldn't work out my schedule, so I let her go alone." The words seemed to come faster, louder, the more he spoke, but he still did not move from his position, slumped over the table.

"I was driving home from the airport when I heard the report on the radio . . ." His voice broke, then recovered, raspier as the tale unfolded. "I thought, 'No, God, it's a mistake.' But I knew I had put her on that plane. I had watched it take off." His shoulders heaved, and Erin longed to reach out to comfort him, but she knew it wasn't the time. Not while he embraced his wife's memory.

"It was a stupid, senseless accident. A collision with a private plane. Too much traffic in the area, and the controller hadn't seen it." He swallowed again, but the lump of emotion in his throat wouldn't be dislodged.

"I swore that if I could, I'd make sure that nothing like that ever happened again . . . that no other husband on earth would ever have to suffer that grief. That's why I asked the NTSB to move me to the field. But along the way since that time, I've learned that I can't stop them all. I can't protect every grieving widow. I can't shelter the children. I can't carry their load of misery on my back and still do my job." He wiped his eyes roughly, leaving them red, and slowly stood up straight.

When he turned to her, the dullness in his expression told Erin that he'd slipped through her fingers once and for all.

"So think of me as the enemy if you have to, Erin, if it makes you handle your own grief better. Think of me as the one you can blame it all on. Because I'm going to tell the truth about this crash no matter what, so that every pilot out there in training will know that it can happen to the very best. That flying takes every ounce of concentration they have, and no amount of experience can substitute for it. And maybe, just maybe, I'll stop one crash, and keep one little kid from suffering like Jason has had to."

Erin's sobs rose up in her throat. It was over. He was dismissing her, telling her that he was playing the game his way and that if she didn't like it, she could hit the road. And while she understood his point and his pain, his dismissal hurt her.

"I wish I had known her," she managed to say. "I wish I had known you then, when you were happy. And I wish things could be different."

He didn't answer, just stared at her with those dull, agonized eyes, those eyes that didn't disappear from her mind even when he wasn't there.

"Despite what you think of me now," she choked out, "I'm still sorry for all the things I said and did. All the wrong conclusions. Next time I'll take more care in checking my facts."

And then she covered her mouth and left him standing in the hangar, surrounded by the sound of those engines rumbling through him like the thunders of hell itself.

CHAPTER TWENTY

The Cessna's engine rumbled beneath Erin, but it, too, seemed like thunder from the underworld.

Her hands trembled as she followed through the mental checklist, mechanically doing what she had long ago been taught to do. Maybe she couldn't forget the life-altering impact of the crash on her life. Maybe she couldn't run from her misery over Mick's sudden absence or Addison's fleeting presence. Maybe she would never be happy again.

But she would not let her flying be one of those maybes she couldn't control. It was likely one of the only bits of her old self she would have left when the report on the crash was filed and others forgot about it and life moved along normally again. She might not have Addison or answers or peace, but she would have her flying. She'd have that if it killed her.

If it killed her. The thought, like a fearful draft of icy air, sent a convulsive shiver through her body. But in its wake came a more rational fear. *It will kill you if you don't.*

She took a deep breath and resolved to make the plane move. One step at a time, she would get it on the runway, then into the sky. Her brain struggled to find some hope, some help, and she grasped for the Scripture verses that had replayed in her mind so many times over the last few weeks. "Perfect love drives out fear." And the one from Second Timothy, where Paul wrote, "For God hath not given us the spirit of fear; but of power, and of love, and of a sound mind." She knew she had that power, that love, and as soon as she took this step, her mind would be at peace again. She would be healed of this fear.

She would just sit here a moment, she told herself. Just a few more minutes, to pull herself together before she tried. She had all the time in the world. No pressure. Nothing at stake . . .

Everything was at stake, Addison thought, diving back into his work with the vigor of a desperate man. He had laid it all on the line, all of it. It was as if he were trying to hurt himself, as if he *wanted* to suffer the emptiness, the loneliness, that he'd had before Erin. It was as if it was some penance he had to pay . . . but for what? For Amanda?

He sat at a table where a stack of documents lay and began scanning the information there again. But the same thought kept haunting him. God required mercy, not sacrifice. He had done his penance. He had hurt. It was time to live again.

He heard the hangar door open and turned around, dreading the need to face another person in his darkest moment. The sight of his father-in-law, his face as stiff and harsh as the gray mustache he wore, only seemed fitting in the context of the moment. Like a prosecutor crossing the courtroom to the defendant, Sid came across the hangar and faced Addison with dull eyes.

Addison was torn between getting up and feigning welcome, and staying where he was. But the look on Sid's face told him this was not going to be a cordial visit. He decided not to get up. "No one told me you were coming."

"The decision was made as soon as I heard you had delayed filing this report again," Sid said. "The Board thought it was high time I put you back in line."

The usual familial friendliness lurking under his cloak of authority was lacking today, and Addison knew he still hadn't gotten over finding out about Erin. "I wanted to double-check the facts," he said. "Call it gut instinct, but I'm not satisfied with the results we've come up with."

"Gut instinct?" Sid snapped. "I'll tell you what I call it. I call it female manipulation. Hormones! You're deliberately delaying things because of that woman you've been seeing!"

"Now wait a minute!" Addison shouted, his anger reverberating off the walls. "You're out of line!"

"No, *you're* out of line, Addison! And I'm here to warn you that someone with your position and your job can't afford to get involved in a dead-end relationship! It doesn't work! It only gets in the way, slows things down, confuses you!"

"The only one confused here is you!" Addison bellowed, coming to his feet. "I'll see her anytime I please, and neither you nor anybody else on the NTSB is going to stop me! There's nothing in my contract that says I can't have a relationship with a woman, or even *marry* her if I feel like it!"

As he stood before Addison, Sid's eyes narrowed with blistering hardness. "I don't need a clause in your contract," he said. "You're not indispensable, Addison. Not even to me. Remember that. I won't let you smear the good memory of my daughter with some kind of cheap affair that alters your good judgment. I'll do anything to stop that."

Addison ground his teeth and struggled not to hit the man, but before he had time to act, Sid had moved across the floor and was out of the building.

Not much later, Addison was sitting on the bare concrete floor of the hangar, leaning back against the corrugated metal wall, when his team came back from dinner. His face was drained and weary, but the deep lines of misery there were more pronounced than the lines of fatigue.

"You okay?" Hank asked.

Addison ignored the question and brought a big hand up to rub his face mercilessly. If Sid thought he could give him ultimatums, he was crazy. As angry as he'd been with Erin, he wasn't about to let either his father-in-law or the NTSB take away his options. He could destroy those himself.

He thought of her tears, her fragile state when she'd left him. Why had he let her go? his anguished heart asked him. Why hadn't he accepted her apology? Did he think he could just forget her, as if she'd never entered his life? Did he think he could use reason to banish her from his heart?

Slowly, as though each limb were sheathed in lead, he pulled himself up and dusted off the jeans that had gone beyond the point of being called dirty hours ago. He leaned against the table next to him, fingered the disassembled parts of the wing, and thought how his life was in the same shape as the mess before him.

"Hey, Addison. Maybe you should eat something. You look a little pale."

Addison again ignored the comment and strode across the room to where his shirt was draped over a chair. He grabbed it up and pulled it on, his expression distant.

"What you need is some sleep."

Addison turned back to his men as he buttoned his shirt, scanning their concerned faces with vacant eyes. "I'll be back later," he said, in a barely audible voice. "Or maybe I won't."

Then he crossed the floor strewn with wreckage and left the hangar to find Erin.

It took over an hour for Addison to track her down. When Madeline said she wasn't home, he had tried the youth center, then the health club, both to no avail. Finally certain that Madeline was covering for her, he'd called her apartment again and demanded to talk to Erin.

"I told you, she isn't here," Madeline said, irritated.

Addison leaned his forehead against the

glass of the phone booth, closed his eyes, and came as close to begging as he'd ever done. "Please, Madeline. I have to talk to her. Make her come to the phone."

"I promise I don't know where she is!" Madeline repeated. "Scout's honor. She hasn't even been home."

Addison turned around in the phone booth, weighing the truth in Madeline's words. He wasn't sure if he believed her. "Is there someplace she . . . someplace she could be that I don't know about? Anywhere at all?"

Madeline hesitated, and Addison knew he'd asked the right question. He held the silence, refusing to give up until she told him. "Yes, Addison," Madeline said finally. "There is one other place she might be."

He found Erin at Pioneer Private Airport, sitting frozen in the small Cessna, its engine running. A sense of overwhelming relief filled him that she had taken this step, even if she'd kept it from him. It was good that she was working to overcome her fear. He hoped it would lift one more obstacle from their way.

Unwilling to upset her concentration, he took a chair in front of the glass panel and watched, waiting for her to move. Sunshine beat down on the runway, and the summer sky was clear. Visibility would be excellent when she flew.

But she never did.

"If you're watching that little lady in the Cessna," a janitor said as he swept the floor near Addison, "you're gon' be disappointed. By my calculations, she's been sittin' there for goin' on two hours."

A look of alarm flashed in Addison's eyes. "Two hours? Has anyone checked on her? Is she all right?"

"Yep," the man said, moving his broom in long, expert strokes. "Keeps sayin' she's about to take off anytime. Just never does."

Addison stood up and grabbed the rail cutting across the glass. Peering out, he could barely make out her shadowed shape in the cockpit, slightly illuminated by the bright lights over her head. The urge to go out there, to apologize, to comfort her, surged through him. But even as it did, he knew it would only make things worse. She had to conquer this herself, just as he'd had to conquer his despair over meeting Jason. Only she could make that plane move.

He watched for more than ten minutes, pacing like a madman as he did, whispering encouragement that she would never hear. "Come on, Erin. You can do it. Just move the plane."

Finally, as if she heard the words and believed in them, she started to roll forward. Addison grabbed the rail again and watched, his eyes alive with anticipation. " 'Atta girl, Erin. Come on. You've got it."

The plane turned onto the runway, then began to move faster, picking up speed as it traveled. Addison's palms sweated on the cold chrome, and his heart hammered the way it had the first time he had flown. "Let go, Erin," he muttered against the glass, his hot breath fogging the pane. "You can do it."

As if following his order, the plane lifted off the ground. Erin was airborne. "All right!" he shouted, paying no heed to the amused janitor, still sweeping across the room. "You did it, Erin! You did it!"

But the glory was short-lived. As he watched, she circled the plane and began descending back to the runway, as if she couldn't get back to the earth fast enough.

Addison's heart plunged to his stomach. "No, Erin," he whispered. But it was too late. Already she was following the runway back to where she'd started.

The plane had scarcely stopped when Addison forgot his decision to leave her alone and burst through the doors, running toward the Cessna.

★ ★ ★

Erin shut off the engine and slumped back in the seat, covering her distorted face with hands that shivered like leaves in an icy wind. Anguished wails ripped from her throat, and tears burned paths through her fingers. She had forced herself to take the plane up . . . but the fear that encompassed her once she was airborne was worse than she'd imagined. "Why, Mick?" she shouted in the small cockpit.

A knock sounded on the window next to her before she could analyze just what she was blaming her dead friend for, and she jumped when she saw Addison standing there. Beneath the overhead lights, she saw the expression of compassion and understanding painted on his features. Erin felt as if God had sent him at exactly the right moment, and relief washed over her like a cleansing tide. She threw the door open and fell into his open arms.

"I couldn't do it!" she rasped, her sobs cracking her words. "I got up, but I could feel the panic coming on. I couldn't do it, Addison!"

"It's okay," he whispered, crushing her racking body against his. "It's okay, babe. I know what you're going through. I went through it myself."

"How did you get over it?" she cried.

"I kept trying. I didn't give up. You aren't going to give up, either. I'm going to help you."

"No, you can't help. I can't escape it. The crash . . ."

"You're not going to crash."

Frustrated and still a victim of the jagged edge of panic, Erin pulled back from him. She shook her head wildly, begging him to see. "No, don't you understand? It already happened, only I wasn't there, and I should have been. It should have been me. It should have happened just as I keep seeing it, and you could have blamed me instead of Mick. No one would have been hurt if you'd blamed me. Not like Maureen and Jason."

The foolish idea destroyed Addison's gentle mood. "Erin, you weren't there! You should thank God for that instead of cursing yourself for being the one who lived!"

Erin moved away from Addison, wind whipping through her hair and her blouse as she left the protective shelter of the airplane. Addison followed her. "You don't understand, Addison. You think you do, but you don't."

"I understand more than you think," he said as she started toward the hangar. "And one thing that is blatantly clear is that you have to overcome your guilt before you can overcome your fear. You have to put it behind you, Erin, and realize that the plane might have crashed whether you were in it or not!"

"How do you know?" she cried. "Maybe I could have thought more clearly than Mick. Maybe I could have kept him from making a mistake! He was used to flying with me! Maybe I could have pulled up when he panicked!"

She caught her breath at the last words and covered her mouth, but too late realized she could never negate the hateful thought. And Addison hadn't missed it. He stopped midstride and stared at her.

"All this time," he said in a neutral voice, "you fought me like a madwoman when I said it was Mick's fault and that he panicked. All this time I've believed you were backed by your convictions. But that wasn't it, was it, Erin? It wasn't my conclusions you were fighting. It was your own. For a long time I wasn't sure he'd made a mistake at all. But you were, weren't you?"

"No!" she shouted. "That isn't what I meant!"

"Yes, it is," he said wearily. "And that guilt you're feeling is more than either of us thought. You're guilty for not being there, that's obvious. But you're also feeling guilty for blaming him, too. You're as convinced as I am that it was pilot error, and you're scared to death that if you fly again, you'll make the same mistakes."

"You have no right to analyze me!" she shouted. "No right! And you're dead wrong!"

He reached for her, but she backed away. "Erin, I'm not condemning you. You just have to see the truth before you can get over the crash. I'll help you."

"I don't *need* your help!" she flared.

He grabbed her arm and shook her, forcing her to hear him. "But, Erin, you can't run from this. It won't go away."

"It doesn't *exist!*" she shouted, jerking away again. "You came up with all this yourself. *You* deal with it. I'm going home."

"Erin, please —"

But before Addison could get the words out, Erin had fled through the hangar and out to her car, like a phantom frightened by its own shadow.

CHAPTER TWENTY-ONE

Erin realized she was growing better at running from herself, from Addison, even from Mick, and the idea shamed her. But as she pulled to a rough halt in her driveway — which was filled with cars she didn't recognize — she realized that she couldn't run from Jason Hammon.

He sat on the front steps, idly examining a small model of a 727 he held, that solemn, older-than-his-years expression still on his features. Erin swallowed and leaned back in her seat before getting out of the car. She hadn't seen him since he'd discovered she'd tricked him, hadn't had to face those gray eyes, hadn't had to own up to her own raging emotions. What would she say to him now?

Wiping the teary evidence of turmoil from her face, Erin got out of the car and ambled slowly to the steps. "Why aren't you in school?" she asked.

"It's summer," he said.

Erin nodded, acknowledging that, indeed, it was. She glanced around for Maureen, then turned back to the boy. "How'd you get here, Jason?" she asked.

"Rode my bike," he said, gesturing toward the small ten-speed leaning against the house. "I wanted to see you."

She sat down on the step next to him and braced her elbows on her knees. She wasn't up to manufacturing a cheerful facade today. Instead, she tried just being herself and getting things out in the open. "Listen, I know I owe you an apology for what I did the other day. It was a dirty trick. I meant well, but I know —"

"It's okay," he interrupted, staring at the model plane again. "I know why you did it, I think."

Erin sighed deeply, feeling that somehow this little boy had grown up way past her, that she had years of living to do before she would catch up to him. She let out a telling sigh and rubbed her eyes. "It's all so complicated, Jason. Everything's so . . . complicated."

She dropped her face in her palm and shook her head, willing back the new flood of tears threatening her.

Jason seemed alarmed at her display of emotions. Tentatively, he reached out and set his hand on her back. It felt stiff, uncomfortable there, as though he didn't know what to do with it once he had made the small gesture. "I'm not mad at you anymore, Erin," he said.

She looked up, tears glossing her weary eyes. A soft, sad smile tugged at her lips as she gazed at him. His gray eyes were wide with sincerity, and somehow the words *did* make things a little better. "Tell me something, Jase," she said. "When did you grow up? I could have sworn that you were just a kid."

He shrugged and removed his hand, embarrassed. "I dunno."

Erin smiled and slipped her arms around his shoulders. Despite his awkward stiffness, she crushed him against her. "Yeah, well, *I* know." She released him and pulled herself up. Holding out a hand, she said, "Come on in. I'll see if I can scare up a snack for us. I'm kind of hungry."

Jason smiled wryly, and Erin felt relieved, for she'd almost been certain that his lips had become set in a permanent grim line. "I wouldn't go in there if I were you," Jason said. "Lois has a bunch of pilots in there, and they're all yelling and fighting. She invited me in, but it sounded a little dangerous. Besides, she didn't know when you'd be home."

Erin glanced at the front door where many of her coworkers were gathered, hashing out the latest demands and grievances on behalf of herself and the other pilots. If she walked in there now, with her eyes all red, the gossip would resume. Already speculation abounded about her relationship with the NTSB official, the enemy, the kind of person pilots respected but would not, under any circumstances, fall in love with.

Defeated, she sank back down on the step. In love? Did it really come as a surprise to her now? And what good did it do her to know she was in love now, when the mere act of feeling only summoned up more emotions she couldn't handle?

"What's the matter, Erin?" Jason asked softly, watching the string of fatigued reactions travel across her face.

"Nothing," she lied. "Guess I'm just tired."

He didn't answer. Instead, he leaned forward, studying the model in his hand. "Erin, I was wondering. Would you mind . . . I mean, would it be all right . . . ?"

Erin looked up at him, her attentive eyes coaxing him to finish the question.

"Well, I really want to learn to fly, and I know I'm old enough 'cause other kids have done it, and Dad promised to teach me, but now . . ." His voice trailed off. "Erin, would you teach me to fly? Dad said you had an instructor's license, that it was how you made your living before you got on with Southeast . . ."

Erin's breath caught in her lungs, and she gaped at the boy. Could it be that she, an experienced pilot, could be so afraid of flying after Mick's crash that she couldn't get off the ground, when his son — a child, for heaven's sake — wanted to follow his father's path into the sky, completely unafraid of what waited in the airways?

"Erin?" he asked, waiting for an answer.

Erin searched for the right words. How could she tell him that she'd lost it, that his image of her was nothing more than illusion? "Jason, I wish I could teach you . . . I do. It's just that . . . I'm probably the worst person you could ask right now."

"Why?" he asked, disappointment flattening his tone. "We're still friends, aren't we?"

"Of course we are. It's just that . . ."

"The plane," he said, anticipating her explanation. "You don't have a plane. But don't worry. Mom said she'd pay for the rental."

"Your mother agreed to this?" Erin asked, amazed.

"Sure," he said. "She's not crazy about it, but she knows Dad already promised and that I mean to do it sooner or later. Dad always said you were one of the best pilots he knew. He would have wanted you to teach me. What do you say, Erin?"

Erin's breath came quicker, like a countdown to disaster, and she covered her mouth to hide her trembling lips. She shook her head idly, realizing that she would have to tell him. Only her mind refused to come up with the right words.

"Is it because you aren't flying now?" he asked. "Because you're in scheduling or whatever? 'Cause, I mean, you could make an exception just for me, couldn't you? No big deal. Just a few lessons."

"It isn't that I don't want to," Erin said. "It isn't that at all."

Jason's eyes cut through to the truth, and a small frown formed between his brows. "Erin, you're not scared to fly, are you? That's not why you've quit, is it?"

His perceptiveness was almost too much for her, but she shook her head in denial. "Of course not," she lied. "It's just that . . ."

"Just what?" he asked impatiently. "You can tell me, Erin. We're friends, remember?"

"I have these dreams at night, Jason," Erin whispered, offering the only explanation she was able to give. "They've shaken me up, and I don't know what to do about them."

Jason paused, as if he didn't know whether Erin had changed the subject or not. "Why do you have to do anything about them?" he asked. "If they're just dreams and all."

"Because if I don't do something about it," she said, "I'll never get my life straight again. And I'll never be able to teach anyone — much less you — how to fly."

"Oh." There was perfect acceptance in his calm voice.

Erin thought a moment, then looked at the little boy who meant so much to her — Mick's son, the symbol of life going on . . . If only she could borrow from his strength to recharge her own. If only he could be the catalyst to bring her back to life. After a moment, she touched his knee. "I'll tell you what," she said. "How would it be if I called your mom from a pay phone or something and asked her if you could come to Pioneer Airport with me?"

His small face lit up like a lamp turned on after ages of darkness. "For a lesson? Today?"

"No, no," she clarified. "Not today. Later, maybe, after I've worked some things out. But not today."

"Then why do you want to go there?"

She glanced down at a fingernail, studied its shape with too close attention, to lessen the gravity of what she was facing. "I have a bone to pick with a little Cessna that's

274

been getting the best of me. If I knew you were inside the building watching, I might be able to beat it yet."

Jason lifted his shoulders. "Sure. I'll even go up with you." He got up and dusted off his pants.

"No," she said quickly. "Not today, Jason. I just need you there . . . on the ground."

"Okay," he said again. "Let's go."

A tense knot of apprehension tightened in her chest as they started back to her car, but Erin knew that Mick's son might be just the one to give her the courage she needed. For he seemed to have more than enough for both of them.

Erin forced the plane forward, not allowing herself a chance to divert down any of the paths of thought that had kept her from flying until now. Jason was inside the terminal, watching without a clue as to the turbulent emotions raging in her now. He probably thought it was perfectly natural to see Erin fly. After all, she was the woman who would teach him.

And so she kept the plane moving, contacting the tower when it was necessary, ignoring the skeptical tone in the controller's voice. He had cleared her for takeoff to no avail too many other times. She would not let Jason know that his father's crash had crippled her. If he could summon enough courage to fly at only nine years old, then she certainly could at twenty-nine.

She would do it for Jason. And for Mick. And for Addison, to prove that he was wrong — dead wrong — about her blaming Mick without realizing it. The crash wasn't his fault. It wasn't.

She waited for clearance to take off, then began her taxi down the runway, picking up speed as she went. Like a manacle, fear threatened to choke her, but she didn't allow herself to succumb to its intimidation. Jason was watching.

She held her breath as her wheels left the ground, and she wrestled the overwhelming urge to put the plane back down, as she had done earlier. Perspiration beaded on her temples and lips, and her heart hammered at life-threatening speed. But still she climbed, because Jason was watching.

"You shouldn't have done it, Mick!" she shouted again as her hands trembled at the controls. "You shouldn't have crashed!"

And on the heels of her soul-deep cry came Addison's words that morning. *You're blaming him, too . . . scared to death you'll make the same mistakes . . .*

Shaking her head in fierce denial, she

reached the outer limits of the airport traffic area, staying away from the busy airways, and skirted out over the Gulf. Her hands trembled at the instruments, and tears came to her eyes.

"You're wrong, Addison!" she shouted furiously.

You have to see the truth before you can get over the crash, echoed his words of that morning. *You can't run away.*

Anger seethed, and she ground her teeth, determined to prove him wrong. But one problem loomed up before her like another aircraft on a collision course.

Addison was right . . . again.

She would have to face the truth soon. But not now.

That's enough, she told herself. *I don't have to put myself through this. I've gotten up, stayed up, so now I can get back down before it's too late.* But her declaration had more to do with her battle with her emotions than it had to do with flying, and that became more clear to her the more distance she flew.

Jason was watching, so she made herself stay up a little longer, disciplined herself to face the realizations flying at her like an ocean wind. Keeping her altitude low, she followed a circular path around the city. More tears carved paths down her face, while truth, like a surgical instrument, carved at her heart.

"I'm sorry, Mick," she whispered. "I'm so sorry."

Sorry. Sorry that you've gone. Sorry for your son. Sorry for the anger. Sorry for the blame . . .

"Oh, my Lord. Is it true?" she whispered. "The blame . . . the blame . . ."

She did blame him, she finally admitted. The horror and disloyalty of that particular truth gripped her, along with the acknowledgment that she was afraid she'd make the same mistakes, crash the plane, kill not only herself but countless others. But a memory from years ago surfaced in her mind. A memory of Mick sitting beside her, his calm, gentle voice admonishing her to depend on herself more than on him. *You're as good a pilot as anybody I know, Erin. Trust yourself . . . trust yourself.*

And Jason was watching.

The sound of the engine purring beneath her seemed to calm her terror a bit, just as confronting the truth seemed to anesthetize her a little, though it still unsettled her. The air-conditioning system began to cool the compartment, making her feel more at ease. Erin glanced out the window, half-expecting a brand-new attack of panic to assault her. She scanned the city stretching beneath her like an enlarged map, and found herself marveling at the beauty of the land, the bayous threading beneath her, the majestic, tree-lined lake. She flew over Promised Land, where Madeline worked, its looming rides and fancy hotels spread out like tiny toys beneath her.

Erin hadn't gone more than twenty miles when the thought struck her full force. She had come as close as she'd come in weeks to feeling complete peace. It was in her grasp.

You're flying. Your palms have dried. You aren't trembling. You aren't going to crash.

And suddenly it didn't matter if Jason was watching. Erin was flying for herself now, for the serenity the act restored to her soul, for the pure joy of soaring through the heavens, knowing that she was in complete control.

"I did it," she whispered to her Creator as tears of joy, not horror, streamed down her face. "I did it. I'm not afraid."

She flew up the coast for fifteen more minutes before turning the plane around and heading back. Jason was probably getting impatient. She radioed the tower, aware of the note of pride in her voice, and got clearance to land.

As her landing gear touched lightly down,

a sad smile came to her face. She had conquered one major obstacle in her life. Now she had to face all the others.

Erin took Jason back to her house and watched as he rode away on his bike, the tentative smile on her face striking a precarious balance somewhere between secretive pride and worried doubt. Yes, she could fly. It would be easier the next time. She would go back later today and take the plane out again, flying until she was able to prove to Addison that she was ready to go back to work.

Pushing the myriad other problems she faced out of her mind, Erin decided to brave the stares and speculation of the pilots and go into the house. After all, she couldn't stay outside all day.

She pushed open the door and stepped into a room that was the battleground for a verbal war. The entire committee of twenty was present — not just the five on the bargaining committee.

"So what are we supposed to do?" one of the senior captains was bellowing, apparently addressing Lois. "They took away our sick days, for pete's sake," he shouted, his arms flailing wildly. "As if it wasn't bad enough that we had a major airline crash just three weeks ago, they expect us to go up *sick,* too, and endanger the lives of our passengers?"

"Just think logically for a minute," Lois suggested calmly to the nineteen men slumped in fatigued positions around the living room. "They think we're abusing our sick leave, and let's face it, some of us have! Besides, all we have to do is get a doctor's certificate to prove we're sick —"

"Forget the doctor's certificate," someone across the room said. "You don't go to the doctor for a simple head cold. The other day Gary Bowman burst an eardrum when he was forced to fly with a cold and couldn't clear his ears. Is that fair?"

"Of course not. I'm just saying that if we ask for something, we have to *give* something."

"A third of our pay isn't enough?" Ray Carter asked. "Half of our rest time isn't enough? Suitable working conditions aren't enough? Because they've taken all of those. If you want to give more, Lois, come up with something of your own to give. I'm fresh out of generosity."

Erin slipped into her bedroom without saying a word, disturbed at the way the meeting was going. The first meeting with Zarkoff was tomorrow, and so far it looked as if the committee members were as far apart in their convictions as the owner was with his employees.

Beside her phone, Erin saw a message in Lois's handwriting. "Addison called this many times." Below the message, Lois had kept a stick count of the calls. They numbered seven.

Erin wadded the note, tossed it into a wastebasket, and stared after it a moment. Her heart told her to call him back, to tell him that he had been right . . . but something inside kept her from doing it. He'd probed too deeply into her soul today, finding her wounds and forcing her to see them. She wasn't ready to be that vulnerable again. Not after she had flown today.

She freshened up and went back out into the combat zone of her living room. Tempers were hotter than when she'd left them.

"What do you guys want to do?" Lois was shouting. "Strike before we've even sat down at the bargaining table? Just give up? Do you really think that man would buckle under to *anything* if we did that? He has scores of pilots working for Trans Western, and he's training hundreds more in Houston."

"We're going to negotiate," a slower, softer-spoken captain assured her. "But his refusal to meet with a professional negotiator doesn't say a lot for his willingness to bargain. We just want him to know that he can't come in here and change things all around and expect us to give in easily."

George Vanderwall, the bitterest man Lois had ever met, shook his head. "I say strike now," he said harshly. "Hit him where his checkbook is and let him know that we mean business."

"A strike would hurt him for a day or two, George. Then it would hit *our* checkbooks, not his," Lois said.

"It's a bad idea to take a woman in there with us on the negotiating team," George informed the others. "It'll be too easy for him to convince her of his terms."

Erin glanced at Lois and saw the blood rush to flood her friend's cheeks in scathing crimson. "Now, wait a minute," Lois said through her teeth. "The membership elected me to this committee for a reason, and that was that I seem to be one of the only ones in this room who has a clear head and isn't thinking with my ego! I'm just as loyal to Southeast as any one of you, and I won't let you tough-talking jerks throw my job away for me just out of some macho sense of principle!"

Erin turned her head away from the others to hide the smile forming on her face. She wanted to cheer for Lois, but it wasn't the time.

For today was a day for silent victories.

Addison lay on his couch in his drape-darkened living room, holding a small tape recorder in his hand. He would dictate his report today, he thought, lay the blame for the crash on Mick, and type it up when he had the energy. There was no use prolonging it anymore. Nothing was going to change.

Just like nothing would change between Erin and him. Their relationship just wasn't meant to be. He closed his eyes and threw his wrist over his forehead. Whoever said it was better to have loved and lost . . . well, he'd never met Erin.

For so long his darkness had been for Amanda. When the drapes were closed and the lights were off and his thoughts were wrapped in intimacy, it had been she that he thought of.

But not anymore. Now Erin loomed higher in his thoughts, in his heart, in his soul, and he couldn't help wondering if, for the rest of his life, he'd think of her when he was down.

Swallowing the emotion in his throat, he heaved a great sigh and clicked on the tape recorder with his thumb.

"On August 7, Southeast Airlines Flight 94, a scheduled flight from Washington's Dulles Airport to Shreveport . . . ," he began.

But it was a poor beginning, for it was the beginning of the end.

CHAPTER TWENTY-TWO

Erin spent most of the next day flying the Cessna, restoring her faith in herself and her abilities. Now, when she thought of flying the 727 again, she didn't panic. The thought actually seemed pleasant. Her tears and trembling had stopped, and life wasn't a plague anymore.

The next step, she decided finally, was to get her suspension lifted and get back to work. But there was only one way to go about that. She would have to call Addison.

She sat inside Pioneer Airport, sipping a cup of coffee, and stared at the pay telephone on the wall. Addison had called continuously yesterday, but Erin hadn't returned his calls. She had called Madeline at home an hour ago, however, and found that his calls had stopped. Addison had given up on her, Erin admitted with dread, and she deserved it.

She leaned her head back on the vinyl sofa facing the runway and closed her eyes. Why couldn't she admit to him that he had been right, that she *had* blamed Mick, and that it took his pointing it out for her to see it?

She'd been busy flying, she rationalized. She would have called him sooner or later, when she gave herself a moment to think. But deep in her heart she knew that she hadn't called because it was so easy *not* to think about the relationship that had been rocky from the first moment they'd met. She wanted to savor the peace that flying had restored to her. Addison had a way of opening her Pandora's box of emotions — and Erin wanted it left closed.

But it was time to call him now, she decided, setting down her coffee with a resolute sigh and standing up. Would he answer? Would he even be home? She went to the phone and, with a shaky hand, dialed his number.

She almost hung up after the third ring, but suddenly he answered.

"Hello?"

She cleared her throat. "Uh, Addison?"

Silence stretched over the line.

"It's me, Erin," she went on. "I . . . I was wondering if you could meet me."

Another pause seemed to last a lifetime, but finally he spoke. "Sure. Where are you?"

She blinked back the mist in her eyes and turned to the window, where she could see Jack's Cessna, positioned and ready to fly.

"I'm at Pioneer Airport," she said. "I've been flying."

"You have?" She recognized the hope in his voice, hope that her mounting such a big obstacle meant she was ready to mount others.

"Yes," she said. "I want you to go up with me, so I can prove to you that I'm over my fear. Addison, I want to go back to work. I want you to get my suspension lifted."

"I see." The words lost the tentative hope of moments before, as though he saw in her request no personal need, no reaching out to him. Only business. Only necessary communication between a commercial pilot and an NTSB official. "Well, I guess I'll be right over, then. No point in dragging this thing out."

The *click* in her ear surprised her, and she held the phone away from her face, as if she could imagine the dial tone cutting her off from Addison's support. Strictly business. Wasn't that how she had wanted it?

She waited inside the terminal until Addison came, sifting through her feelings. What *did* she want from him? A nice pat on the back? A good report to her chief pilot? No. She wanted to share this little bit of joy with him, wanted an excuse to see him without saying it, wanted a hint of his affection, though she wasn't quite sure where she wanted to take the relationship from there. She'd been so angry yesterday, and anger wasn't something that went away just because she discovered it wasn't justified. She knew she was clinging to her ire like armor, but she wasn't sure why she needed that kind of protection from Addison.

When he walked through the doors of the terminal, she felt her defenses drop. He was wearing the same shirt he'd been wearing on that first day he'd come to her door and taken her to the lake and sat out there beside her, asking questions in his gentle, painstaking way. If she hadn't fallen in love with him on that day, she had certainly come to like him against her will. Addison was a hard man to dislike. Even when she tried.

He stood before her, face expressionless, hands hidden in the pockets of his jeans, and he shrugged. "I'm here. You ready?"

She nodded, chagrined by his detachment. "I guess so, if you're in a hurry."

"No hurry," he said coolly.

She tossed her empty coffee cup into the wastebasket and stood up. "Well, like you said. No point in dragging it out."

He followed her to the plane, got in, and didn't say a word. The quiet was like a chilling arctic wind. Silence filled the cockpit as she followed her checklist, preparing for takeoff. Her hands began to shake again.

Finally, Addison had to break the silence. "You said you'd already taken her up?"

"Yes," she said. "Most of yesterday and all day today."

"Yesterday?" he asked, surprised. "What did you do? Come back after you left me here?"

The distinct choice of words took her aback for a moment, but she recovered and answered the question as coldly as it had been delivered. "Yes."

She turned on the engine and continued checking the instruments.

"Well, at least I'm good for something. I can make you so mad that you forget how scared you are. Should I try it again? I'm sure I can come up with something. It's been coming so easy lately."

Erin hated the sarcasm in his voice and refused to take the bait. "No need," she said. "I'm not afraid anymore. You'll see."

"If you aren't afraid, why are you still shaking?"

Erin looked at him, furious in spite of herself. "I'm shaking because your new attitude is making me nervous, that's why. I don't know how to act around you."

He bit his lip, as if in contemplation, and nodded. "Well, I can see your problem. One minute you're leaning on me and letting me comfort you, and the next you won't even return my calls. Does sort of leave one not knowing how to act."

Erin's face stung with unexpressed rage, but she refused to give in to the fight he was trying to provoke. She radioed the tower and began taxiing down the runway, defiance dictating her expression. "I'm going to fly this plane, Addison, and no matter what kind of intimidation you use, you aren't going to stop me."

"I wasn't trying to intimidate you," he said quietly. He looked out the window, rubbing his stubbled chin as his face softened. "I'm sorry."

Erin didn't acknowledge the apology. Instead, she concentrated on her orders from the tower, acquired permission to take off, and began working toward the speed that would lift them into the air.

Addison didn't say a word once they were up. Instead, he watched her carefully. She savored the quiet and took them over the lake, letting the familiar calm seep into her soul again.

"You're really doing it," he whispered after ten minutes or more, when he could see that she was in complete control. "I can't believe it."

She wet her lips, which had suddenly gone dry, and cut through a misty cloud hanging low over the water. "I told you."

"Tell me this," he said, all traces of bitterness in his voice gone. "Was it really your anger at me that provoked you into flying?"

She could hear the pain in his voice, as if he hoped she would say no, that his influence was only positive. "Yesterday, when I left you, I felt like my life had gone totally berserk and that I had lost control of every aspect of it. I thought I was going insane."

"And what happened?" he asked quietly.

"Jason asked me to teach him to fly," she said. "And I thought that if a nine-year-old boy could still want to fly after his father had crashed, then why couldn't I?"

She kept her voice low and steady, her emotions as firmly under her control as her aircraft. "So I brought him to the airport. I forced myself up to prove to myself, and him . . . and, yes, you . . . that I could do it. And I did."

"Yes, you did," he whispered. "I'm convinced. I'll make sure your suspension is lifted immediately."

"Thank you," she said, but somehow there was no joy in her heart. Removing this obstacle only severed one of the ties that had bound them. It meant that there might very well be nothing left between them.

She landed the plane without a word, then pulled it back into position. Neither made a move to get out.

"Why didn't you return my calls?" His question cut through the silence.

"I told you, I've been flying."

"There's a phone here," he said. "You could have called."

She sighed and propped her elbow on the door.

"Why did you run out on me yesterday?"

"The things you said . . . ," she began. "I didn't want to hear them."

He shifted in his seat in order to face her. "I wasn't being malicious. Don't you understand that? I was just trying to make you see yourself. Make you face some important things."

"Well, it worked," she said wearily, turning back to him. "Are you satisfied? You made me face those things. That I blamed Mick, just like everybody else did. That all the years he'd proven himself to me didn't matter, that a handful of circumstantial evidence could change my mind. You made me face the kind of friend I am, Addison, and I resent it."

"Erin, you're the best friend anybody

could ever have. You fought like a Trojan for Mick. If *anybody* could have changed my mind about him, it would have been you."

She peered out the window, seeing far beyond the runway.

"But how could I change your mind when I wasn't convinced?" she asked without inflection.

"You couldn't have changed my mind regardless of how you felt," he said. "Erin, don't you know by now how stubborn I am?"

Erin continued gazing out the window. "You tear me to pieces," she whispered after a moment. "One moment with you I'm flying, the next I'm sifting through my own wreckage. I don't know how to live like that, Addison. I need some peace."

"The wreckage is almost behind us," he whispered.

She nodded and turned her sad, resigned eyes to him.

He pulled her into his embrace, holding her as though some monster might come at any moment and rip her out of his arms again.

No monster came. Just the sweet spirit of love that had almost been discarded, only to be rediscovered at the last moment.

Addison's first professional task at the airport that day was to talk to Bill Jackson, Erin's chief pilot, about lifting her suspension. When that was taken care of, he went back to the hangar, where his crew was already hard at work combing through the disassembled pieces of the wreckage for the second time. Hank, Addison's flight-control specialist, was absorbed in his work, piecing together the complex elevator system, the section that acted as a steering mechanism for the plane.

Everyone but Hank looked up when they heard Addison's footsteps on the concrete. He scuffed toward where most of them worked, his head hung low. "I guess I don't have to ask if any of you has found anything," he said.

Murmured negatives followed from each of the men. Hank, however, seemed too engrossed in the elevator to answer.

"Hank, come on over here. Let's talk."

Hank still didn't look up. "Give me a minute, Addison. I'm trying to figure something out."

Addison gave a questioning look to the others. "Has he found something?"

"There isn't anything to find, Addison," one of the crew members maintained. "Our first conclusion was the right one."

Addison paced slowly to the instruments

displayed on the counter, touching one of them. "I'm beginning to think you're right. Maybe it's time to file the report."

"And go home," Horace added anxiously.

"Yeah," Addison muttered. "Home."

The men watched him with steadfast interest, waiting for his "maybe" to become something more definite, something they could tell their families. Suddenly, Hank spoke up again.

"Uh, Addison, come here a minute. You might want to take a look at this."

Addison stepped over several pieces of seared metal until he was beside Hank. "Whatcha got?"

Hank frowned and gestured toward the reassembled pieces. "I don't know. Maybe something, maybe nothing. Just like you said, we've been trying to piece together the elevator system . . . And take a look at this."

Addison looked where Hank was pointing, saw that two pieces were broken apart at what should have been their attachment point. Hank pried out a bolt about four inches long, broken in two pieces. "I found this. It was easy to overlook before."

Addison took the bolt, his frown cutting deep fissures in his forehead. "The problem," Addison said as he studied the pieces, "is determining whether the bolt broke as a result of the crash or before it."

"If it broke before it, we've got a case," Hank said.

"That's right," Addison said, excitement filling his eyes. "A broken bolt in the elevator system could affect the steering. It could very well have caused the crash." Addison stood up and took the bolt to a table where microscopes lay under stronger light. "This bolt is sheered," he said. "And it's chalky at the break." He held it under a magnifying glass and examined it closely as his heart began to pound harder. "There's some corrosion inside . . . a little rust . . ."

"Sounds like a fatigue break," Hank said. "A stress break brought on by the crash would be shiny and stretched. But if it's corroded inside, it's probably been ready to break for a while."

"You're right," Addison agreed, leaning back from the microscope with a smile on his face. The other team members gathered around the table, intent on seeing the bolt for themselves. "If it broke *before* the crash, and the push rod broke loose, Mick Hammon had absolutely no control over the elevator. Right up until the last minute, he would have thought he was pulling the plane up. But the elevator wouldn't have connected. If that was the case, there wouldn't have been one blasted thing he could have done to save the aircraft."

"So he would be completely exonerated," Hank added. "If that's, indeed, what happened."

Addison peered into the microscope again, then backed up to allow each team member to see for himself. "Man," said Horace, who'd done the most complaining in the four weeks they'd been there, as he examined the broken bolt. "We almost made the poor guy look negligent."

"Almost," Addison said, the gravity of their oversight becoming more and more apparent as his heart filled with righteous purpose. "But not quite."

He put the bolt in a small bag, tagged it, and handed it to Hank. "I want you on the next flight to Washington. You're going to hand deliver this to headquarters for metallurgical analysis. Tell them I want the works — spectrographic, microscopic, destructive. I want to know everything there is to know about this bolt, and I want it fast."

"Sure, Addison," Hank said, eyes dancing. "I'll call you as soon as I hear."

"Rush it," Addison called, as Hank started out of the hangar. "The sooner we know, the sooner we can wrap this up."

As Hank disappeared from sight, the team

erupted into congratulations and laughter. Addison accepted their handshakes and backslaps, but his mind was already on his next step. For the first time since this whole investigation had begun, he might just have some good news for Erin.

CHAPTER TWENTY-THREE

Addison was at home that night, waiting for Erin to bring over Chinese take-out food, when Hank called with the results.

"You'll never believe this," Hank said, his voice solemn but anxious. "Not only were we right about the bolt being the cause of the crash, the metallurgical analysis showed that the bolt was counterfeit. Who knows how many others were in that plane?"

Addison sprang from his chair. "Counterfeit! Are they sure?"

"Positive," Hank said. "They even took the pieces of the bolt and subjected it to measured stress to see at what point it would break. Addison, it broke at a much lower tensile pressure than it was supposed to."

"Where did it come from?" Addison asked bitterly.

"We don't know for sure," Hank said. "But they think it was probably made outside the States. They said they've been seeing more and more of this lately, in all sorts of applications."

Addison sank back into his chair again. "I've heard about it," he agreed, his voice barely audible as the implications of their discovery filled him with dread. "They've turned up in military tanks, ships, even the space shuttle. Apparently they're made cheaper and somehow get rated at higher stress levels so they'll sell for more money." He leaned forward, grounding his elbows in his knees as the truth sank in. "Why didn't it occur to me before?"

Hank's response was quick. "Don't be so tough on yourself. We haven't seen this in our investigations before. At least we can officially clear the captain."

"Yeah," Addison said, pulling himself up again and setting a pace pattern across his rug. "He's clear. But it's a lot easier to make recommendations about future training programs to prevent panic than it is to find a solution to this. What do I say? 'The National Transportation Safety Board recommends that in the future only authentic bolts be used?' If we can't tell which ones they are until they break, where does that leave us?"

"You're right, Addison. There's no solution yet. But at least now we're aware of the problem."

"What good is that if hundreds of people wind up dead?" Addison yelled. "*I'm* the one who had to probe the families and

301

friends like a vulture looking for spicy little clues to what may have snapped in the pilot's mind, when it was a stupid bolt that snapped! I'm the one who has to see the pain on those people's faces and carry the guilt and responsibility for my conclusions. And who is really affected by those conclusions? Does it prevent any crashes? No. We have to just sit back and wait for another bolt to snap somewhere at a critical point in an approach. It stinks, Hank!"

"Maybe so, Addison." Hank's voice was grim, but he didn't sound as defeated as his boss. "But it's our job." He paused for a moment, then, as if uncomfortable with what he was about to say, went on. "And, speaking of our jobs, Sid is here with me. He wants to talk to you."

Addison flopped down onto the couch, bracing himself for more rage, more fury. Sid would still be angry and passing orders as if he were some Little League coach and Addison a nine-year-old player. Addison wasn't in the mood.

"Addison," Sid said, when the phone had exchanged hands. "You did a good job. I owe you an apology for being so hard-nosed about the delays. I guess your instincts served you well this time."

"They always do," Addison said, a dull

edge to his voice. "You should know that by now."

"Yes, well . . ." Sid cleared his throat, paused a moment, then tackled what was really on his mind. "I want that report tomorrow. You can deliver it in person, and then you're off to Albuquerque —"

"Albuquerque?" Addison asked. "What are you talking about?"

"I'm talking about the crash that happened this morning in Albuquerque. Midair collision of two light engines. Should be pretty cut-and-dried. Can't blame that on a bolt."

Addison raked his big fingers through his hair. "Albuquerque," he repeated miserably. "Cut-and-dried." He sighed, and racked his brain for a way to keep from leaving Erin so soon. He wasn't ready. It was too early.

"Right," Sid said. "There was a survivor, so it's pretty simple. The pilot's girlfriend can give you all the information you need. She's in the hospital, but we can get you permission to question her. I suspect there were drugs involved."

"You want me to question a woman who just lost her boyfriend and her friends and is hospitalized herself?" Addison asked.

"Of course. It's the typical scenario."

"I don't go by typical scenarios!" Addison

shouted. He lowered his voice, expelled a ragged breath, and went on. "Besides, I can't be there tomorrow. I'll send my report on with one of the team members. I still have some loose ends to tie up here."

"Wrong," Sid told him. "You'll bring it yourself and then you'll go on to Albuquerque. This isn't a request, Addison, it's an order."

"But I told you, Sid. I can't get away —"

"Loose ends can be cut off," Sid bit out. "Especially when there isn't room for them. You had your fling, Addison. It's time to come back to the real world. And in this world, there's no room for that woman."

Addison sprang up, as if facing the man in person. "There will be room for her if I make room!"

Sid chuckled mirthlessly, leaving Addison cold. "You don't understand," he said. "I can't keep working with you while you dangle that woman under my nose. You have a choice, Addison. Either her or your job."

"You can't force that on me," Addison shouted. "There's no rule against an NTSB investigator being involved or even married!"

"I told you before, I don't need a rule," Sid warned him, his voice quivering with emotion. "All I have to do is pass along that you've become difficult and resistant to the NTSB's procedures, and you can stand in the unemployment lines. It's a promise, Addison."

For a moment, Addison was too amazed to speak. Instead, he stood with his mouth open, trying to gauge the intent behind the bluff.

"Be sensible," Sid went on, his voice feigning reason. "This is no life for a family. You travel constantly, and when you get where you're going, you're totally absorbed in your work. Next time, she won't be connected with the crash. Next time, she'll be left out of it, and you won't be able to spend time with her even under the pretense of work. Take my word for it. There isn't room in the field for marriage. I'm thinking of her as much as you."

"Your consideration stuns me," Addison said caustically.

"I'm right. You know I am."

"Let me get this straight," Addison said through his teeth. "I just want to make sure I know where the lines are drawn. You're telling me that either I get rid of Erin or I lose my job. Is that it?"

"The choice is pretty straightforward," Sid said smugly. "You can make an impact in this job. You have no idea how many accidents you've helped prevent. Even now, you can get on this bolt thing and make sure that something is done to find these counterfeits. When it was *your* wife who died in a crash, you knew how important it was to keep things like that from recurring. Get your thinking back in perspective, Addison. Don't forget the grief that we both suffered when that tragedy happened. You've saved hundreds, maybe thousands, with your recommendations. Your work is too important to throw away on a little infatuation."

"So that *is* what you're saying?" he repeated. "That it comes down to an ultimatum?"

"I'm not an ogre," Sid said, his voice full of emotion. "You're like a son to me. You're all I've got. I just want to see you do the right thing. If you turn your back on this job, then Amanda's death was useless, wasted. Through working in the field you've had the chance to make some sense of it all, to use that in a positive way. Don't bury that in a lot of useless emotions. Use your head, man. You need this job as much as we need you. You can no more walk away from it than I can."

"I can go over your head," Addison threatened. "You can't do this."

"Go over my head, then," Sid said quietly.

"And if you're right, and my word doesn't pack the weight it used to, then I'll go. There won't be room here for both of us."

The phone went dead in Addison's hand, leaving him staring at the receiver, defeated, as if it were an explosive about to destroy his life.

He hung up the phone and paced frantically across the carpet. How could it come down to this? His job or Erin? Sid knew his job had been his whole life since Amanda had died. Addison *was* his job, just as Sid was. Sure, there was a possibility that his superiors would veto Sid's ultimatum, but if Sid quit the NTSB, where would that leave him? Would he take refuge in a dark house again, hiding out from the world because there was no one else to care? If Addison allowed that, wasn't that in itself a betrayal to Amanda?

Besides, Sid wasn't crazy. At least not in his normal work affairs. It was just when it came to his daughter . . . to Addison . . . to the prospect of another woman taking Amanda's place in Addison's life.

No, the choice was up to him. Would he leave the NTSB? The prospect sank uncomfortably in Addison's heart, though a voice somewhere inside asked what good there was in keeping his job, when stupid things like counterfeit bolts caused crashes.

Rage over that particular injustice threatened to choke him again. How could that accident have been prevented? And why had so many people had to suffer and die? His investigation had hurt Jason, Maureen, Erin . . .

Erin. What was he going to do? Sid's words came back to him, his warnings about relationships and the nature of his job ringing a little too true. He didn't want a long-distance relationship. They'd drift apart, learn to hate each other.

But if he didn't have her, his job would seem empty and lifeless. He'd hate *himself* and Sid and the whole NTSB. And soon he'd wind up seeing the victims and survivors as statistics, fact machines, from whom he could get answers in exchange for nothing.

First things first, he told his frantic mind. He'd tackle one problem at a time. First, he had to deal with Maureen and Jason. He went to the phone, punched out Erin's number, and felt his anger and confusion subside a little at the sound of her voice. Was there really a choice, after all? "Hi, babe," he said, forcing his voice to sound lighter than he felt.

"Hi. I was just on my way out the door."

"Look, about the Chinese food." He stalled, trying to decide how much to tell her now. "I'm not really hungry. I was thinking, maybe we could eat later."

"You don't want me to come?" she asked. The disappointment in her voice made him smile.

"No, I still want you to come," he assured her. "I . . . I was just thinking. Why don't you run by the Hammon's house and get Maureen and Jason to follow you? Something came up today, and I need to talk to all three of you."

There was a long silence between them. Finally, Erin spoke, a note of dread in her voice. "I'll bring them," she said.

Addison knew she waited for him to tell her if the news was good or bad, but for the life of him, he wasn't sure which it was. "I'll be out on the bayou behind the condos," he added quietly. "I need some air."

It wasn't difficult to sense the despair in Erin's voice. "All right, Addison," she said. "We'll see you soon."

CHAPTER TWENTY-FOUR

The night breeze was pleasantly cool and playful, and Addison enjoyed it after the heat of the hangar. He looked out over the water behind his apartment complex. He found a rock, kicked it into the water, and gazed out over the dusk-darkened bayou. Banishing thoughts of his ludicrous choice from his mind, he concentrated on telling Maureen and Jason the results of his investigation.

What would he say to them? How did he apologize for overlooking a malfunction in the airplane and laying the blame for all those deaths on the man who was father, husband, friend? How did he explain the senseless use of a cheap bolt?

It had all seemed so simple when he'd transferred to field work for the NTSB. He'd had a purpose. He had really believed his investigations and subsequent recommendations had prevented countless crashes. But had they really? Or had he just been deluding himself, because of his wife, into thinking he had an effect on other lives?

And if, rather than Erin, he chose the job, where would he go from there? Albuquerque? Would it be any different there? Deaths and destruction? Few, if any, living witnesses? Grieving family members or friends who tried to keep him from reporting anything negative about their loved ones? Thousands of shattered and burnt pieces of wreckage that he and his crew were supposed to assess inside and out? And from there he'd go to yet another state, another crash, another set of lives that would never be the same.

Even if he could make himself go over Sid's head, find a way to have both Erin and the job, what would it do to Erin, to be in love with a man who confronted disaster on a daily basis? Already, he'd had a sample of how things could be. In the wake of almost every moment of joy between them came rage and fighting, then days of anger before the cycle started again. The rage was always due to his job. Yes, he realized that this job had been different, because it had focused on someone she loved. But the nature of all of his cases were the same. They were all accidents. There were often deaths. And there was usually someone at blame. Would she come to resent him the more she saw what his job entailed? And what about the constant separations, the profound distractions, the intense work on each and every case?

He heard his name called behind him, and he turned back to the apartments and saw Erin walking toward him, followed by Maureen, who folded her arms defensively across her stomach, as if to say, "Don't hurt me any more; I've had enough." Jason followed, hands hidden in his pockets.

He met the trio halfway, got the greetings out of the way, then sat down on the grass skirting the water. Erin sat next to him, facing the pond, in the same way she had on that first day they'd spent together at the lake. Little had changed, he thought. They were still talking about Mick.

"I asked Erin to bring you here," Addison began, a bit too slowly, "because we . . . that is, my team and I . . . came to a definite conclusion about the crash today. There's no more doubt in our minds. We have evidence now that we didn't have before."

Jason stood up and took a few steps toward the water, keeping his rigid back to the other three. Maureen's eyes misted over, but her brave, tired expression didn't waver. Erin frowned down at the grass, plucking blades with one hand.

"You don't have to walk away, Jason," Addison said quietly. "Your dad's cleared. It was absolutely not his fault."

Jason swung around, and Erin looked up.

"Then what was it?" Maureen asked, confusion distorting her face. She wore an expression of disbelief, as if she couldn't quite comprehend that the nightmare had ended.

Addison laid his face in his hands and rubbed his eyes. "It was a malfunction on the airplane."

Erin wasn't going to let the statement go that easily. "What kind of malfunction, Addison?"

"In the elevator system," he said. "It wouldn't engage. Mick thought he was steering the plane, but nothing was engaging."

"Why?"

Addison looked at Erin, knowing he would have to provide details. But just how much should he tell her? The faces turned attentively toward him, waiting for an answer. "Because the plane had been built with some counterfeit bolts. One of them snapped just as Mick was making his approach."

Maureen placed her hand over her mouth. "Oh, no," she whispered.

Jason went to his mom's side, knelt in the grass, and set a hand protectively on her shoulder. His face was weary and drawn when he regarded Addison. "Then . . . Dad didn't know what was happening? He never had a chance?"

Addison shook his head slowly. "I'm

afraid not, Jason."

Erin stared at Addison as the implications of the discovery became clear in her pilot's mind. "How many bolts like that were in the plane? All of them?"

"I don't know yet," he said. "I'm going to have them all analyzed and recommend that every plane built by that manufacturer at the same time have spot checks to determine where other counterfeit bolts might be. I'm sure there'll be a full-scale investigation."

He turned back to Maureen and Jason, a look of deep regret in his eyes. His voice dropped in pitch, and his tone became intimate, like that of a friend. "I owe you two an apology. I intruded on your privacy, turned your lives upside down, made things pretty bad for you at the worst possible time. I hope you'll forgive me."

Maureen wiped her eyes with the heel of her hand. "There's nothing to forgive," she said. "You did your job, that's all. If anyone else had been investigating, he probably would have stopped at uncovering the obvious." Her voice wavered, but she forced a smile and held out her hand. "What we owe you is our gratitude."

Addison took her hand in both of his own, savoring her authentic thanks. It was odd, because no one associated with a crash had ever thanked him before. After a moment, Jason held out his own hand, the gesture more that of a man than a boy. "Thanks," he said simply. Addison shook his hand, unable to escape the dreadful feeling that he'd given them both something entirely new to grieve about.

"If you don't mind, I think Jason and I need to be alone for a while," Maureen said, her pale face drawn as she came to her feet. She wiped her eyes again and wrapped her arms around her son who seemed so much stronger than she was.

Addison and Erin watched until they were out of sight.

"You can take the tape now," he almost whispered, setting his eyes on her, memorizing her soft lines and the sculpted perfection of her face. "I promised you could hear it when the investigation was over. It's in the apartment."

Erin turned back to him, gauging his mood in the waxing moonlight. "Thank you, Addison."

He laughed mirthlessly. "For what? For giving them — you — some new injustice to grieve over?"

"No," she whispered, moving closer to him. "For giving them back their pride and

315

the untarnished memories of Mick that they had before. Anyone else, any other investigator, would have given up the investigation long before you did. They never would have found the truth."

"I upset them," he said, gesturing to where the two had gone out of sight. "Did you see how upset they were? And so are you. I can see it, Erin."

"You're right," she said. "It's a matter of the better of two evils. Neither conclusion alters the fact that Mick crashed, that he's gone —" Her voice broke off, and the moonlight caught the tears in her eyes. "But the fact that it wasn't his fault does make a difference. You've got to believe that."

Pulling herself to her knees, she slid her arms around his neck. "I love you, Addison," she whispered.

He leaned his head against hers and closed his eyes, his body shaking with the emotion rising up inside him. After a moment, he whispered, "I never thought I'd hear those words again. And I never thought I'd say them. But I love you, too."

He kissed her, struggling to keep his volatile emotions from getting out of hand and forcing him into making snap decisions that would change his life. He needed time to think, time to weigh one loss against another. The kiss broke, and she reached up to wipe the mist under his eyes. "I thought it would be over when I discovered the truth," he said, his voice rasping. "I thought I could file the report and wash my hands of it. But it never ends. It just gets uglier and uglier. Tomorrow morning I have to go back to Washington, come up with recommendations to the FAA for something to be done about those bolts . . ."

"Tomorrow?" She released his neck and sat back on her heels to face him. "You're going back to Washington *tomorrow?*"

The hurt on her face broke his heart. "It's headquarters, babe. You knew I'd have to go back. They're impatient for me to be available for the field again."

"Addison, we just got started. I don't want you to go."

"It's my job," he said dismally, repeating the words that had become so distasteful to him over the past few weeks. "I have to go."

She widened her eyes to keep from breaking into tears. This couldn't be happening. Not when everything was coming together. Not when she was beginning to feel good again. She sat stiffly, as though a rigid spine could give her courage. "Then . . . then I'll come with you. I'll get a transfer to Washington. Then we could see each other when you're in town."

Addison shook his head, the effort deepening his own pain. Sid's warnings began to take shape, setting their love on shakier ground. "Except that I won't be there for long," he said. "As soon as I get back, they're sending me to Albuquerque, and after that, who knows? It depends on where the next accident happens."

He saw that Erin tried to smile and not surrender to panic just yet. She blinked back the tears forming in her eyes. "Well, I guess I'll just have to fly to wherever you are on my days off. I usually have three days off at a time, unless Zarkoff changes that. It would be something."

"It would be nothing." Addison stood up, took a few steps away from her, turned back, and studied her as best he could in the growing darkness. She looked so broken, he thought, and he had broken her. Somewhere the hurting had to stop. "I'd be working, having to concentrate on my investigations, probably depressed at the discoveries I was making. You'd be depressed, too, and neglected, and it wouldn't be fair."

He ground his teeth and kicked a stone, sent it rolling a few feet away. "Aw, Erin. I want more than a casual relationship whenever we can spare the time. An afternoon here, an evening there. It won't work. It couldn't work that way for either of us."

Erin scrambled to her feet, and he could see the fight rising inside her. "It *does* work, Addison. All the time. It's the nature of a pilot's job to be away a lot and to take advantage of the time he has. Lots of pilots I know have adjusted, Addison. We can, too."

"*Pilots* adjust," Addison said. "They fly off on a trip, come back, and all's well. But not guys like me. When I go off, I'm buried in wreckage for weeks. I take the recorded voices of victims to bed with me at night. I rack my brain trying to dig through to the truth. In every town there's a Maureen . . . a Jason . . ."

"And an Erin?" she bit out painfully.

"No," he said quickly. "Not an Erin. But in this town there was, and for a big percentage of the time, she hated me for what I do. You won't forget all that just because it's someone else's life I'm profiling. You'll still think it's callous, and we'd wind up fighting and, finally, drifting apart."

Erin no longer tried to conceal her pain. Tears fell over her bottom lashes. Her lips quivered. "Then . . . then you're telling me that it's over? That there's no use? That it was fun while it lasted?"

No, he thought miserably. *It can't be over. Not like this.* He caught his breath, cleared his throat, and struggled with the truth. She had to know. "Erin, listen to me. I'm just saying that it's going to be complicated. The truth is that I've been given a choice. You or the job. My father-in-law is my boss, and he's pulling the strings. I have to work some things out, Erin. Some very important things. I need some time to think."

"I can't believe it," she whispered, amazed. "It isn't a choice between me and your job that man wants from you, Addison. It's a choice between me and your wife, isn't it?"

"Maybe in his mind, it is," Addison admitted quietly. "Not in mine, though."

Erin turned away from him, wiping away her tears.

"Erin," he whispered. "Don't turn away."

"Don't turn away?" she echoed, flabbergasted. "Me? Tell me one time that you aren't saying good-bye."

His expression became clouded as the sky before a storm. "I can't tell you that," he whispered. "Not until I've reevaluated some things, made some decisions. I feel like my work isn't finished. It's too important to leave my job without thinking long and hard about it. I feel tied to it. Please try to understand."

She stood motionless, desperately trying to absorb the shock, desperately trying to cope. "I understand," she lied, her voice wobbling. "Of course you have to think. Reevaluate everything . . . people depend on you . . ."

"Erin, I don't want to lose you. There's got to be an answer. I'll think of something."

"I have to go," she whispered, then turned and hurried back to the parking lot.

Addison didn't move to go after her as Erin ran through the grass. There would be time for that later, he prayed, when he found some concrete answers, some peace, some resolve. But not now. He had nothing to offer her now, except confusion and more despair.

CHAPTER TWENTY-FIVE

Good-byes. They were getting harder all the time, Erin thought as she sped home, the tape of the crash lying in her lap. She had gone into Addison's apartment for the last time and taken the tape that had preyed on her mind for so long. Then she'd simply walked away.

But she wouldn't think about Addison now. Not when her life was on the verge of coming together. Not when everything was working out. She was flying again, and Mick was cleared.

Somehow, none of that mattered when Addison was fading from her life. But did he have a choice when people were dying because of substandard materials? When the country needed men like him to fight for their safety?

Almost defiantly, she pulled the tape out of its protective box and jammed it into her tape deck. Her neighborhood came into sight, but she kept driving. Night began to invade the car, lending an eerie quality to the cockpit static that came across the speakers.

And then came the sound of Mick's voice, as if he were right there next to her.

She drove aimlessly as the tape played, listened and embraced the calm confidence in his voice, the idle conversation with the first officer who'd replaced her, and with the flight engineer. She smiled when he made a comment that if "Erin weren't so hardheaded, that bump she took in the accident might have done some damage."

She found herself driving down Biscayne Boulevard, and wondered how she'd wound up there. Still she drove aimlessly, listening to her friend, her captain, engaged in the business of flying a plane.

The car seemed to head toward the airport of its own accord as the tape played on. She heard the routine checklists being exchanged, weather reports gathered, transmissions to approach control. Her muscles tensed with apprehension, and her heart twisted with misery as Mick got closer to the point where the tape would end.

Just before Mick began his descent, tears streamed down Erin's face. "It's a bolt, Mick," she whispered aloud. "Just a stupid little bolt. You can't even fix it."

She heard the first officer calling out the descending altitudes, the mention of the plane being below the glide path, the frantic cry to "Pull up! Pull up!"

And when there was nothing else to be heard, Erin pulled her car off the highway and slumped over the steering wheel. She was suddenly weeping for the losses she'd encountered in the last few weeks; weeping for the losses yet to be encountered; weeping over the guilt for believing, like everyone else, that Mick had panicked.

When the worst of her misery was spent, she leaned her head back on her seat and looked out the window. The taillights of a commercial jet caught her eye, slowly making its way through the pitch-dark sky.

With the eye of her heart, she could almost see Mick in the cockpit, smiling down at her and offering her a thumbs-up. *It's okay, Erin,* she could imagine him saying. *It's okay.*

A sob rose up in her throat as that feeling of forgiveness from him, and from herself, overwhelmed her. Silently, she returned the thumbs-up gesture. "Good-bye, Mick," she whispered. "Take good care of him, Lord. I can't wait to see him again."

She dragged a Kleenex out of a box on the floorboard and blew her nose, then wiped the tears from her face. Still looking up at the sky, she whispered, "What now, Lord? I thought I could see your plan forming. I thought it was all working out. That the crash had led me to Addison, and so there was some way that it all worked for good. I thought I saw your hand."

She sobbed harder, her heart pleading with God for some sign that he heard her. "I know you're still answering prayers, Lord," she whispered. "You answered my prayers about Mick's guilt. And you answered my prayers about my flying. Could you just answer this one, too? Could you work it all out, somehow, so that I don't have to say good-bye to Addison?"

Silence filled the car, except for the quiet sound of her weeping. As peace descended over her, her tears slowed, and she wiped them away and blew her nose. She took in a deep, ragged breath and leaned her head back against the seat, watching the sky as that peace poured like warm honey through her. A shooting star arced across the sky, and she sat up straight, watching it disappear. God was listening. He had heard.

And she would trust him, whatever his will was in her life.

She started the car and waited for a space in the traffic.

That peace stayed with her as she pulled back into the flow of life again. She had managed to say good-bye to Mick once and for all. And she was leaving it up to God whether she had to say good-bye to Addison.

Without actually making the decision to do so, Erin wound up at the airport. She went to the Southeast Terminal, to Frank Redlo's office, and knocked on the casing to the open door.

"Come in," he mumbled.

He didn't look up until she'd come all the way inside, and he smiled. "I took a chance on your being here," she said. "I wanted to talk to you."

Frank checked his watch, saw how late it was, and rubbed his bald spot wearily. "Yeah, I'm still here. I was kind of waiting to see how the negotiations went. The bargaining committee is meeting with Zarkoff right now."

"I know. Lois is on the committee. I thought I'd wait for her and see how it went myself. Meanwhile . . ."

"You wanted to come see if you could still have your job back," he said smugly.

She nodded. "Exactly."

Frank shifted in his chair and leaned his elbows on his desk. "The next time I tell you what's best for you, you'll listen to me, won't you? Storming in here, telling me you want to quit . . ."

"I was confused, Frank. And I was terrified. I'm over it now."

"Are you sure, Erin? To tell the truth, you don't look so good."

Erin realized that she must, indeed, look awful after all the tears she'd shed. But fear of it being too late for her career invaded her hopeful heart. "Didn't Addison Lowe talk to you? He said he was coming here today —"

"He came," Frank said, nodding. "Talked to Jackson, and the chief says it's time to put you back on the schedule. Says you've been tearing up the airways with Jack Griffin's Cessna."

She tried to smile. "Yeah. I'm ready to go back to work, Frank."

Genuine pleasure softened the otherwise harsh lines on his face. "I'll put you back to work this week, Erin. It'll take a while to work you into the schedule, but I want to hurry before we find ourselves with a strike on our hands. Otherwise it could be a long time before you fly again — that is, if you even have a job left. You need to get back to work before the strike, so you can prove to yourself and everybody else that you can do it. If you have to wait until the strike's over, you might lose your courage again. Let me get to work on it, see where I can schedule you. I'll call you as soon as I've gotten you in."

She stood up. "Thanks, Frank. I really appreciate your standing behind me."

He shrugged, embarrassment making him resume his gruff facade. "It was nothing. I just don't take kindly to losing my pilots. I only hope I'm not about to lose the whole lot of them. I just might, if Zarkoff doesn't ease up."

"Don't worry," she said. "If anybody can get Zarkoff to change his mind, Lois can. It'll be all right."

CHAPTER TWENTY-SIX

But Erin's faith had precarious footing in the bargaining room that evening. Zarkoff sat like a hostile king on his throne at the end of the table. He was nursing a cigar whose smoke wafted through the room like a toxic fog designed to keep his subjects in line.

But the "subjects" were anything but passive. The five on the bargaining committee sat rigidly in their seats, unwilling to let the intimidation of his apparent indifference sway them.

"The first thing we'd like to address," Ray Carter began, "is the issue of pay cuts. Our pilots have accepted pay cuts in the past, but this amount is —"

"Non-negotiable," Zarkoff said, tapping his cigar ashes out on a tray and ramming the stub back into his mouth.

Ray glanced up from his notes. "Pardon?"

"The pay cuts are non-negotiable. Let's not waste time here. What's the next gripe?"

Stunned faces looked at each other, and Lois leaned forward. "Mr. Zarkoff, you can't be serious. That's what we're here for. To negotiate."

Zarkoff yanked the cigar from his mouth and leaned forward on the table, his blistering gaze directed at Lois. "Look at me, honey. Do I look like I'm kidding?"

"But if you won't even talk, what are we doing here?"

Zarkoff focused his piercing gaze on Ray Carter. "Was there anything else, Mr. Carter, or is your committee just going to sit here whining?"

Ray's jaw took on the hardness of granite as he bit out his next words. "Perhaps we could come back to the issue of pay cuts in a while. Maybe you feel more comfortable right now talking about work conditions. We're particularly concerned with the cuts in sick leave and the longer hours."

"Non-negotiable," Zarkoff said again.

Ray slumped back in his seat, a look that was a mixture of both warning and astonishment on his face. "Don't do this, Mr. Zarkoff. You'll regret it. I swear you will."

"Oh?" Zarkoff asked, looking amused.

Lois jumped up, unwilling to let Ray lead them right into a strike. "Mr. Zarkoff, our members are getting angry. If you don't give us a few concessions, this committee can't be responsible for what they might do."

"Are you people threatening me?" Zarkoff asked, amused.

"Yes."

"No."

Ray's and Lois's answers came simultaneously, but Ray shot her a scathing look that said, "Let me handle this." Lois bit her tongue.

"Yes, Mr. Zarkoff," Ray said. "We are threatening you. There's a lot at stake here. To you, it's just another takeover, a bigger profit. To us, it's our livelihood."

Zarkoff studied his cigar. "And what a livelihood it is," he said. "Some of you people have earned a hundred eighty thousand a year."

"That was a long time ago," George Vanderwall piped in. "Since then, we've watched our pay be chiseled on until it's almost half of what we used to make."

"It's difficult to get public sympathy when you're still making a hundred grand, Mr. Vanderwall."

"We don't *all* make that much," Lois argued. "Some of us make substantially less. The point is, when we came to work for this airline in good faith, years ago, we had certain salaries and built our lifestyles in accordance with those salaries. There's no security anymore. If we take a twenty-five percent cut, those pilots who were once earning a hundred eighty thousand and are now down to a hundred thousand will only be making seventy-five thousand. They have mortgages, Mr. Zarkoff. College expenses for their children. Are you saying that they're wrong to have counted on their salaries and expected their dedication to this company to at least be repaid with a little security?"

Zarkoff chuckled, the raspy sound chilling her blood. "My heart bleeds for you poverty-stricken souls," he droned. "Well, I can see you people feel pretty strongly about this. If that's the case, then I guess you'll just have to do what you have to do."

Ray Carter's eyes flashed fire. Lois's flashed alarm. "What are you saying, Mr. Zarkoff?"

"I'm just saying that if you people want to strike, nobody's stopping you. That way you can make your little statement, and I can get on with running my airline."

"It's our airline, too," Lois said. "Are you seriously willing to jeopardize the safety of the passengers by bringing in new trainees to fill our cockpits?"

Zarkoff's grin was all satisfaction. "I have three hundred pilots completing training in Houston right now. They can be here in an afternoon, and we won't have to cancel a single flight."

"You lowdown —"

"Ray!" Lois stopped the words coming out of his mouth and willed her face not to reveal the rage she felt. "Mr. Zarkoff, don't you have the slightest concern for the people who have given their lives to this airline?"

Zarkoff stood up, his bulky frame dominating the small room. A cloudy haze of smoke hung like a royal aura over his head. "My concern is in making this into a profitable company, and if you people don't want to play the game, then there are hundreds of others who will. And I assure you, none of them will expect to start at a hundred grand or even seventy-five. It's about time for a housecleaning, anyway. Now, if you'll excuse me, the press is outside waiting for a statement. I'll be sure to pass along how pleased I am with the way negotiations turned out."

Lois and the other four committee members gaped at him in shocked silence while he gathered his things.

Erin waited with several others outside the bargaining room, which was really the pilots' lounge, for the meeting to break up. It was too early, she thought. They hadn't been in there that long, and there was a multitude of problems to be hashed out. But Erin didn't want to go home. She wanted to wait for her friend so she'd have Lois to confide in. She wanted to spill out her heart about Addison, to hear her friend's no-nonsense advice, whatever it might be. So she waited.

The wait was not long. In moments the door opened. Zarkoff was the first one out, still wearing the Attila the Hun expression he had worn the first day she'd seen him. Others filed out with grim faces.

When everyone had left the room except for Lois, Erin went inside. Lois was still at the table, her head buried in her arms, and her papers scattered around her.

"Lois?" Erin asked.

Lois looked up, misery evident in every line of her face. "Oh, Erin. It was awful. We blew it."

Erin sat down across from her roommate. "What happened?"

Lois leaned back and focused on the ceiling. "He wouldn't budge. He said every issue we brought up was non-negotiable. Finally, when we were getting nowhere, and tempers were rising, he said that if we didn't like it, we were certainly welcome to strike. He said he'd replace every last one of us before the day was over if we did. And Erin, I know he will."

"That's it? No bargaining? No discussion? No nothing?"

"No. We're sunk, Erin. Those pilots are going to demand a strike, and we're all going to lose our jobs. I can't cross the picket line if I'm on the negotiating committee! And you . . . you haven't even had the chance to fly yet since your suspension! What are we going to do?"

Erin propped her chin on her hand and shook her head balefully. "I don't know, Lois. How long do you think we have?"

"Are you kidding? I expect a strike vote by tomorrow. The most time we have is two or three days. I don't know how to make them understand that he *wants* us to strike."

"Maybe it's the principle of the thing," Erin said. "Maybe they're all willing to lose their jobs to keep from working under his conditions."

"It sounds real idealistic," Lois muttered. "But when those bills come due and their kids start needing shoes, let's see whose principles are strongest then."

"You're going to fight it, then? Try to hold off the strike?"

"I can't do that, Erin," Lois said, defeated. "Not without some solution. What I have to do is find some other way. Some way to wake that man up."

Erin felt exactly the same sentiment, but not about Zarkoff. What she needed was some way to get through to Addison, but she feared it was too late. He'd already cast her off. And she couldn't talk to Lois about her problem now. Not when Lois's own concerns were so immediate, so burdensome.

Both downhearted, the two women went home, feeling like they might each wake up the next day to a world collapsed or entirely changed. They only hoped that Madeline's usually high spirits could inject some life into their own.

CHAPTER TWENTY-SEVEN

Addison beat out the last few lines on his laptop. His report finished once and for all, he sat staring at the wall for a moment, trying and failing to conjure up some happiness.

Feeling like a soldier who'd just come in from frontline battle, he turned off the table lamp, casting the apartment into bleak darkness, and went to the couch. He sank down, lying on his back, and stared at the ceiling above him.

What was he going to do about this impossible choice he faced? What was he going to do about his professional life? What was he going to do about Erin?

It was frightening, even contemplating quitting the NTSB, when it had been such an anchor to him since Amanda's death. It had been his vengeance for his wife's crash. It had been his purpose for going on.

Now the purpose seemed hollow and futile. The loneliness was still there, as well as his need for human love, in larger doses than three days at a time. He needed Erin, not in fragments or phone conversations. He needed her always.

Summoning all his courage, he considered the possibility that it was time for some other man to fill his shoes, someone else who had a debt to collect, a passion for the illusive lives he may or may not save in his work, a need to feel he was doing something, however naive that feeling may be. Maybe that person could take up the cause and see it through, finish the work Addison had started. Maybe it was time for him to go back to piloting in one form or another. He'd watched Erin get her wings back. Was it time he sought out his own? Was it time to end this dark phase of his life and enter a much brighter one centered on love instead of disaster?

Not certain which way he should turn, he chose to fall on his knees and take the matter to God.

Erin sat on the couch between Lois and Madeline that night, desperately fighting her urge to go to bed and cry her heart out. But Lois needed her. They watched the news, waiting to see the press's interpretation of the contract negotiations, but all Erin could see or hear was Addison's face as he'd told her he needed time to think.

Pain twisted like a knife inside her, carving out a growing hollow that she doubted would heal. She now knew how difficult it had been for Addison to get over his loss of Amanda, for she had lost Addison, not to death, but to circumstance.

"Here it is!" Lois said as the Southeast logo appeared on the screen. She leaned over to turn it up. "Listen."

". . . after the recent takeover by Trans Western. Collin Zarkoff, sometimes dubbed the Lee Iacocca of the airline industry, had this to say about negotiations that took place at the Southeast headquarters tonight."

The film clip showed Zarkoff standing proudly out in front of a Southeast aircraft, as if it were his own personal creation. He smiled, projecting a different image than his usual grim-faced persona, and he played to the press like a master. "I believe the Southeast pilots and I have come to an understanding tonight," he assured the reporters. "We had a nice little talk, got some things aired out, and I think they realize that I have nothing but the best in mind for this airline."

"Will there be a strike?" Carl Logan, a well-known field reporter, asked.

Zarkoff set his massive arm around the interviewer's shoulders and chuckled as if they'd been lifelong buddies. "Well, you know, I'm not holding my breath, Carl. We both laid our cards out tonight, and I think we each know where the other stands."

"The man should go into politics," Lois muttered through her teeth.

"He can't. He's making too much money with his airlines."

"The media people love him," Lois went on. " 'The Lee Iacocca of the airline industry!' If they only knew."

Erin hugged her knees to her chest. "Maybe you should tell them. Might hamper his good-natured image a bit. Give them a view from the other side."

"Yeah," Lois sighed, "but how? He's been playing this game a lot longer than we have."

The telephone rang, startling them both, and Erin couldn't help bounding toward it.

"It's probably one of the union members," Lois said. "The phone'll be ringing off the hook tonight!"

Erin ignored the speculation and grabbed the phone, praying it was Addison. "Hello?"

"Erin? It's Frank," the caller said, dashing her hopes. She lowered herself to the chair beside the telephone and tried to hide the disappointment in her voice.

"Hi, Frank."

"Listen," he said. "I just heard the news and I'm anticipating a strike vote tomorrow. We've got to get you up before then so you won't be counted as inactive when things start happening. So I'm scheduling you for the eleven o'clock flight to Washington, D.C., tomorrow morning."

Washington? she thought dismally. That was probably the flight Addison was taking. She closed her eyes and pinched the bridge of her nose.

"Erin? You're not having second thoughts on me, are you? I have enough problems . . ."

"No," Erin said quickly. "I'll be there. Count on me."

"I will," he said.

When she hung up, she sat staring at the phone for a minute, thinking of the irony — the absurdity — of her piloting Addison's flight.

She stood up, sighing from her soul, fighting the tears threatening her. "I have to go to bed," she told her roommates. "I have to fly to Washington tomorrow."

"Thank goodness," Lois said. "That'll get you back on the payroll. Now if we can just keep from snatching you back off it in a strike."

Lois watched Erin rush to her room, wishing from the depths of her soul that she could help her in some way. But there was nothing she could do to lift her friend's spirits. When Madeline had gone to bed, Lois got on her knees and prayed for her friend. Then she prayed for the negotiations she seemed so helpless to influence.

Just before she started to bed, Lois unplugged the telephone. To Lois, the silence was sweet relief from the barrage of questions she faced. To Erin, the silence was reinforced certainty that she and Addison were finished.

To Addison, Lois's act resulted in an unanswered ring sounding uselessly against his ear, making him sure that his hesitation, his confusion, had driven Erin away, and that she wouldn't answer his call if he were the last man on earth. Still, he kept trying to get through well into the night, until he drifted into a restless sleep.

CHAPTER TWENTY-EIGHT

It felt good to be back in uniform, but the relief seemed secondary to the heavy-heartedness Erin felt the next morning. Addison hadn't called. He'd had all night to think, to reevaluate, and whatever he'd come up with, it hadn't warranted a phone call.

Lois followed behind her at the airport, quietly absorbed in her own thoughts about the union meeting and strike vote that were slated to take place that morning. Erin had the deep need to tell her friend what had happened with Addison, that the relationship was over and that she couldn't remember what life had been like before he'd entered her life. What would it be like without him now?

That was the worst thing about going on with life when others made their exits. No longer would Mick be there on the long trips, to banter and joke with, to confide in, to turn to. No longer would Addison be there to fill the yawning void in her heart.

But she couldn't tell Lois that, not when both their careers hung in the balance. Lois was carrying union responsibilities on her shoulders like a delicate time bomb. In just a few hours they might not even have their jobs left. But that was secondary to her losing Addison.

Take the job, Lord. Just give me another chance with him.

Lois got her an absentee ballot, since she'd be on her flight by the time the meeting began. She waited, preoccupied, while Erin voted against the strike. Erin dropped the vote through the slit in the locked box and studied her friend. Lois was staring at the stack of ballots as if they would come alive and riot against her. "You okay, Lo?"

"Yeah," Lois whispered. "Just a little nervous. I'm just praying all the pilots who won't be here will have sense enough to use these absentee ballots or the computer votes they can make through other hubs. And I'm praying they'll cast the right vote." Her eyes lost their glaze, and she glanced at Erin.

"What about you? How are you holding up? First flight and all . . ."

"I'm fine," Erin assured her. "Just fine."

Lois took a heavy breath. Her haggardness testified to her lack of sleep the night before. "Look, don't let any of this distract you today. There's nothing more you can do, now that you've voted. Just pretend nothing unusual is happening and concentrate on that flight, okay?"

Erin smiled at her friend's concern. "I will. Don't worry."

Lois glanced up the corridor. "Well, I guess I'd better go start lobbying. Maybe I can change a few minds in the time I have before the meeting."

Erin watched Lois head toward a cluster of pilots in the coffee shop. She couldn't help being grateful for a moment alone with her thoughts.

Erin checked her watch, saw that she still had plenty of time before she had to be at her gate, and she made her way upstairs to the pilot's lounge. It was still empty because of the early hour, so she went in and closed the door behind her. She crossed her arms and ambled over to the windowsill. Through the glass she could see the maze of runways lined with planes waiting for clearance to take off.

Again, the irony of her situation struck her. Addison would be on her plane this morning. She'd be overcoming one complication in her life while another one became more deeply rooted.

Erin closed her eyes and fought the tears. *No crying today,* she thought. She was done with tears, at least in the light of day, when such evidence of upset could be interpreted as fear and paranoia. She would only cry when she was alone, at night . . . there would be plenty of time and solitude for tears then.

Blurry images of Addison in the short time she'd known him came to mind. Addison that first day on the lake, talking about the loss he'd known and the understanding he had of her feelings. Addison slamming the racquetball for her, helping her to vent her pain constructively. Addison with paint smeared on his face. Addison eating a Sonic burger. Addison pulling her out of the plane and holding her. Addison kissing her with elegant, eloquent longing . . .

Somehow, in the sequence of those images, she couldn't imagine him saying good-bye. The image just wouldn't come.

She opened her eyes and stared at the sky, at the wispy clouds in the distance. She was finished with fear today, she thought, and somehow, she would manage a dignified good-bye if that was, indeed, God's will.

Addison stacked the pages of his long report in his briefcase, closed and locked it, then turned back to the bed to finish packing his suitcase. He should have gotten pictures of Erin, he thought. Something to take with him, to remind him that she was real when he woke up late in the night and missed her so badly that he wanted to die.

Erin, why did you unplug the phone?

The misery in his heart forced him to manufacture conclusions. She had washed her hands of him. She wasn't home. She had decided it was over. *They* were over.

He loaded his bags and briefcase into his rental car, locked the rented condominium for the last time, and sat behind the wheel, staring straight ahead without starting the engine. But it *wasn't* over, he told himself. Not while he still had breath . . . not while he still loved her.

He turned on the ignition with new purpose and drove to Erin's house, determined to make her understand what he really wanted. Hope quickened his step as he trotted to her door. He knocked hard and waited.

When there was no answer, he realized that her car was gone. Had it been gone all night?

Defeated, he went back to his car and stared down at the airline ticket lying on the seat next to him. *Father,* he prayed with a sick feeling in his heart. *If I could only have one more day. See her one more time.*

He'd come back after he'd filed the report, tied up all his loose ends, confronted Sid once and for all. Maybe he'd convince her then how much he loved her. All he had to cling to now was the prayer that by then, it wouldn't be too late.

Addison made it to the gate just as the passengers were boarding and got in line to offer the flight attendant his boarding pass. Idly, his gaze drifted out the airport window to the plane that would take him to Washington . . . but not home. Nowhere felt like home anymore.

He handed the flight attendant his pass and started up the long ramp to the 727. With each step, he felt a little more disconnected from his heart.

He reached the door of the plane and glanced, unseeing, at the uniformed pilots standing at the door of the cockpit. He noticed the flight attendant smiling greetings as passengers boarded. He stepped inside and brushed past them. Suddenly something . . . her violet scent, her very presence? . . . snagged his attention. He turned around and saw Erin, her eyes wide, as she watched him walk toward his seat.

He stopped cold.

"Erin?" he asked, jamming the aisles as passengers tried to get by. "Are you flying to Washington?"

She nodded, but someone pushed him further down the aisle. He slipped into his row in first class, dropped his briefcase on the seat, and looked at Erin again.

"I didn't know . . . I'm glad . . ."

He saw her mouth twist into a grim line, and she turned and disappeared inside the cockpit. He'd follow her, he thought, just as soon as the aisles were clear and he could get out. He'd go after her, tell her that he needed one more chance . . . that he couldn't live without her.

But there didn't seem to be a right time. She was distracted, he thought, for this was her first commercial flight since the crash. She didn't need him disorienting her, possibly upsetting her, when there was no place to run. He settled back into his seat, fastened his seat belt, and leaned his head into the aisle to see into the cockpit. From the back, she appeared to be calm, efficient, ready to do her job.

The aisles cleared when everyone was boarded, but the door had not been sealed yet, and the cockpit was still open. The captain and the flight engineer sipped coffee at the entrance to the plane, talking to the flight attendant, who smiled, oblivious to the fact that Addison's world was about to end.

Finally, unable to stop himself, Addison

yanked off his seat belt, got up, and bolted toward the cockpit, determined to see Erin. Jack, the captain, stopped him at the door.

"Hey, you can't go in there," he said, an edge to his voice. "Is there something I can help you with?"

"No," Addison said.

Hearing his voice, Erin turned around, and their eyes connected with electric force.

"I . . . I'm Addison Lowe," he said, tearing his gaze from Erin and extending a hand for Jack to shake. "NTSB. I need to talk to Erin."

"Yeah, I remember you," Jack said, not taking his hand. "You're the one who got her suspended."

"I need to talk to her," Addison repeated. "It's important."

"Sorry, pal. It'll have to wait."

Addison's eyes beseeched Erin again, and finally she stood up. "It's okay, Jack. I'll just be a minute."

Reluctantly, Jack backed out of the doorway, allowing Addison to step inside the cockpit. "Thirty seconds," he said.

Thirty seconds, Addison thought frantically, as they stared at each other with pain in their eyes. *Thirty seconds to set things right for the rest of our lives.*

"How . . . how do you feel? Everything

okay with flying today?" he asked, wondering why the least significant things to say always came to mind at the worst times.

She nodded and lifted her chin. "I can't help thinking there's a certain poetic justice in your helping me get my wings back so that I could fly you out of my life." She turned back to her controls. "Now, if you'll excuse me, I'm flying this leg, and it's time for you to go back to your seat."

"Erin," he said. "You don't understand. We need to talk."

"Later," Jack said from behind him. "It's takeoff time now."

Miserably defeated, Addison backed out of the small compartment, allowing the captain and second officer to go inside. Slowly, he went back to his seat. The cockpit door closed, cutting off his view of Erin.

Addison closed his eyes and hated himself for letting her get away.

"He's had all the chances we're going to give him," Ray Carter shouted at the hundreds of Southeast pilots who had turned out for the strike vote.

"But we need our jobs," Lois pointed out calmly. She and Ray and the rest of the bargaining committee had taken their places at the front of the room. "If we strike —"

"Not if, *when*," Ray said. "What do you expect us to do? The man won't even talk. You can't negotiate with someone who refuses to meet with a professional negotiator and who won't even discuss the demands of his own employees. This calls for drastic action!"

The pilots came to their feet, shouting agreement that a strike was the only way to resolve things. Lois covered her face with her hands and braced herself for the inevitable.

"I move that we call a strike vote!" someone in the first row shouted.

"Seconded!" several others yelled simultaneously.

"All in favor of our voting whether or not to strike, say aye," the president demanded.

"Aye!" a chorus of pilots sang out.

"All against."

A much smaller scattering of ayes sounded across the room. Lois looked longingly at the box of absentee and computer votes, and prayed that they would change things, or that the members in favor of voting didn't represent those in favor of striking.

"Then we'll begin the vote now," the president said, with a strike of his gavel.

As the voting process began, Lois had a sinking feeling that she had lost the battle.

Despite the turmoil in her heart over Addison, Erin had no trouble flying the plane that morning. Even when they entered a cloudy region and encountered rain, her confidence in her flying never wavered. She found herself settling in comfortably with the easygoing captain at her side and the flight engineer, Scott, behind her.

"Well, we're almost there," Jack said cheerfully. "How does it feel to be in control again?"

"Feels great," Erin said, genuine enthusiasm in her voice. "I just hope it isn't snatched away as soon as we land. A strike vote could put an end to flying."

" 'Fraid so," Jack commiserated. "But at least you won't have to sweat it out without having first proved yourself."

The approach procedure began, complete with weather reports that were relayed to the passengers. The three pilots busied themselves with the checklists they were required to follow before preparing to land, working as smoothly together as if they had been a team for years.

Erin forbade herself to count down the moments until she would have to say goodbye to Addison. Instead, she counted the miles from the airport, the pounds of fuel, the altitude. She maintained her diligent effort of flying the plane while Scott and Jack followed the necessary approach routine.

All three crew members in the cockpit concentrated on specific duties. Erin flew the plane, feeling calm and confident, but at the same time knowing the little twinge of caution that made her the capable pilot she was. Jack watched the airspeed and the altitude, calling out deviations. Scott managed the aircraft systems and monitored the holding speeds, range of the aircraft, and fuel flow.

"Southeast 81, you're cleared for approach," approach control radioed. "Contact the tower at the marker."

Erin reached the marker, the point a few miles from the end of the runway that emitted a tone over the radio, and she noted the glide slope coming toward the center of its instrument. *This is where it went wrong for you, Mick,* she thought. *This is where the elevator broke.*

She pulled the power back and started her descent. Routinely, she called for her landing gear.

The usual reply of "down and check three green" never came. She glanced toward Jack, waiting for his response while he tried to engage the gear. After a moment, he shook his head. "The gear must be jammed. I can't get it."

Erin's heart lurched. "What?"

"The landing gear must be stuck. I can't get the lights to indicate that they're all down."

Without waiting for further explanation, Erin stopped her descent and began climbing again, waiting for her captain to instruct her further. She felt a fleeting moment of panic, but it was banished by years of training and preparation for an emergency of this kind.

"Uh, Tower, this is Southeast 81," Jack radioed, in that professional, calm voice that made the problem seem routine. "We're having trouble with our landing gear. Need a few more minutes."

"Roger, Southeast 81," the tower responded. "Climb to two thousand feet and go back to approach control."

Erin followed the commands of the tower, and Jack radioed back, "Okay, going up to two thousand . . ."

When they'd reached the desired altitude, Erin held her breath and prayed they'd be able to correct the problem. Surely, it was a lightbulb out, she thought, knowing it was unlikely. She listened, holding her breath, as approach control set them in a 360-degree holding pattern while they worked on the problem.

"Erin, engage the autopilot," Jack ordered.

Erin obeyed quickly, and they began trying to find the source of the problem. Scott went down to the forward electronics bay to see if he could visually determine if the gear was down and locked. He wasn't able to tell.

Together, they tried all three methods of getting the landing gear down: the normal hydraulic extension, the emergency hydraulic extension, and the manual hand-crank system. All failed.

Jack leaned back in his seat, his eyes working over the instrument panel, not missing a thing. "Okay, folks," he said in a voice so matter-of-fact that one who didn't know better would think he was discussing a minor inconvenience rather than a potential disaster. "We're going to have to make an emergency landing."

Erin cleared her throat and tried to wrestle with fear. She was a professional. Pilots had landed without landing gear before. She had tackled this very problem in simulated flight when she was training . . . they would be fine. "I . . . I've never done this before in an actual flight," she whispered.

"Well, neither have I," Jack confessed,

"but if we go by procedure, we'll be okay."

"You'll fly?" Erin asked hopefully.

"No," he said, and her worry increased. "I think it would be best if you flew to touchdown. That way I can keep one hand on the thrust reversers. When the throttles are idle, I'll be able to grab the thrust reversers and pull them back."

Erin eyed the three horizontal levers attached to the throttles and acknowledged that his plan was sound. Even if it meant that she was responsible for getting the plane to land on its metal belly rather than wheels that wouldn't come down. But there was no time to argue.

"Meanwhile, I can keep my left hand here" — Jack gestured toward the tiller, a small steering wheel — "so I can control the plane as soon as it's on the ground. Understood?"

Erin forced out a hoarse "Yes."

Fear had to be shelved in some dark chamber in the back of her mind as preparations for touchdown became foremost. The flight attendants were notified to prepare the cabins for an emergency landing, and the tower was radioed. Ambulances, fire trucks, and maintenance crews were told to stand by. Detail after detail was taken care of efficiently and quickly.

Once preparations were under way, Erin never had a moment to let paranoia affect her performance. Despite what had happened to Mick, she was determined to do her part to get the plane down safely. There were too many lives at stake to lose her courage now. Mick hadn't had an option; Erin did. She could either rely on her training and self-confidence, or she could let the plane tumble to a fiery stop, taking countless lives . . .

Back in Shreveport, Lois stayed in her chair as the meeting broke up. The members had voted overwhelmingly in favor of a strike. If nothing miraculous happened between now and midnight tonight, she couldn't report to work tomorrow. As easy as it would be to cross the picket lines, she knew she couldn't do it. She was union, just like the rest of them, and wouldn't consider diluting the power of their statement. Not even if it meant her career.

She gathered her papers and stood up, facing Ray Carter. "Well, you win," she said in a flat voice.

"I hope we all win," he answered.

Realizing it was futile to continue the conversation, she started to leave the room when Frank Redlo came barreling in. "Thought you'd want to know, Lois. We just got word that Jack and Erin's flight is having landing-gear problems. They're gonna have to make an emergency landing."

Lois stumbled back, her mouth slack. "Oh, not Erin."

Ray Carter frowned and leaned back against the table, shaking his head balefully. "She'll freak. That plane is doomed."

Lois's teeth clamped together, and her blue eyes flashed fiery diamonds when she swung to face him. "Erin Russell is as capable as you are of getting that plane down safely. Maybe more capable!"

"Wanna bet?" he asked.

"Yeah, I'll bet," she said, her face glowing. "I'll bet my whole career on it. What have I got to lose? You just threw it away for me, anyway."

With that, she stormed out of the room, determined to win that bet and make Ray Carter eat his words.

Addison sat in first class, staring in confusion out the window. Something was wrong. First he had felt the plane descending, making an approach, and suddenly they'd pulled up. They were farther now from the airport than they'd been before. He unbuckled his seat belt and stood up, intent on going to the cockpit to find out what was wrong.

Before he could reach the aisle, the senior flight attendant came out of the cockpit, her face a peculiar pallid shade.

"What's up?" he asked.

She turned away from the other passengers and lowered her voice to a whisper. "There's been a problem with the landing gear, Mr. Lowe. We're going to have to make an emergency landing. Jack said to tell you that he might need your help organizing the evacuation when we land."

Addison's eyes flashed in the direction of the cockpit door, as if he could see through it to Erin. "I'll do anything they need me to do," he said. "But can I go in the cockpit for a minute?"

"I'm sure it's fine," the woman said. "The jump seat is vacant. Excuse me, I have to go prepare the other flight attendants . . . and the passengers."

Addison hurried forward to the closed cockpit door, opened it, and stepped inside. The three pilots seemed too preoccupied with the emergency to notice him. "I heard about the landing gear," he said quietly, so as not to disturb Erin's concentration. "Anything I can do for now?"

Erin glanced back at him over her shoulder, but Jack answered. "Not right now, unless you know some way to repair the landing gear from here."

Addison sat down in the jump seat, the empty seat usually occupied by off-duty pilots flying from hub to hub. "Sorry," he said. "I don't have a clue." He leaned forward, his worried eyes pinned on Erin.

"How're you doing, babe?"

The easy endearment made her look back at him, and Jack glanced at them both, surprised. "I'm fine," she said. "No problem. I'm going to fly to touchdown."

His face must have revealed his discomfort, because she added, "Don't worry. I can do it."

"I know you can," Addison said gently.

A radio transmission came from the tower, and Jack answered it. The flight engineer excused himself to go reassure the passengers. Addison stood up and moved closer to Erin. He set his hand on her shoulder and began a deep, eloquent massage that soothed more than her muscles and performed a healing ritual in her heart.

"You get us down safely," he whispered. "I've waited too long for you to lose you like this."

She turned around to meet his eyes, and he saw the questions there. Had she really believed he was going to walk away?

"Stay up here for a while if they don't need you yet," she whispered, searching his eyes for what she needed so badly to find.

"How are we on fuel?" Jack asked Erin, shattering the moment.

Erin broke her visual embrace with Addison and checked her instruments. "Low," she said. "We can't hold much longer. We need to get her down."

Scott came back into the cockpit, his young face struggling to hide his worry. He'd probably only been with the company a few months, Addison surmised, probably counted most of his flights as uneventful. Addison hoped that tonight Scott would have a story to tell his friends. He hoped they all would. "The cabin's almost ready. I told the flight attendants that we'd warn them over the PA just before touchdown. Some of the passengers are upset, but it's relatively quiet back there." He turned to Addison, his mouth twitching slightly. "Addison, could you cover one of the wing exits? You know what to do if we have to evacuate."

Addison stood up, nodding his agreement while his mind considered the possible scenarios they faced. There could be a damaging impact, countless injuries, fatalities, a panic among the passengers that could cause more injuries. If there was fire, there would be little time to get everyone out before an explosion could occur. "Did they reseat the children and elderly near the exits?" he asked.

Scott took his seat, his eyes intent on the instruments that would guide them to safety. "Yeah. And we have two pregnant women and three lap babies. We tried to seat them where they could get out first. They'll need help, though."

Addison's eyes gravitated back to Erin, his haunted gaze meeting hers as if for the last time. Why couldn't he be in two places at once? his heart asked. Why couldn't he stay here with her, the strength of his will making the plane land safely, while still doing what was needed of him in the cabin? "I'm going back there, babe," he said. "You can do it."

As if sensing his hesitation in leaving her, Erin tried to lighten things up. "If I don't," she teased, "are you going to write me up? It's a little nerve-racking handling an emergency with an NTSB official aboard."

"Ex-NTSB official," Addison clarified, then left the cockpit before the import of his words could sink in.

Erin stared at the door for a moment,

puzzled. Surely, he hadn't said what she thought he had. "What did he say?" she asked Scott.

"He said, 'Ex-NTSB official.' Must have quit or something."

Despite the task that confronted her in the next few minutes, Erin couldn't help the smile that lifted her heart, renewing her strength. Had he taken Sid's ultimatum seriously and chosen her? Her battered spirits rose, and with renewed determination she turned to the job of getting the plane — and all those frightened people — on the ground. Too much was at stake to mess up now. She just might have a future, after all.

CHAPTER TWENTY-NINE

Lois paced in the pilots' lounge, torn between terror at Erin's situation and the belief in what she had told Ray Carter about Erin's abilities. Erin could do it. She could get that plane down without hurting anyone. All of the Southeast pilots had been trained for such emergencies. Until Mick's crash, Erin had always been one of the coolest, clearest-headed pilots she'd known. And she was all right now. Lois would not allow her doubts to cloud the confident picture she tried to visualize.

Several other pilots sat around the lounge, discussing the plight of the union should the strike actually be called at midnight. While most of them had voted in favor of it, no one was thrilled about not having a paycheck for what could be weeks. Or — if Lois was right, and they all knew she could be — they might never get one again.

"If there was just some way we could make Zarkoff show his true colors to the press," one of the pilots said. "Maybe then we could get a little public sympathy on our side instead of his."

Lois crossed her arms and continued pacing, silently agreeing that a little help from the media wouldn't hurt.

"Can you believe he made it sound like we'd all come to some nice understanding last night? When the jerk wouldn't even *talk* to us?"

"What we need to do is tell *that* to the press," someone said.

"We tried. But they're only interested in how he's whipping Southeast into shape. The only way to get attention our way is to have some ace . . . something that puts us on top for a while . . ."

Lois spun around as the seed of an idea sprouted. "That's it," she said. "That's what we'll do."

The pilots focused on Lois, whose eyes were wide with eagerness. "*What's* it?" someone asked.

"Just imagine. One of the things Zarkoff wants is to look good, and the way he does that is by making us look bad. But what if the press saw Southeast pilots act in an emergency situation and come out heroes?"

"You mean Erin's flight?"

"Yes!" Lois stopped cold, her thoughts reeling. "I'll call the Washington press and tell them all that a Southeast plane is about to make an emergency landing at Dulles

Airport. Then when Erin and Jack get the plane safely on the ground, on live national television, no less, we'll be on top. The press will be covering us, instead of him!" She picked up the phone book and began scanning columns as she spoke. "We'll work them from this end, and I know Erin and Jack can handle things from that end. We're all worried enough about our jobs to take a chance when we see one!"

There was excited chatter in the small lounge as Lois punched out the number of Washington information.

"There's just one problem," one of the pilots said. "What if it isn't a heroic landing? What if they don't make it?"

Feverish heat suffused Lois's face at the suggestion, but she decided she wouldn't think about that possibility just now. There was no room for doubt. Only faith in what her friend could do.

"It's raining," Erin told Jack, her voice as calm as his, though inside, she trembled. "How bad is visibility?"

"Just above minimums," Scott responded. "It won't make things easier."

"This isn't supposed to be easy," she said, feeling confident despite the obstacles she faced. "Jack, it looks like it's the right wing that doesn't have its gear down. I'm going to try to land on one main wheel, to minimize the danger of fire and damage to the plane, okay?"

"That's just what I'd do," Jack agreed. "Remember, there's not enough fuel to make a missed approach if visibility gets worse. Just use your instruments."

"I will," she said.

Radio contact continued between the cockpit and approach control, while Erin concentrated on her task. Memories swept through her mind like images in a familiar nightmare, but this time it was no dream. Despite such thoughts, Erin reminded herself that God had not given her a spirit of fear — fear came from another source. God was with her, watching over her, following his plan. He would give her the power to save these lives, to save the plane . . . she could do it.

Adrenaline pumped up inside her when approach control cleared them to land and Jack began counting down her descent. When they passed the five-hundred-foot mark, she heard Scott sound the four chimes that warned of the landing. He made a quick announcement on the PA that it was time for the passengers to brace themselves.

Calmly, Jack continued calling out her altitude. "Four hundred, three hundred, two hundred, one hundred fifty . . ."

Erin put every ounce of concentration she possessed into lifting the right wing and lowering the nosewheel as they closed in on the ground. She felt a jar as the left gear touched down, and she set the right wing tip down as gently as she could.

From there, Jack took over, pulling back on the thrust reversers to slow the airplane down. They could hear the scraping of metal outside, feel the drag of the right wing. The plane shook with the flammable pull of friction, but the pilots didn't waver from their plan. After a moment, they scraped to a stop.

Erin sat, paralyzed, for no more than a split second as reality sank in. They had landed without fire, without major damage to the plane, without injuries. Just a bumpy landing. Nothing more. Behind her, she heard the passengers erupt into cheers.

"You did it," Jack said, his voice hoarse and breathless, his emotion evident for the first time since the flight began.

"*We* did it," she corrected. A sense of success, of accomplishment, flooded her, leaving her tingling.

"I'll finish up here," Jack told her, unable to help smiling. Perspiration trickled down his face, revealing the fact that he'd been just as tense as the others. "You evacuate the passengers out the aft air stair. We won't be needing the slides this time."

Erin wiped her own face and followed Scott into the cabin, where Addison, having already anticipated the type of evacuation that would be ordered, had opened the exit and begun letting the shaken passengers out down the ladder.

When he spotted Erin, love and pride filled his eyes. He left the door and whisked Erin up into his arms, crushing her against him. "I love you, Erin," he whispered. "I knew you could do it, but man, was I praying."

They were scarcely inside the airport when the press descended upon Erin, shouting questions left and right about the landing. Holding fast to Addison, for physical and moral support, she answered each query, until she saw the small monitor set up at the side of the room. There she saw Zarkoff being interviewed at the same time in Shreveport. He smiled like a proud father. It was apparent that he'd watched the landing on the television the reporters had provided for him, and now he bragged of the abilities of "his pilots" to handle any situation.

Erin recognized a network reporter near her and seized the moment. "Did the Southeast pilots vote for the strike today?" she asked.

"Sure did," the reporter answered. "How do you feel about that, Miss Russell? Does it lessen your satisfaction over this heroic landing?"

"Yes," she admitted. "It scares me to death. Zarkoff will replace us with less-experienced pilots. He's already warned us. I'd hate to see a plane full of trusting passengers encounter this kind of emergency again and have inexperienced pilots with little training try to land safely."

A female reporter raised her voice above the others. "But Miss Russell, Mr. Zarkoff contends that he tried to negotiate, but that your demands were unrealistic."

"Tried to negotiate?" she asked. "He absolutely refused to meet with a professional negotiator, and when he met with our bargaining committee, he refused to discuss a single issue they brought up. He told them that his first offer was his final one and that if they decided to strike it would actually save him money!"

The press shot out more questions at that revelation, and Erin answered them as honestly as she was able, knowing that this was one battle Zarkoff was going to lose.

In Shreveport, Lois stood in the background, looking anxiously at the monitor that showed Erin in Washington, standing up for the Southeast pilots like a pro. She turned to Zarkoff, whose face was as red as an overripe tomato, and listened to the questions the press threw at him.

"How do you respond to Miss Russell's accusations?"

"I'd say that it's all a misunderstanding," he said. "I don't want a strike. I value my employees here."

"But wouldn't it, indeed, save you money to bring in less-experienced pilots and pay them less?"

"Well . . . theoretically, but —"

"We're talking realistically, Mr. Zarkoff," a hard-nosed reporter pressed. "Did you negotiate with those pilots or not?"

"It was a misunderstanding," he maintained, smiling smugly. "I think we can meet again, come to some understanding to end the strike. I'm willing to make a few concessions. My pilots are worth it."

"What kind of concessions?"

All the reporters turned around when they realized that Lois was the one questioning Zarkoff now. She stood with hands on hips, her head tilted skeptically. "Concessions in pay? In work conditions? In sick leave? In hours?"

He rubbed his face and cleared his throat, as obviously uncomfortable as she'd ever seen him. She etched the picture on her mind for future reference. "All of them," he assured her on national television. "Mark my word. We'll work this thing out. I don't want to lose even one of these capable pilots."

Lois stepped back from the crowd and sank against the wall as the press closed in again. The plan had worked, she thought. And things were finally looking up.

At Dulles airport in Washington, Addison was finally recognized as the NTSB investigator who'd investigated Mick's crash. The press pounced on the irony that he'd been on the plane during the emergency.

"How do you evaluate the handling of this emergency?" a reporter asked.

"It was handled expertly," he said. "Even better than I could have hoped."

"Do you think the crash a few weeks ago would have been avoided if more capable pilots had been flying?"

There was a hush and all eyes — including Erin's — became fixed on Addison. "That flight was piloted by one of the most capable pilots in this industry," Addison said. "Mick Hammon would have saved that plane if it had been humanly possible. It was a failure in the elevator system that caused the crash, and the initial speculation that it was the captain's fault was absolutely in error. Mick Hammon acted appropriately and with dignity."

Erin couldn't help adding to that, her voice wobbling with conviction. "If not for Mick, I wouldn't have landed that plane so accurately today," she said. "He taught me everything I know about good piloting under pressure."

At the youth center in Shreveport, Jason Hammon stood alone in the large gym, shooting the basketball with all his might, watching the ball fall freely through the hoop to come back to him. His hair was wet with perspiration, and his face was a hot shade of red.

"Hey, Jason," Zeke called from the doorway, his voice echoing from the walls. "Erin's on TV. Something about an emergency landing. Come on. Hurry!"

Erin? Emergency landing? Jason's heart jolted. He grabbed the ball and looked back at Zeke, saw the look of urgency on his face.

Still holding the basketball, he shot out the gym doors, Zeke fast on his heels, and went to the room with the television. At least twenty kids were gathered around, listening as Erin and Addison praised Mick, suddenly making him into a hero.

"Who's this Mick guy?" Zeke asked innocently.

Jason's shoulders straightened, and he lifted his chin with the first pride he'd felt in weeks. "Mick Hammon was my dad," he said.

"Get outta here," Zeke said. "You expect me to believe —"

"Believe it," someone in the crowd said.

Jason glanced through the throng of kids to find his ally, the person who could prove to Zeke that he was, indeed, Mick's son. The crowd parted, and he saw T.J., the bully who'd picked a fight with him before, standing across from him.

Jason's muscles tensed and his heart raced. Adrenaline pushed through him like a drug that made him capable of greater things than his size could have mastered.

"That was his dad, all right," T.J. said, his cold eyes riveted into Jason's. "He came to our school on career day."

"Wow," Zeke said, oblivious to the mounting tension in the room. "You must be proud of him. What Erin and Addison said was on national TV. You're famous . . ."

Jason didn't hear the words. His attention was completely on T.J., who was standing only a few feet away from him. His eyes narrowed.

T.J. hooked his thumbs into his front pockets and took a step toward him. Jason's hands coiled into fists. T.J. took another step. Then another.

Just when Jason expected the first remark that would send him swinging, T.J. offered a tentative smile. "So, you gonna just stand there holding that ball, or are you gonna play? I got a buck says you can't dunk as good as you can paint."

Jason's defenses lowered a degree, but he held T.J. in cold scrutiny a moment longer.

"Come on, man," T.J. said. "Just one game."

Quiet settled like a thick fog over the room. Jason wet his lips, took a step toward T.J., and tossed him the ball. "You're on," he said, as a smile tugged at his lips.

At home, Maureen sat on the couch, watching Erin and Addison on television, tears of relief tumbling freely down her face. It was over. No more nasty phone calls, no more cruel remarks for Jason at school, no more wondering why Mick hadn't done things differently.

Now, Mick, too, was something of a hero, and his family could go on with their lives.

CHAPTER THIRTY

As soon as Jack made it into the terminal, Erin and Addison were able to slip away. Holding her hand, he pulled her into a quiet lounge a short distance down the hall.

He drew her into his arms, holding her as if they were lovers who'd been separated by years of war, as if one of the planes on the runway outside would separate them again in mere moments. With eyes closed, they swayed in time to the soft music of love only the two of them could hear.

"I thought I was going to lose you," he whispered, his voice shaking. "I thought I wasn't meant to find happiness."

She gazed up at him, her amber eyes melting under his. "Then why did you pull back yesterday? The choice seemed so hard for you."

Addison's hands framed her face, stroking back her hair. "I was a wreck, Erin. That bolt thing pushed me past my limit, and then Sid's stupid ultimatum . . . I didn't know what was right anymore. It was like when you couldn't fly. You didn't trust your power to do anything. I knew I loved you, but I didn't know if that was enough."

She laid her head against his chest, feeling his heartbeat on her cheek. "Did you resolve it?" she asked, holding her breath. Whatever his answer, she thought, she would be there for him, help him work through it, as he had done with her. Nothing seemed as bleak now that she knew he truly loved her.

His sigh drew the breath out of her. "I had to think about my job, Erin. It made me miserable to think about going back to Washington and then Albuquerque and then who-knows-where else. I couldn't face little secret fragments of time with you, so that I could have my career and our relationship. I wanted more. And I was so confused about my job. It's been my whole life for a long time, Erin. I didn't know if giving it up was the right thing. Sid made me feel like I was turning my back on Amanda if I walked away from the NTSB to be with you. But he was wrong, Erin. He was wrong."

Erin turned her face up to his, confusion widening her eyes. "In the cockpit, you said you were an ex-NTSB official. You don't really have to quit, do you? Couldn't you go over his head, tell somebody what he did to you?"

Addison shook his head. "I'm quitting," he told her, and the sudden peace in his eyes told her he'd made the only choice he felt good about. "Sid gave me a choice, and I made it. Amanda wouldn't have wanted me to be alone, or to chase after vengeance for the rest of my life. I've had enough of the depression and the digging and the drilling of victims' families and friends. I want to feel good about what I do, and I haven't felt good about this for a long time. It's an important job, but there are others who could do it justice. I want to be with you, Erin. And after seeing you work today, seeing your competence and control, I want to get back into piloting."

Erin caught her breath as she pressed splayed fingers over her mouth.

"I want you to marry me, babe," he whispered, pressing his lips against her forehead. "Be my wife. God gave us a gift. Let's keep it."

"Marry you?" She stepped back and looked at him through a blur of tears. The strength of his sincerity was there in his eyes, as binding as her own. "Oh, Addison, yes!"

Crushing her in his arms, he smiled down at her, knowing that they were safe together in each other's love. For the rest of their lives, they would be there for each other, whenever broken wings needed mending.

About the Author

Terri Blackstock is an award-winning novelist who has written for several major publishers including HarperCollins, Dell, Harlequin, and Silhouette. Her books have sold over 3.5 million copies worldwide over the last twelve years, under two pseudonyms.

With her success in secular publishing at its peak, Blackstock had what she calls "a spiritual awakening." A Christian since the age of fourteen, she realized she had not been using her gift as God intended. It was at that point that she recommitted her life to Christ, gave up her secular career, and made the decision to write only books that would point her readers to Him.

"I wanted to be able to tell the truth in my stories," she said, "and not just be politically correct. It doesn't matter how many readers I have if I can't tell them what I know about the roots of their problems and the solutions that have literally saved my own life."

Her books are about flawed Christians in crisis and God's provisions for their mistakes and wrong choices. She claims to be extremely qualified to write such books, since she has had years of personal experience.

A native of nowhere, since she was raised in the Air Force, Blackstock makes Clinton, Mississippi, her home. She and her husband are the parents of three children — a blended family which she considers one more of God's provisions.

The employees of Thorndike Press hope you have enjoyed this Large Print book. All our Large Print titles are designed for easy reading, and all our books are made to last. Other Thorndike Press Large Print books are available at your library, through selected bookstores, or directly from us.

For information about titles, please call:

(800) 257-5157
To share your comments, please write:

Publisher
Thorndike Press
P.O. Box 159
Thorndike, Maine 04986